Angus

&

Liliana

What Cuba could be

A novel

by Mike McCarty

First printing, 2016

Printed in the United States of America
Set in Book Antiqua 11pt

Angus & Liliana

ISBN-10: 0-9903948-2-4

One Leg Out Productions.

Cover design by the author

For

Colleen

Disclaimer

Angus & Liliana is a work of historical fiction. Apart from well-known actual people, events, and locales that figure into the narrative, all names, characters, places, and incidents are products of the author's imagination or are used fictitiously.

~ANGUS and LILIANA~
Chapter I
Havana to Connecticut

Havana, Cuba 2007

"If I'm still alive after this, another day I will tell more."

"Oye Lydia ¿Cómo estás? ¿Cuáles son las noticias?"

Many times a day Lydia hears the question: ¿Cuáles son las noticias? – *(What's the news?)*. Each time she answers: "Si estoy todavía vivo después de esto, otro día mi lengua será más floja."
(If I'm still alive after this, another day my tongue is looser.)

Lydia spends her days across from the Hotel Sevilla in Havana, Cuba. The cars drive up and call to her and they wait, they wait out of respect as she slowly makes her way to them.

"Gracias," come back tomorrow and the news will be better," she will often say.

Lydia is old and she moves slowly. She walks with as much side-to-side motion as she does forward progress. Lydia has sold her newspapers here since before the revolution. Her encounters are brief, just enough time for a predictable exchange of greeting and her "Granma" newspaper for centavos.

Lydia has seen all the characters of the past – Batista, Fidel, Che, all have passed before her, most have come and gone.

"Hola Lydia ¿Cómo estás?

"Muy bien, gracias," always hopeful she predicts: "I think tomorrow the news will be better."

No one has ever asked more of Lydia – the newspaper and a brief hello, that's all she has ever known. No one has ever taken the time to ask for more.

Across the street in the hotel dining room Liliana looks out the window as she waits for her lunch appointment. From her table she can see Lydia as she goes about the business of selling her newspapers.

"Father, *¿Cómo estás?"* and she kisses his checks as he joins her at the table.

"It feels like rain," her father says, "my shoulder is telling me that rain is near."

"Which do you notice first, Father, the clouds above, or the pain in your shoulder?"

"How cynical you have become, my daughter?"

"Do you know Lydia, the newspaper lady?"

"Everyone knows Lydia," as he opens his paper to read.

"Yes, I know, we stop for our paper, but have you ever had a conversation with her?"

"Like everyone else I'm on my way to somewhere else. Why do you ask about Lydia?"

"I was just curious. I was sitting here watching you buy your paper and thinking that she must have many stories to tell. Maybe I will walk over and talk to her."

"She will be like most Cubans; she will have a story, but she will be reluctant to tell it. There is no doubt that a lot of history has passed before her eyes. She has sold newspapers there for as long as I can remember. I doubt anyone has ever taken the time to talk to her.

You have always had a soft spot for old people, Liliana. This is a good trait and something I am counting on."

"It's just that if we wait for others to tell the story of Cuba it may get told by the wrong people. Soon we may need people like Lydia. She may be the treasure that is hiding in plain sight."

Connecticut, USA

Coming out of the tunnel it would need all its speed to manage the grade ahead, steam billowing up, the unmistakable *chugging* sound reflecting off the mountain wall, the Southern Pacific locomotive known as "Daylight" strains to make the grade. Now on top it would be clear sailing through the tall grass prairie and beyond. The train gives a long *whistle* as it again comes up to speed.

Next to the tracks sits a crystal vase, and from this vase rises a single white lily whose petals are dusted with yellow gold. Beside the lily is a long stemmed rose, a single red opening bud with petals tinged in pink.

Near the vase, and to the sound of the train whistle, moves a nude female form striped in black and white.

"Angus."

"Yes, Lily."

"I'm feeling tension."

"What kind of tension, Lily?"

"You know, the usual kind."

"Didn't we talk about this? You said you wanted to be a zebra so I'm doing my best to make you a zebra."

"I know, Angus, but your brush on my skin and the train whistle is creating tension and driving me crazy."

"Well, if you keep writhing around like this you're stripes are going to turn into circles. Is that what you want?"

"I want relief, Angus."

"You're peaking way too soon. We have all morning."

"I can peak many times before noon, Angus."

"You see? Now look at my white stripe, it's merged with the black and created grayness. Now I have to wipe off. Here, here's something that may give you some relief while I finish your backside. You know I'm no artist, but if I start something I like to finish."

"Angus."

"Yes, Lily."

"Will you help me place it properly?"

"Lily, let me work the backside while you work the front. I think you can find its proper place."

"Angus."

"Yes, Rose."

"When will you finish with Lily? You promised to play train and tunnel with me."

"You girls give me too much credit. I'm one man doing the job of artist, train conductor, and Lord knows what else as the morning progresses.

"Angus."

"Yes, Rose."

"The flowers are a nice touch."

In the woods of Connecticut away from the highway lives Angus Calumet Quin. His is not a modest house by any means and with sufficient grounds that one could consider it an estate. Still, it's not near as grandiose as those across the bay in the Hamptons. This house, along with his 6,000 square foot apartment on Park Ave. on the upper east side of Manhattan, have been Angus' operating theater since becoming a partner with Fortney, Quin, and Hurst Financial, LLC.

In the basement of Angus' Connecticut home is an extraordinary model train set. This elaborate miniature train community comprises hundreds of square feet and is raised onto a platform table with skirting all around. There are train stations, forests, towns, water features, as well as bridges and mountain tunnels. It has every manner of locomotive and rolling stock operating on main and parallel tracks. There are modern locomotives as well as antique steam engines. It is very impressive.

Angus knows the lore of the train, the history, even the name of the things that pump round and round and make the wheels turn. Angus' father was a train conductor and had imbued his son with the sights, sounds, and smells of the train and the track. The well-played song of a train whistle and the clack-clack of wheels on the track had left a lasting impression on young Angus. Even the smell of the train yard could be brought up from memory.

On rare occasions Angus' father would wake young Angus at 4:30 AM to accompany him on a trip from Chicago to St. Paul, or perhaps to Council Bluffs, Iowa.

"Angus."

"Yes, Rose."

"When will you be through with Lily?"

"Well, Rose, I have only the belly of the zebra to do."

"What was that noise?" asked Rose calmly.

Angus rushes to the basement door and listens ... "Oh Shit!" exclaimed Angus. "It's my son and granddaughter. He said they wouldn't be here 'till tomorrow. Here, Lily, Rose, quickly, get under the skirting and be still. I'll try and get them to the other end of the house as quickly as I can. Please, don't relieve any tension until I give the OK. OK?"

"OK, Angus. It's kind of dusty under here."

"Hey you guys," greeted Angus. "Hey Thomas, Eva, I thought you were set back until tomorrow."

"Hi, grandpa, look what I got," shouts Eva, as she holds up a new train car.

"Things got spun around and we ended up on our original path," explained Thomas.

"Great then, you guys want to go upstairs and grab a juice?" offered Angus with a bit of urgency.

"No, grandpa, I have a new train car that I want to show you. Can we put it on the train and watch it go around?"

Unfortunately, the flap in the skirting was directly beneath the train switching yard and control station. Without perfect coordination this could be the kind of story that would be told and retold for generations.

"Yeah, that new train car was all Eva talked about all the way here," added Thomas.

"OK then," agreed Angus. "Let's get that car on the tracks and see how she rolls. A couple of laps around then we'll get a juice. I tell you what, Eva, I'll find a spot for your car on the track and you go over to the tool shelf and look for a coupler that looks like this. OK?"

"Angus, I need to pee," whispers Lily from behind the flap.

Angus quickly rips off the grain storage bin from the landscape and shoves it through the skirting. What could make this worse?

"Sound," shouted Angus, "We need some sound to go with this new car of yours."

With the flip of a toggle switch the entire wall to the right of the control station became a video screen showing footage of a vintage steam locomotive barreling down the tracks. Angus turns up the volume – chugging steam and blaring whistles would provide cover for the sound of zebra pee hitting the bottom of a toy grain storage bin.

"Hey Dad, what's with the black and white paint?"

"Oh, that. I was going to make a poster for the employees at work but I forgot the poster."

Fortney, Quin, and Hurst Financial, LLC, known on the street simply as FQH, though not a household name was instrumental in designing many of the financial instruments known variously as *credit default swaps, mortgage backed securities*, and *collateralized debt obligations*. These concepts sprang organically from the minds of unchecked capitalists with poor, or no government oversight, and primarily from the mind of Angus Quin. These financial instruments, in concert with *subprime mortgages* guaranteed by the Federal Government through Fannie Mae and Freddie Mac, were instrumental in creating an environment that had become a virtual powder keg of risk.

FQH did a tremendous volume of business packaging and selling these products. And while others were merely becoming millionaires, for his efforts, Angus Quin had amassed a serious fortune.

The Connecticut woods stimulated Angus' substantial imagination and financial creativity, whereas Manhattan was where he turned the bolts and screwed the nuts, or was it the other way around?

The mission was always clear: *make money*. And with the increasing emergence of powerful technology coupled with the absence of proper regulation it was the perfect storm environment for Angus' keen mind. To Angus it was like finding money on the ground.

After a few laps around the track Eva's new car was sufficiently broke in.

"What train is that in the movie, grandpa?" asked Eva.

"That's the Union Pacific 844 charging on at 70 mph. It's heading south through Nevada. It's a beautiful thing isn't it, Thomas – relentless …, like your mother. Have you spoken to your mother lately?"

To this question Angus received a kick to the knee from behind the skirting. A kick that said – don't get yourself bogged down in meaningless conversation. You're still on safari here!

"Let's all move up to the kitchen and get some juice. Did you guys park in front or around back?"

"In front," responded Thomas. "Is that a problem?

"Well, there are some gardeners that will be leaving soon and I don't want them blocked in."

This was as much instruction as it was an explanation.

Thomas and Eva were now being safely herded to the kitchen far away from the basement exit.

"I have grape or apple. What's your pleasure? Thomas, have you spoken to your mother lately?"

"It's been a few weeks. I think she's in Switzerland, Lucerne, I think."

"That looks like your gardeners heading out now," observed Thomas.

"They'll be back; they're just taking a break from the rigors of horticulture.

You know, Thomas, there are some serious changes coming. Changes in the financial system, major changes and some could be catastrophic."

"What do you mean, like a depression?"

"The extent of the damage is hard to measure but it will reach far and wide throughout the system. You should put yourself into cash for the foreseeable future. Not all at once but gradually work toward cash or treasuries. You should tell your mother to do the same. She's not likely to contact me anytime soon.

"Really, is this your own analysis or do you have some inside knowledge?"

"The only knowledge I ever have is inside, but it's clear to me that a hard fall is coming. And when it comes FQH will be held up for close scrutiny and myself in particular."

"You haven't done anything illegal have you dad?"

"When the system collapses and fortunes are lost legality will be a moving target for politicians scrambling to cover their ass. Sorry, Eva, that was a bad word.

The timing is difficult to call but when it comes it will make a loud noise. I want you to understand that when it does blow up my heretofore public anonymity could suddenly change and you may see our name in the papers or on the nightly news. Don't be alarmed."

"This all sounds pretty ominous, dad, can I help in any way?"

"The best thing you can do is protect yourself by slowly moving into treasuries. If someone ever asks you why you did it you can tell them that you just wanted to be safer – your contacts in Florida told you that there was a housing bubble and you wanted to avoid any undue risk when the bubble burst. Do you still own that condo in Sarasota?"

"Yes, we go down in November and then again in the spring. What's going wrong with the financial system?"

"There are millions of ARM's, adjustable rate mortgages that were set below the market. And there were directives given by the government through Fannie Mae and Freddie Mac to downplay credit worthiness. Now that these rates are starting to adjust upward the homeowners are defaulting on their mortgages at a rapid rate – people can't afford the homes they were encouraged to buy.

Millions of those risky mortgages have been bundled and scattered all over the world in the form of securities paying attractive returns. FQH, along with others have packaged these mortgages and made fortunes."

"So the Florida housing bubble is real."

"As a result of all this manipulation home prices have risen artificially creating the bubble. You remember the 'Dot.com' bubble of 2000? Well, now we have a housing bubble. And Florida, along with a few other markets, has experienced rampant speculation. Florida is on the top of the bubble.

It's a perfect storm that's coming from multiple directions and for a variety of reasons. In fact, I would sell your condo and don't quibble too much over the price.

And don't be alarmed at the crap you may read or see on TV. Sorry, Eva, that was another naughty word."

"That's alright grandpa, you should hear what Ben says at school."

"What does he say, Eva," wonders her dad.

"The other day he called Valery a 'bajina' and the teacher made him say I'm sorry to the whole class. He hung his head down the rest of the day."

"Well, sorry can be a bitter pill," agreed Angus, as he starred out the window through the Connecticut woods.

~ANGUS and LILIANA~
Chapter II
Welcome Aboard

"I want you to take the tender back to Miami then take a taxi to the corner of Hillview and Osprey. It's not far from the harbor. On that corner you will find a market named 'Morton's.' I want you to pick up sixteen New York strip steaks at Morton's meat market. Tell them you're picking up for Angus Quin, here's my card. They will also have 5 magnums of Mixon Vineyards Cabernet waiting there with the steaks. I've written it all down here along with my phone number. Put these items aside, we won't use them until after we leave Key West."

These were Angus' instructions to the sous chef. He then moved on to resolve other details - his guests would arrive shortly.

"Welcome aboard. Welcome," greeted Angus from the main deck foyer of "The Vegetarian Coyote," a 50 meter yacht anchored just off Key Biscayne, Florida. "Welcome guests, all. Please join the others in the main salon, or anywhere you like. The ship is yours to enjoy, welcome."

From the mainland guests were being ferried to the yacht by the Vegetarian Coyote's tender affectionately known as "Bernice." Bernice made several trips this afternoon from the dock of the Ritz Carlton Hotel on Key Biscayne.

"Greetings everyone, greetings, if I could have your attention please. Yes, please gather here in the main lounge as best you can. Can you hear me in the back over the roar of the Coyote engines? You know the Coyote claims to be a vegetarian but clearly the caterer didn't get the memo. There are a wide range of delights offered on the hors d'oeurvre platters, please enjoy and stuff your pockets. Hopefully everyone has now arrived.

Fortney, Quin and Hurst welcome you to its annual financial symposium. Our little get together is designed to increase your caloric consumption, and take some of the edge off of the daily grind. I see old friends and a few new faces; we have financial professionals from all over the country on board. Byron Hurst is with me here; Philip Fortney drew the short straw and is watching over things back in New York.

I confess that I don't know all that much about boats. I was part of the advance party that arrived a couple of days ago and I've been taking care of little details, but mostly I've been relaxing on this beautiful ship. Is it a ship, or a boat? I don't' know which. I asked the captain where Byron was yesterday and he told me he'd gone to port. Well, naturally I headed straight for the bar. I love a good port. Then I find out that port is the left side of the ship. If you're going to call one side port why not call the other side Sherry? No, it's port and starboard. For further clarification please see the captain. They tell me his family's maritime lineage goes back as far as the early twenty-first century. So, we've got that going for us.

My point is you don't need to know anything about boats to enjoy yourself while on board. And remember, if you need anything at all just wink at one of the 14 crew members. Don't, however, wink at the captain. He's had much too much to drink and he doesn't need any more distractions.

I do love this boat life. I may retire to a boat. Hopefully I won't have to learn to tie all those knots. I'm not sure who actually owns this boat. The papers go through Costa Rica then to Panama and over to Minsk then back to Costa Rica where you have to see a woman named Lupita. No matter, we pirated the ship ten days ago off the coast of Somalia so it will be some time before the owner catches up. Imagine Byron with an eye patch. I do love this boat life.

As you all must know by now we are going to have a raffle tonight. The twelve lucky winners will accompany me on the Vegetarian Coyote overnight down to Key West. Believe me we have all you need for the journey, including one of these beautiful Vegetarian Coyote robes being modeled here by able sea person Elizabeth and able seaman James. Elizabeth and James will walk among you so you can feel the goods – the goods being the robes, not Elizabeth or James.

The remaining "losers," as we shall refer to you when you're gone, will go with Byron and be attached to a cable and dragged through shark infested waters back to the Ritz Carlton to spend the night. From there you will be transported to Key West by private charter where we will again meet up. You can of course opt out of the raffle if you don't fancy the bacchanalian experience we have planned for you as the Coyote travels south.

We are here to enjoy. Maybe in Key West we'll discuss things of substance, but I wouldn't count on it. Thank you all for coming and hopefully the hurricane will change course and miss us, I kid about that. I'll be in the Lizard Lounge if you need me. You will find it located on the left side of the boat as you walk from the steering wheel toward the caboose. Thanks again, I shall now return to port – a nice tawny port, I think. My intrepid partner Byron Hurst would like to say a few words, Byron Hurst, ladies and gentlemen."

"As Angus said we will be ferrying back to the Ritz starting at ten PM. If for any reason you need to leave sooner please let me know. We'll have two more tenders operating besides Bernice.

And a note about this yacht: The Vegetarian Coyote was built by Guildship, the prestigious Dutch ship yard and first commissioned in 2004. The ship is state of the art throughout and is powered by twin 2,000 horsepower diesel engines. It is gyroscopically stabilized so precisely that you can enjoy a game of pool in the billiard room.

The ship is ably directed by Captain Rolf Jorgens and his crew of fourteen. And to the question: What's a boat like this cost? Well, I'm told that if you sold your jet, your

Lamborghini, and your polo ponies you would still need to come up with a sizable sum of money just to cover the down payment.

Thanks for coming. The Vegetarian Coyote will be sailing for Key West at midnight and I'll see you all in Key West tomorrow evening."

The evening progressed in predictable fashion. People gathered in small groups to discuss what they knew: yields on treasuries vs utilities, portfolio strategies, the strengths of Paul Volker vs Ben Bernanke.

Elizabeth and James were sufficiently groped, pinched and proposition as they passed through the crowd showing off the Coyote's robes. And the weight of the liquor was being more evenly distributed throughout the ship.

Karen from Santa Barbara, a teacher's union pension fund manager, and Ken, a state regulator from Pacific Palisades were discovered by the ships engineer on the floor of the engine room. Imagine, you're a couple of hours away from a suite at the Ritz Carlton and you're caught on the deck of the engine room between two 2,000 horsepower diesel engines. This is what liquor can do to judgement. However, spontaneity is usually not part of the personality inventory of those that crunch numbers all day so you've really have to applaud this behavior.

Angus had counseled the entire crew to intervene only if the guests were involved in safety issues.

At 8 o'clock the personal gift bags were handed out to those who could be found or wakened (a complete search and inventory by the crew would come later). These bags were not unlike those handed out backstage at the Oscars. They were personalized as to male and female and in some cases held items of a more personal nature selected for certain guests by Angus himself. Among other things there was Jasmin noir eau de parfum by Bulgari for the ladies, and there was the Bulgari fragrance: "MAN" ostensibly for the men. One bag contained a book of poetry by Ogden Nash, while another held a collection of Shakespeare sonnets. These gifts were a reflection of Angus' personal relationship with some of the guests. Another contained a CD of Billy Holiday's "Lady Sings the Blues," and yet another lady received a single poem on parchment:

"The Highwayman," by Alfred Noyes.

The last lines of the poem read:

> And still of a winter's night, they say, when the wind is
>   in the trees,
> When the moon is a ghostly galleon tossed upon cloudy
>   seas,
> When the road is a ribbon of moonlight over the purple
>   moor,
> A highwayman comes riding –
>   Riding – riding –
> A highwayman comes riding, up to the old inn-door.

These personal touches, which no doubt arrived with perfect pitch, were not left to secretaries, or otherwise picked out at the last minute while in the airport gift shop. These were details conceived and executed by Angus with care and forethought. Angus Quin believed in the power of personal touch.

The examination of these bags brought us right up to the time of the raffle.

"Ladies and gentlemen, please, may I have whatever amount of attention you can muster at this time," this announcement coming at nine o'clock from Angus who had been operating out of the Lizard Lounge on the left side of the boat. Angus was not a heavy drinker which made him perfect for the task at hand – herding drunken guests.

"You should find in each of your gift bags a raffle ticket. This ticket has a number printed on it. If you cannot find your ticket, or if it has been swept overboard by a restless, wayward wind, please raise your hand and another will be provided to you. If you do not wish to participate in the raffle raise your hand and you will be beaten and tossed overboard. But seriously, if your number is called and you just want to weasel back to the Ritz please call out your intention so that we may call another number. There are a finite number of berths on board and the captain informs me that we cannot all spend the night on board. Unlike in our line of work – there are rules. I will bunk on a couch with my blanket and teddy that I brought with me from Connecticut."

Angus had to call sixteen numbers to get his 12 overnight passengers. The dozen consisted of 7 women and 5 men. Apparently there were four guests that for reasons unstated could not, or would not dare, remain on board. The lucky twelve were taken by crew members to their respective berths to get settled in and refreshed before meeting back in the lounge at 11:00 donned in their gifted Vegetarian Coyote robe.

When the final inventory of drunken human flesh had been tallied, which meant searching every nook and portal on the ship, Bernice departed for the mainland and the Ritz Carlton for the last time.

Angus, now curled up in a blanket on the couch, waited for the raffle winners to reappear in the lounge as he watched on the ships big screen TV one of his favorite old movies: "The Train," with Burt Lancaster. Not only was this a terrific story, it had much to do with the details of old trains.

Slowly, the raffle winners began to arrive with the exception of 3 women and 2 men. These, as it was relayed by the staff, had passed out on their beds and could not be roused.

"The movie is almost over," Angus told his guests. "Burt Lancaster is about to whack this Nazi bastard that was trying to steal all these great paintings away from France.

He had this boxcar filled with all the great names: Renoir, Gump, etc. There, another Nazi bastard dead on the tracks. I love that movie.

So, we are now 7 left standing, or at least reclining," observed Angus. "Congratulations. I've ordered Diet Dr. Pepper cocktails and buttered popcorn. While we wait on the popcorn you may remember Elizabeth and James from earlier in the evening. Elizabeth and James were not selected merely for their ability to model robes, no indeed. What you are about to witness has been seen by only a handful, well, maybe hundreds, of privileged individuals. James, in addition to his obvious robe modeling skills plays a mean flute, and Elizabeth was trained by gypsies in a far off land."

With a wink from Angus, Elizabeth dropped her robe to reveal an extraordinarily well toned, almost completely naked body. Elizabeth, AKA Shakira, begins a Middle Eastern belly dance to the rhythmic styling's of James' flute. Shakira danced and writhed around and between the guests touching and taunting as her belly and hips intermittently became disjointed from their normal connecting parts. Her hips were in such a state of gyration that the integrity of the ship's gyroscopic stabilizers was called into question. When Shakira had completed her performance one more guest had succumbed to sleep.

"You know," said Angus, "a flute without holes is not a flute. Think about that."

"Angus, do you have more planned for this evening?" asked Lois, secretary to a big shot that could not make the trip. This was Angus' policy: if you can't make it – you must send your secretary.

"If I were to retire now would I miss the elephants diving off the bow?"

"Now why didn't I think of that," Angus said as he slapped his knee, "I will include that in next year's financial symposium."

"Do you think there will be a next year, Angus?" asked Roger, interjecting a serious note to the conversation. The other's ears perked up.

Angus pondered the question for a moment.

"Do you remember the Elliot Wave?" asked Angus.

"Yes," responded Roger after some thought.

"Refresh my memory," requested Jim, a relatively young fund manager from Kansas City.

Angus began: "The Elliott Wave theory was developed back in the '30's by Nelson Elliott. His theory was developed for the purpose of predicting financial markets. Later Elliott discovered that his theory closely matched the Fibonacci Summation Series. Fibonacci numbers also show up in the so called 'Golden Mean' or 'Golden Ratio' (1.618). It's said that the golden ratio shows up in the drawings of Leonardo da Vinci.

More recently, back in the '80's, a market prognosticator named Robert Prechter brought the Elliott Wave and Fibonacci theories back into public view. There are many books written on the subject and you can quickly find yourself in the weeds if you're not completely interested, but one of the principles of the Elliott Wave theory that has always fascinated me is – *crowd psychology*.

Elliott's theories can be extended to all basic human endeavors. We move between the excesses of optimism and pessimism in predictable sequences, at least Elliot thought so. And when the excesses of either reach their peak they then move back toward the opposite excess. As human behaviors correct away from one excess they never stop at the moderate norm, but instead race past it toward the opposite extreme. And so we, as imperfect humans, are in a constant state of travel between two extremes:

Our too liberal politics beget politics that are too Conservative, and then back again.
We have too many eggs in our diet, oops; cholesterol is not really the problem – eat more eggs.
We have too little financial regulation; we will soon have too much financial regulation.

We run screaming from one excess straight to the opposite extreme.

An Elliott "Super Cycle Wave" could be cresting now, my friends."

Those gathered were hanging on Angus' every word; not unlike a drunk staring at his car keys. Angus was after all the fox schooling the chickens. He couldn't very well say: those products you've been buying from me are crap and will ultimately be your ruin. So instead Angus gave them the Elliott Wave theory. A more sober group might have gotten the drift of Angus' explanation, but when the alcohol wears off these folk will have no idea what just transpired. No one had the nerve to say: Hey, Angus, would you mind running that by me one more time?

The jest of Angus' story was that just maybe – chartering a $75 million dollar yacht for hundreds of thousands of dollars a week to entertain clients might be viewed by Elliott as emblematic of an eminent reversal of fortune.

For Angus it was time for the elephants to jump off the bow, and then came a much needed interruption as Angus noticed the first officer of the ship standing conspicuously near.

"Yes," spoke Angus, giving the officer the opportunity to speak.

"Captain Jorgens wishes to advise that in accordance with our midnight departure schedule we will be getting underway for Key West in ten minutes."

"Thank you," responded Angus, "have the captain proceed as scheduled. And remind me, when will we arrive in Key West?"

"We should arrive between 1 and 2 PM tomorrow," responded the first officer.

"Angus."

"Yes, Lois."

"Is there a story behind the naming of the boat? The Vegetarian Coyote seems a curious name."

"Actually, people use all sorts of names for their boats. It's not always the name of their wife or daughter. In this case the name comes from a children's book. The author of that children's book is the owner of this boat. And that beautiful design on the robes, the Coyote with the rabbit, that was done by the famed Spanish artist Carlos Ygoa. Who knew children's books paid so well?"

"I've heard of Carlos Ygoa," responded Lois, "I love my robe and I'm never taking it off. I'm going to wear it to work."

"I do love this boat life," added Angus. "You know this boat is for sale. I think every luxury yacht is for sale. The game is this – you build, or buy a yacht, you immediately put it up for sale and for charter. You reserve a few weeks a year for yourself but the rest of the year you give over to a charter management company who charges a few hundred thousand a week plus expenses for charter. So, you have some cash flow, you have a great vacation destination, and if it sells you make a million and start all over again. Not a bad racket."

The motion of the Vegetarian Coyote could now be felt as they headed southwest at twelve knots.

~ANGUS and LILIANA~
Chapter III
Key West and Beyond

While the north remains frozen the winter months in
south Florida are glorious. And in the spring the air is full
of the smell of bougainvillea and orange blossoms. There
is a constant freshness to the air like you get in the mid-
west just before a thunder storm. People stream in to
Florida just before Thanksgiving and in some precincts
the population doubles. They come from New York,
Michigan, or Canada, and they come from Europe and
South America. You can hear any number of languages
spoken in the sidewalk cafes. Then sometime around
Easter everyone gets the memo and leaves. Florida is then
given back to the locals to suffer through those few
dreadful months of summer and to live on the money left
behind by the snow birds.

Key West, however, is a different kind of animal. It's
different from Florida proper, and it's different from the
world proper. Key West is one of those places like New
Orleans for Mardi Gras, only the silliness never stops. Six
toed cats and beautiful sunsets – welcome to Key West.

Through the night The Vegetarian Coyote made passage
southwest toward Key West.

Angus and Robert Starr sat privately on the upper aft
deck as they sipped morning coffee. The sun was up but

not by much and the rest of the raffle winners were sleeping in. Pacing at a steady 12 knots the Atlantic Ocean was somewhere, without a marker, turning into the Florida Straits, and then on to the Gulf of Mexico. In the distance could be seen the string of Keys passing by to their north: the famed Key Largo, Islamorada, Marathon, and then smaller Keys like Duck Key, Conch Key and Boot Key.

As the salty morning breeze swirled past them, engineered by the Coyote to slip past and not disrupt, Angus spoke to break the calm: "I do love this boat life. We're going to spend a couple of days in Key West but this is not our final destination. The guests will remain behind but Byron and I will continue on south. Robert, we're going on to Cuba to meet Philip and we'd like you to join us."

Robert Starr was the managing partner at Pinnacle-Starr Brokerage and head of the mergers and acquisition department. Robert had brought many IPO's to market as well as the mergers and acquisitions of some of the country's most recognizable multinational corporations.

"What's going on in Cuba, Angus? Can you just sail right into the harbor there?"

"There are a string of keys just off the mainland to the east of Havana. On these barrier islands there are several resorts set up to lure mostly Europeans. You know

Philip's family has been connected to Cuba since before Castro. Something is brewing in Cuba and Philip has his finger on it. Philip wants you to join us in a meeting with some of the Cuban principals. We'll anchor off shore and hold the meeting on board."

"This sounds very exotic, Angus. Should we expect Vito Corleone to be in attendance?"

"That wasn't Vito that was Michael. And I doubt we'll see that solid gold telephone. I really don't have any more particulars except that we will arrive Wednesday in the afternoon and Philip will then join us from one of these resorts. He will brief us at that time and Wednesday evening the four of us will have dinner and a meeting with these Cubans. I'm told there could be as many as five Cubans and at least one is very high up on the Cuban totem pole. Will you be able to stay on board for a few more days?"

Robert reflected for a moment then looked at his watch and said: "Let me make some calls, Angus. I'll get back to you later in the morning. Sailing on to Cuba; I've always wondered what the inside of a Cuban prison looked like."

The two remained seated soaking in the vision of the Coyote's foam trail as it disappeared behind them, as their coffees were again warmed by the invisible yet ever present staff.

The Coyote anchored in sight of Key West on Sunday. All those that made the trip from Miami were invited back on the yacht for sunset drinks and hors d'oeuvres. Then it was party time back at Key West. All those that were capable did the bar crawl and saw Hemingway's six toed cats.

Early Wednesday morning the Coyote quietly lifted anchor and headed south. The captain was given GPS coordinates for anchor 2 km off shore from the Paradisus Veradero Hotel and Resort 140 km east of Havana. The Paradisus was one of several resort hotels along a stretch of barrier islands. Foreign (ex-American) tourists provided much needed hard currency to the otherwise – poor as a church mouse – Cuba.

The plan was for Angus to take Bernice, the ship's tender, and collect his senior partner Philip Fortney at the resort dock at 3:30 pm sharp. They would then return to the ship for a briefing regarding the evenings schedule and topics of discussion. By two o'clock the Coyote was close, maybe too close. This was supposed to be a protected meeting but sometimes the word doesn't get to everyone in the loop. So the Coyote held back, they would precede to the rendezvous no sooner than they absolutely had to.

At 3:15 the Coyote was holding on the provided coordinates as Bernice pulled away and headed for shore. On board were Angus and Bernice's most capable pilot. On yachts of the size and scope of The Vegetarian Coyote tenders can be substantial crafts in their own right. Bernice was thirty-four feet and could do 35 knots. These tenders are designed to transport the yacht's owners and guests safely and comfortably to shore. Many ports are incapable of providing berthing for yachts of the Coyote's size, so they must anchor offshore and use the tender for transport to shore.

As Bernice approached the shore the scope of the resort became obvious. The pilot followed his nose into a manmade protected cove. Here they found Philip standing alone on the dock.

By four o'clock the plan had gone without a hitch and the foursome of Robert Starr and the three partners: Philip, Angus and Byron were relaxing at the bar on board the Coyote.

"What are we looking at here, Philip?" asked Robert.

"I've asked the captain to take us a bit further off shore until later this evening. Our guests are expected sometime between six and seven and I'll get a heads up fifteen minutes prior to rendezvous. Meeting times in Cuba are taken as a 'general vicinity of' the time stated.

I'll give you some background while we wait. I've been coming to Cuba since I was a boy. My father spent a lot of time with Ernest Hemingway here in Cuba. Hemingway's Finca Vegia estate is just outside Havana. My father and I would travel to Cuba from Miami to spend time either at the estate or on Pilar, Hemingway's fishing boat. During those trips back in the late 40's early fifties my father would sometimes leave me at Finca Vegia while they were off together drinking daiquiris at The Floridita bar, or shooting pigeons at the Club de Cazadores.

Hemingway had a maid during those years and this maid had a son named Enrique. Enrique and I played together many times during my father's outings with Hemingway. Enrique and I have stayed in touch and been friends ever since. It's just one of those relationships that happen in the course of a life. And over the years Enrique Fuente has become a very influential figure here in Cuba. Enrique will join us later along with three or four others. I've met the others except for one, a person said to be very close to the Castro's.

Enrique suggests that things are going to begin changing in Cuba very quickly. It's true that Fidel's demise has been predicted every year for the last 50 years but there is that unmistakable fact – nobody gets out alive, and Fidel was born in 1926. Fidel has outlived all of his contemporaries, but Mother Nature will not be denied. The news will soon break that Fidel has just entered the hospital for a serious operation and has ceded power to his brother Raul.

The real substance of our meeting is unknown to me so we'll just play the gracious hosts and see what's on their minds. We'll have some drinks then dinner and at some point the story will unfold."

The Coyote was the perfect place for such a meeting. In Cuba there is always intrigue, always that which you could never have anticipated. Fidel's regime hadn't survived all these years by accident. And when meetings are held, well, there should be caution.

"Well, Philip," Angus said, "you have my attention. This is a good one; you couldn't chase me off this boat now with a Cuban cattle prod. Normally we'd be back in New York watching the snow fall, and look at us – we're waiting off shore Cuba for a delegation of Cubans who ostensibly need us for some purpose. You've got me, Philip, I'm not going anywhere."

"Think about it, Angus," responded Philip, "why does anyone need people like us? What do we ever have to offer? We know money. We can't fix your car or your washing machine, we know money. The four of us, we deal in complex money matters all day long and we tend to down play the importance of what we know, what we do. It's possible that Cuba could be heading for a rapid change. I don't think Enrique would put us in this position if it weren't something worthwhile. I've been coming to this island all my life. I've always held out the hope that real change would come. Maybe this is a beginning and maybe we can be part of it. To love Cuba you have to be a romantic and to this I plead guilty."

Byron added, "I have to agree with Angus, I can't wait to hear what they have to say."

"I made my decision in Key West," said Robert. "This is the most excitement I've had since Boston won the pennant in '04."

The group was then abruptly approached by captain Jorgens.

"Yes, captain," acknowledged Philip.

"We have been joined by three military type speed boats. They appear to be at rest one hundred meters to port."

"Are they stationary?" asked Philip.

"Yes, they appear to have taken up positions and are holding in place," responded the captain.

"Thank you, Captain, please have the first mate advise if these boats alter their position or make any aggressive moves towards us. And in the mean time you might review your procedures for emergency broadcasts."

"Well, there you have it," said Byron, "I wonder if they will allow my wife conjugal visits with Cuban prisoners."

"Would that be prisoners in general, or you in particular," asked Angus.

"Oh, not me," responded Byron, "I was just thinking about sending her down here to have sex with Cuban prisoners as a humanitarian gesture, like a Peace Corps thing. Maybe this will help reduce my sentence."

"Have you discussed this with Virginia? I think a program like that would be well received within the Cuban prison system. You could have Virginia on posters with the slogan: 'Give piece a chance.' You should make a poster like that, seriously."

"Do you think we should make contact back home, Philip," wondered Robert, putting an end to the nervous banter.

Angus went to the port side and could see the three "rib" style dark colored boats scattered by 50 yards left, right and center, each boat had at least 2 occupants. They were as the captain had said – stationary. Angus then returned to the group.

"These are not attack dogs, these are guard dogs. I think these boats are here for our protection," offered Angus. "If they had a different purpose they would be more curious."

"Until they tip their hand in some aggressive way we'll just have to hope for the best," surmised Philip.

"We should have the captain point the Coyote's laser at them," Byron figured, "and if they make a move he could burn a small hole straight through each boat. As they begin to sink we'll make our escape," Again a bit of nervous humor coming forth from a mostly serious group.

Philip motioned to the ship's butler who was always standing by just out of earshot.

To the butler Philip said: "When our guests arrive there will be a formal introduction and I'd like to have the captain introduced with the four of us with some part of the crew in the background."

"I understand," said the butler, "I'll advise the captain and arrange for the crew to be available in the lounge."

"I understand that some of the crew speaks Spanish. Is that true?"

"Yes," responded the butler. "I too am fluent in Spanish."

"Good, I would like to have one of you nearby at all time in case we have any translation issues."

Philip continued, "We'll greet them in the foyer then direct them to the main deck lounge where we'll exchange introductions. When that's complete the crew can go back to their duties. I would like for you to personally take drink orders from our guests once they are seated. At that time you should advise each guest that we are serving steak and ask how they prefer it cooked. Also, be prepared to offer an alternative menu should anyone object. The chef already has our preferences. I can't imagine that we will encounter vegetarians but you never know. I'm thinking that they may be tired of great seafood.

Advise the chef that you will call for our dinner seating a half hour after drinks are served. Look to my approval before you make the 'dinner is served' call. I may delay our dinner seating slightly depending on the conversation. Have the kitchen prepare for six additional guests although I anticipate only four. That's ten plates total.

"Do you understand these instructions? Do you have any questions?"

"I understand," responded the butler.

"Good, thank you that will be all. It's nice to have good help," said Philip as he relaxed back into his chair.

Good, professional wait staff understands that what a client wants more than anything is precision, precision in all things great and small. The kind of wait staff that exists on a chartered yacht must adapt quickly to new, unfamiliar clients, the type of clients whose expectations are high having paid hundreds of thousands of dollars for a single week's charter.

Philip Fortney had orchestrated more than a few get-togethers in his time as founding partner of the firm.

"I'm going to make a call back to the office," announced Byron. "Out of 52 employees surely someone will be working."

Everyone then relaxed and contemplated what surprises the evening might bring.

At 7:05 Philip's phone rang.

"Good, so these boats we see are with you? ... I see" he was heard saying as he hung up, "they are departing the dock now. Our companion boats are friendly."

Philip motioned to the butler and advised him that the guests would be arriving momentarily.

The seas were calm so when the guests arrived it was an easy transition from the smaller boat to the 164' Coyote.

Greeting the guests at the gangway was first captain Jorgens with a hearty: "Welcome aboard," sounding much like the Scandinavian sailor that he was.

After the captain, next in line was Philip who offered sincere greetings to all and a warmer embrace for his close friend, Enrique. Angus and Robert waited in the lounge as Philip led the Cuban guests with the captain following close behind. There were three gentlemen and to the surprise of all one lady. Following behind was a member of the Cuban's crew who carried boxes of cigars. This crew member then returned to the boat which now held alongside the Coyote's starboard side. The other three "guard" boats also remained in place for the remainder of the evening.

All were now standing in the lounge of the main deck. The American contingent lined up to port and the Cubans to starboard. It was Philip who first spoke:

"To our lady guest, gentlemen, allow me to first introduce the able captain of our ship: captain Rolf Jorgens. Captain Jorgens will now take his leave and return to his duties at the helm. My name is Philip Fortney; I am the founding partner of the firm Fortney, Quin and Hurst Financial. Also, I would like to introduce Angus Quin, senior partner of our firm, and next to Angus is Byron Hurst, our managing partner. On the end we have Robert Starr, managing partner of Pinnacle-Starr Brokerage. To the man we come to you from New York City."

When Philip had finished his introduction the lady stepped forward.

"My name is Liliana Beltran and I would like to introduce to you your guests for this evening. First, Señor Ramon Nicolas Beltran, close advisor to Generalissimo Fidel Alejandro Castro Ruz, next, General Roberto Fulgencio Cienfuegos, Revolutionary Army Airborne Brigade for the district of Havana, and next, Enrique Maduro Fuente, longtime friend and advisor to the Castro family. We all speak and understand English very well with the exception of General Cienfuegos, who's English may need help from time to time. I will be staying close to the General throughout the evening to provide translation when necessary."

When Ms. Beltran had completed her introductions Enrique Fuente stepped forward and spoke:

"I wish to thank my longtime friend – since we were young boys – Philip, and your associates for coming to Cuba. Please accept these fine cigars as a small token of our appreciation and friendship."

Angus spoke up to say: "I would like to personally accept these cigars. In fact, I would like to accept one right now."

"Please, everyone, come and relax," coaxed Philip, "This Vegetarian Coyote yacht is ours to enjoy, and these crew members are here to assist you in any way. Come, sit."

At these instructions the crew left the room and everyone found a chair and made themselves comfortable while Angus busied himself opening one of the boxes of cigars.

"They won't let us smoke here in the lounge, but on the deck is OK. I do love a good cigar. What type of cigars do we have here?" inquired Angus, unable to take his eyes off of Ms. Beltran as he rolled one of the cigars between his fingers. *'Who is this beautiful Cuban woman: Liliana,'* thought Angus to himself as he feigned interest in the cigars.

She was indeed a distraction. Her skin was the color of light brown tobacco leaves. She had dark hair, and full, expressive lips. She was dressed in a tailored suit with slacks that took a long time to reach her ankles. Was this her only function – to provide language backup for the General? Angus told himself that he should try and focus elsewhere. It is quite possible that every man in the room was having this same internal dialogue.

With Angus' eyes fixed upon her Ms. Beltran took this as a question to the General. Ms. Beltran repeated Angus' question discretely to the General in Spanish: "Sr. Quin quiere saber qué tipo de cigarro."

The General then spoke up proudly in broken English: "Si, the cigaro es 'Cohiba Behike,' vitol es 'BHK 54' very special."

For Cubans cigars are a proud part of their identity. A Cuban cigar is recognized worldwide as the best of the best. For a country that has little else to brag about, cigars are ever present throughout the culture.

"Cohiba celebrated its 40th anniversary in 2006 with the addition of this 'Behike' line," added Enrique, "these were some of the first boxes produced."

"My goodness," Robert said, "this will be a real treat after dinner on the open deck."

"Here, Robert," offered Angus, "take a look at this cigar. It's a work of art. Even the box is a thing of beauty."

"I would like to offer a more complete introduction, if I may," said Señor Beltran. "It is no coincidence that Lilianna's name and my own are the same. Liliana is my daughter. Liliana is a trained translator and works for the Cuban government in this capacity at the U. N. She holds a diplomatic passport. Liliana studied Language Arts in Spain and Engineering in the United States. And as you can see she gets her looks from her mother."

And so, the mystery woman is revealed, somewhat. She is now, if possible, even more intriguing.

"And where did you study engineering, Ms. Beltran?" asked Robert.

"I attended Cornell University," responded Liliana.

"And you had no difficulty getting into Cornell from Cuba?" wondered Byron.

"I was able to make my transition from The Complutense University of Madrid. I had been a resident of Spain for three years so they accepted me as a Spaniard."

"So you are familiar with our state of New York," added Philip.

"Yes, I enjoyed my time there very much."

The butler then nodded to Philip indicating that Dinner was ready to be served and Philip indicated his approval.

"Dinner is served on the main aft deck," announced the Butler to the group.

With this announcement everyone made their way to the covered open air dining table on the main aft deck.

There were two wines served with dinner: 2003 Mixon Vineyards Cabernet Sauvignon and the 1990 Domaine des

Baumard Quarts de Chaume Chenin Blanc. The menu consisted of a shrimp and avocado cocktail followed by a potato and leek soup enhanced with sharp Wisconsin cheddar cheese and garlic butter croutons. The entrée was prime dry aged New York strip steak served with a grilled asparagus triplet dressed with vinaigrette of minced shallot, minced apple, honey, French mustard, rice vinegar and canola oil. And if there was room the chef offered mignardises consisting of various bite sized candies, cookies and tarts. These dessert treats were served with a dark roast coffee.

The chef was rightly brought to the table to take his bows as the butler offered everyone at the table a cigar from the box that Angus had opened. No one turned him down, including Liliana. It is not uncommon for women to smoke cigars in Cuba. The group decided that the chef should be awarded the distinguished "medal of cigar" which consisted of – a cigar.

After dinner the group stood at the rail and stretched giving the staff time to clear the table. As Angus was considering a maneuver to Liliana's position on the rail it was she that joined him and spoke.

"It's a curious name, don't you think? Do you think there is a coyote that would not eat meat?"

"There is a story about a scorpion and a frog, do you know it?" asked Angus.

"No, tell me a story," responded Liliana.
"A scorpion approached a frog on the bank of a river and asked the frog if he would let him ride on his back to the other side. Well, said the frog, if I do that you would sting me and I would drown. But if I sting you, said the scorpion, we would both drown. After more discussion the scorpion convinced the frog to take him to the other side. When they got to the middle of the river the scorpion stung the frog and they both drowned."

"But why did the scorpion do this?" wondered Liliana.

"Because it was his nature."

"So we should be skeptical of this coyote," surmised Liliana.

"We should be cautious, I think."

"It's a good story, Sr. Quin."

"Please, call me Angus."

"Very well, Angus, the night air and the wine make me want to believe this coyote."

Everyone was reseated and was joined by a glass of 1970 Fonseca Vintage port to compliment the cigars.

"What a beautiful cigar," said Philip.

"What great lips!" thought Angus.

"Gentlemen," spoke Ramon Beltran, "now that we have finished that delicious meal and our cigars are lit I would like to explain the purpose of our visit. We don't need to discuss the many differences between our countries. These arguments are old and lead nowhere. I would like instead to talk about the future, the future of Cuba."

All those in attendance inched up in their seats in anticipation of what they knew must be the evening's payoff.

"First," Senior Beltran continued: "if you will indulge me for a moment, I would like to tell you a story, a story of a young boy. On September 26, 1960, Fidel Castro gave a speech to the U. N. General Assembly in New York City. These were tense times and the entire world was watching. Fidel made sure that everything about the trip was contentious starting with his choice of hotels: The Theresa Hotel in Harlem. While there Fidel met with Malcolm X and the poet Langston Hughes and other controversial figures of the time. His speech at the U. N., which lasted over four hours, was very condemning of the

United States and it created much animosity among your politicians.

This was a very import time in history. The very night of Fidel's speech there was held the first televised debate between Richard Nixon and John F. Kennedy. And only a few days later Nikita Khrushchev pounded his shoe on his desk in the U. N. assembly. All these milestones in history narrowed into only a few days. And only a few blocks away from the United Nations building, on September 30, 1960, the New York Yankees beat the Boston Red Sox 6-5. My father, who was part of Fidel's delegation, and I were at that game in Yankee Stadium.

What I saw, but didn't fully understand at the time, was the power of sports. For a 12 year old boy from Cuba it was a magical experience. On that day I saw Whitey Ford, Yogi Berra, Clete Boyer, Mickey Mantle, Roger Maris and Ted Williams. My father had to drag me from the stadium. The sights, the sounds, the smells, the fans screaming, well, it left a permanent mark on that young boy, a mark that remains to this day.

A few days later in October the Pittsburg Pirates would beat the New York Yankees in the seventh game of the World Series. This seventh game won by a walk off home run by Bill Mazeroski at Forbes Field in Pittsburg. This seventh game of the 1960 World Series, said to be the greatest game ever played, was heard by me on a small radio back in Cuba."

Robert Starr was so caught up in the story he couldn't help but blurt out: "And that home run is the only walk off home run in history to win a game in a World Series."

"You are right, Robert," said Sr. Beltran.

"Sorry for interrupting," apologized Robert, "please continue.

"A few months later, in January of 1961, President Eisenhower severed all relations with Cuba. And we have lived with this situation ever since. Now, there may be a light of encouragement coming our way. I have no more patience with politicians and their talk, talk, talk. I am told by Enrique and by others that the people on this boat have the kinds of skills necessary to accomplish my dream, my dream for Cuba and her people."

Everyone inched a bit closer in their seats as Sr. Beltran paused for effect.

Angus finally asked: "And what is that dream, Sr. Beltran?"

"Baseball!" responded Sr. Beltran.

"Baseball?" said Philip.

"Yes, baseball."

Those that had been out on the edge of their chairs suddenly, and collectively, relaxed back in their seats.

"Please," urged Sr. Beltran, "stay with me a while longer. What I am proposing is this: to be built on the outskirts of Havana, the greatest baseball stadium the world has ever known. This stadium will host the Chicago White Sox and the New York Yankees, the Los Angeles Dodgers and the Baltimore Orioles, and even the Yomiuri Giants of Tokyo. Imagine a harbor full of boats, an airport with planes from all points on the compass, and a stadium filled with screaming Cubans, Americans, Brazilians, and people from Canada to Argentina. Do you know who loves baseball more than Americans? Cubans, Dominicans, and Venezuelans! The list of Cuban players that have found their way to U. S. teams is long and distinguished. No longer will this be necessary."

Señor Beltran's voice was rising with passion.

"Do you not think that with a free Cuba and a world class stadium that every team in major league baseball would not want to make the trip to Havana? For years they traveled to Montreal, Quebec.

There has been built, I think, over all these years, an irresistible mystique regarding Cuba; a curiosity and even sympathy for the Cuban people. What better than the competition of baseball to bring our two people back together, to heal these wounds of the past?

What we need is a stadium, a world class stadium. In the states you might sell municipal bonds, or you might levy a tax on the citizens to pay for your stadium. These schemes won't work here. What I want from you is a plan that will work. Some means to get from here to there. And for your troubles you will receive a generous percentage of the enterprise.

When you think on these matters you will encounter many questions, many barriers. I ask that you allow your creative minds to look beyond these historical limitations. We are approaching a new age in Cuba. The failed ideologies of the past will soon be nothing but an ugly footnote to history. There will be problems but a new generation of Cubans is standing by ready to lead.

What I am suggesting is a consortium, a consortium between partners such as your firm, other contributors to be named, and the new Cuban government. The legalities will obviously be finalized at a later date, but our minds, gentlemen; our minds are free to go forward.

What I propose is for you to go back to New York and think on what I have proposed. Think about what will be possible when Cuba is free. In a couple of weeks I will send my daughter to New York City. She will discuss with you your thoughts. If you do not wish to be involved then I say thank you for the drinks and for the delicious meal and I wish for you a good life. But, if you feel that we have reason to proceed then I promise to you tonight that I will devote all my energy and resources to accomplish this goal. Tonight you may have heard only the word baseball, mi amigos, but I assure you there is much more.

And if you will indulge me further, as I conclude, I would like to show you a picture."

At this point Sr. Beltran motioned to his daughter who pulled from a satchel a photograph which she passed to Philip. The photo was then shared with the rest of the group.

"This, gentlemen, is the Trogon, the national bird of Cuba. It was chosen because its colorful plume is the same as the Cuban flag. This bird, also called Tocororo lives only in Cuba. It's a beautiful bird, no? It is said that the Tocororo cannot live in captivity, dying of sadness if caged. I want to see this bird on uniforms playing in the World Series in Havana, Cuba."

And with the drama of someone who might have witnessed a few of Fidel Castro's speeches over the years Ramon Beltran rose to his feet and thrust his glass into the air. His voice rose as he said:

"And so I stand and raise my glass to you. I salute your skill and your imagination, and I salute your ability to recognize an opportunity: Salute, salute, salute.

The Coyote left late that night for Miami. The three Cuban speed boats stayed with them until they got to international water. The four passengers agreed that they would not discuss Sr. Beltran's proposal until they got back to the City, instead, allowing his comments to churn and simmer in their minds.

"It's hard to leave the Coyote behind," said Angus, as they boarded the private jet for home.

Life is good on Wall Street these days: planes, yachts, bottled water. The plane in question was a Gulfstream G280 with a seating capacity of 10, a range of 3600 miles, and a cruise speed of Mach .80, or 528 mph. This ride will clearly beat peanuts in coach on a Miami to New York flight.

"A person could get used to that yacht life very quickly," agreed Robert, "maybe we should put together a package. We could sell 26 shares, each share representing 2 weeks on a yacht that we purchase. I'm told that the operating expenses amount to about 10% of the yacht's value each year – that's salaries, insurance, fuel, etc. Then again chartering is not a bad way to go. I don't know what Philip gave for a week on the Coyote, but the good news is you can pay the tab and walk away."

"The Coyote pulled in $350,000 for the week," offered Angus. "Then there's fuel, food, tips. It will top off at around $425. I'll take 25 shares of that package and I'll give you and Alice the one odd week. And what about that Liliana, is she a hazard or what?" I'd hate to have to stare at that as a married man, whew."

"I don't know what you're talking about, Angus; however, did you happen to visually measure the inseam of her slacks? I made it to be 34 inches."

"You are wrong, my friend. It was clearly 34.25 inches, and I would love to do a more in depth evaluation – including a metric conversion."

"Angus, have you considered that this woman might be some kind of bait?"

"How cynical are you, Robert Starr? Clearly she is as pure as the water that flows down the East River. She is a solid 8.5 speed that's for sure. I make her to be about 35. I am now going to close my eyes and divert my mind away from her for the remainder of this flight. I have that kind of discipline."

Thirty seconds later …

"It was her lips that caused me the most trouble."

"Angus, she's probably married to some Che Guevara type and has 3 screaming kids."

"You know, I don't think these are the Che Guevara types. I think these are the Andrew Carnegie, J. P. Morgan types. I think these people are capitalists. It is an intriguing situation," as Angus closed his eyes again.

"I'm going to go up and talk to Philip about when we can meet and discuss all this."

"Let's do this, Robert," said Philip, "tomorrow is Friday and we've all been gone for days. Let's all take tomorrow and the weekend to think about this and meet in our office Monday – say two o'clock. That will give us some time to catch up on business. Does this time suit you, Robert?"

"I'll know more when I get to the office. Let's stay with your plan and if something gets in the way I'll get back with you tomorrow."

"Would you tell Angus and Byron? We'll be landing soon."

One of the benefits of traveling in your own private plane is that you can use the smaller airports. Teterboro airport is located in the New Jersey Meadowlands and is a relatively quick drive to mid-town Manhattan. Commercial planes are not allowed at Teterboro.

"Sure, Philip, I'll tell them."

"What's the plan?" asked Angus.

"We're going to let this ride until Monday at two o'clock in your office."

"Well, I assume that Philip knows how to get in touch with these Cubans."

It was back to the business of finance for all involved. Work product doesn't stop just because you've been away on a yacht eating asparagus triplets with vinaigrette that lacked garlic and smoking great cigars. Being a partner has its perks.

"Mr. Quin," interrupted Rosemary, Angus' secretary. "You're two o'clock meeting is underway in the conference room."

"Thanks, Rosemary, I'm on my way."

The four were now gathered and it was time to lay out their thoughts. It had been almost four days since the encounter on the yacht and all were eager to get, and to give, opinions.

"Gentlemen," began Philip, "I'm going to make a few comments then I'll throw it open for discussion. I have been blessed in my life to work on some very interesting projects, but looking back I can't remember a single one that comes close to this. The scope of this, when you let your mind wander, is unfathomable.

As usual when there is great opportunity there is an equal counterbalancing risk. To get involved in these matters is to put ourselves in the middle of international politics. Is this our forte? Do we know these waters? As things exist today we will be bucking not just our own government's policies but those of Cuba. So, on one side we clearly have a 'unique opportunity,' but let's also place on the negative side of the ledger 'politics.' Fortunately, measuring risk/reward is what we do here.

I'd like to think that my affection for the island would not cloud my judgement. I'm not going to recuse myself from participation, but I think I need to hear what the rest of you have to say? Who would like to start?"

"I'll take a shot at it," responded Byron. "On the positive side I think your assessment of the opportunity reflects that of my own. To say that this could be huge doesn't really do it justice. It could be a ball stadium today, but as Beltran alluded there could be more here than just baseball. On the negative side I can see where a project like this could easily consume our firm's resources. We have people in this office that are highly specialized individuals who sometimes work 10-12 hour days with what we already do. Would this be an 'All In' move for FQH? Do we gear up another division? I'm not sure how Robert's firm stands but I'd be surprised if it were not similarly situated."

Byron's comments were somewhat predictable, coming from an operation manager's perspective. Byron was closest to the day-to-day problems of the firm.

"Really, though, baseball stadiums, adjustable rate mortgages, what's the difference? We don't do a walk-through of each house in our portfolios. We package up *stuff* and we sell it. That's what we do. I'd like to hear someone else's take."

"Take your shot," said Angus, looking at Robert.

"Sure, I'll give it a go. We are similar as to our resources, Byron. I think any organization that operates efficiently operates on the edge. But 'unique opportunity' may be the understatement of the twenty-first century. All of us here are risk takers, that's what we do and we're all pretty good at it. And most of the time we're operating on a gut level. Let's try and pin down who these people are then go forward with a healthy amount of skepticism. Also, it's no secret here that I am a rabid baseball fan. Like you, Philip, hopefully this won't cloud my judgement, but what Beltran said about every baseball team in America wanting to go to Cuba is absolutely true. But this truth is way down on the list of considerations. Would they line up at a McDonalds in Havana? Would they like to drive down the road in a brand new Corvette? Absolutely they would. Would they pack into a state-of-the-art stadium? No doubt they would. The issue is getting from here to there.

Angus then speaks up: "You nailed it, Robert. Who are these people and how deep do they go? The questions that keep coming up in my mind are these – is Mr. Beltran mad as a hatter? I'll concede that the potential is huge. My question is just who are we dealing with? Shouldn't we answer that one question before we jump into this 'unique opportunity?'

Does anyone in this room have a connection at the State Department? Do we have anyone that we can talk to to get a feel for who we're dealing with? I would also like to know how Fidel is feeling."

"Ha," remembered Robert, "my sister works at the State Department in DC. Why didn't I think of that?"

"Gentlemen," spoke Philip, "it should be noted that anytime we speak to anyone beyond these walls we should be guarded. Our queries should be couched in vague, unspecific terms."

"Call me paranoid," added Angus, "but the four of us just landed in Miami having come, without permission, from Cuba. I think all of us should be careful while we're snooping around, and what about Captain Rolf, what's his story if someone taps him on the shoulder?"

Philip then helped put their minds at ease in this regard: "When I met with the captain regarding the crew's gratuity I had a 'theoretical conversation' with him regarding this very subject. I suggested that, theoretically, we were going from Key West to the Cayman Islands, but the autopilot malfunctioned and didn't recognize that Cuba was in the direct path. When we unexpectedly came upon Cuba we were joined by three Cuban navy patrol boats, and later boarded by Cuban authorities. We discussed our mistake with them and watched as they did a cursory search of the ship. We then sat down with them and had coffee and enjoyed a bit of conversation. They were gracious and in a short time we were back underway. Our confidence in the ships navigation system now in question we decided to forgo our trip to the Cayman Islands and return directly to Miami. I suggested that he might have a technician take a look at the autopilot."

"And will this be the captain's story?" wondered Angus.

"Captain Rolf is a principled man, theoretically. I managed to assuage the captain's indignation with what would be considered an outrageous tip, but it was the 3 Cuban cigars that brought the deal home."

"You didn't get where you are for no good reason, Philip Fortney," allowed Angus only half joking.

"OK, let's summarize," began Philip, "I think we all agree that we shouldn't dismiss this Cuban situation outright. Byron, I acknowledge your concerns regarding resources and when the time comes we'll address that. Robert, will you make contact with your sister at State? And remember; keep your comments as vague as you can."

Byron then offered what would surely be helpful information: "I have here the actual names of the Cuban's on the boat. I wrote them down when we were on the boat figuring with all those vowels we might not remember them with the passage of time. Here is the list:

- Ms. Liliana Beltran, no specific title, interpreter, UN delegation, diplomatic passport
- Ramon Nicolas Beltran, close advisor to Fidel,
- General Roberto Fulgencio Cienfuegos, Revolutionary Army Airborne Brigade for the district of Havana,
- Enrique Maduro Fuente, Philip's friend and advisor to Castro family.

"That's good work, Robert" said Philip.

Robert then advised: "Fella's, I'm going to be in California all the rest of the week. We should probably not wait until I get back before we start this investigation. Ms. Beltran will be here in 2 weeks."

Angus then suggested: "Robert, if you will provide your sister with these names I will arrange to meet her on the northeast corner of the Mall in DC, Wednesday at 4 PM. This is beginning to sound like a real thriller."

"Alright, my sister's name is Naomi and I'll call her tonight. I'll ask her to meet you and I'll get what color dress she will be wearing."

"Well, let's all be very careful with this," advised Angus, "until we know what direction we're heading. We don't want to be put on some list over something that proves out to be a wild goose chase. Let's just be thoughtful in our actions.

Philip do you have any control over Ms. Beltran's itinerary? I'd like to set her up at the Waldorf. She may be our best source of information. I find that people's guard comes down more easily when they're surrounded with the trappings of luxury."

"I'll work on that," responded Philip.

The trappings of luxury? The Waldorf Astoria would fall comfortably into that category.

"And while we're all together," added Angus, "I know you all have your finger on the current economic situation. The Fed's numbers released at yesterday's FOMC meeting confirms to me that we are heading for real trouble. I will also admit that at this point in time I don't know what we can do about it. We are knee deep involved and there's no way to back out at this point. My suggestion is to get defensive as best you can and hope for the best. The more this situation spins out of control the more I see that train from Calgary to Vancouver. Someday I'm going to make that trip."

~ANGUS and LILIANA~
Chapter V
Park Avenue

"Willard."

"Yes, Mr. Quin"

"How long have you been the doorman here at the hotel?"

The hotel in question was the Waldorf Astoria. The Waldorf Astoria, 301 Park Ave., New York City occupies an entire city block in the heart of midtown Manhattan, between Park and Lexington Avenues and 49th and 50th Streets. And even though Angus owned a townhouse only eight blocks away he spent enough time at the Waldorf to be known on a first name basis. There was the historic Bull and Bear Bar, cited by the New York Times as one of the three greatest bars in the world. There was the Peacock Alley restaurant, and then there was the occasional tryst.

"I've been the doorman at the Waldorf for going on 22 years."

"And we've been acquainted for at least a dozen of those years, right?"

"I take your word for that, Mr. Quin; I know it's been a while."

"And every time you call me Mr. Quin I say, no, please, just Angus, right?"

"That's right, Mr. Quin."

"Willard, do you think that you will ever call me Angus?"

"You know I can't do that, Mr. Quin."

"I know, Willard. I just like to pull your chain. Do you know if Nancy is working the concierge desk today?"

"I believe she is, Mr. Quin. There she is now. She must have been on a break."

Angus slipped Willard a twenty dollar bill as he did every time he spoke to him. A door man at the Waldorf can offer invaluable assistance from time to time. Angus would invent some premise to solicit a bit of information so not to appear to gratuitous. It's the exchange of information that warrants the gratuity. It's the giver's predictable, repetitive action that greases this flow of information. And as Homer Simpson once noted: "Knowledge is power."

"Thanks, Willard, I see her there. Have a good day, Willard."

"You too, Mr. Quin."

Angus proceeded through the lobby of the hotel toward the concierge desk.

"Good morning, Nancy, how's the eggs benedict today?"

"I'm sure they're superb, Angus."

Nancy didn't hold quite so tightly to the hotel protocol. She too had known Angus for years. And by the way, eggs benedict was invented at the Waldorf by Oscar Tschirky during his 50 year career with the hotel. Mr. Tschirky also invented the Waldorf salad and Thousand Island dressing.

"Farm fresh eggs I trust?"

"Yep, brought in fresh each day from upstate somewhere."

"Nancy, I'd like for you to do me a favor. I'd like for you to arrange a nice bouquet of flowers to be sent to Ms. Birnbaum's suite. Word is she's not feeling well. How well can you feel at 87? And put on the card: Missing you at Sunday brunch, anonymous admirer, Angus. And book me a suite for four nights starting a week from Thursday – the usual fresh flowers and the satin sheets. Have them put all this on my corporate account."

There are some people who hold permanent residency at the Waldorf. Many celebrities through the years have maintained suites there. Frank Sinatra spent a million dollars a year to keep his suite at the Waldorf between 1979 and 1988. In fact some of the suites are named after their famous guests, like: the Winston Churchill, the Cole Porter, the Duke and Duchess of Windsor suite. Herbert Hoover lived in retirement at the hotel for 30 years.

"Would you like any particular flower this time, Angus?"

"No, I do like it when they arrange a lot of different kinds of flowers together. Maybe a few bunches like that."

Angus then shook Nancy's hand and held it longer than was required. He then discretely passed her a one hundred dollar bill without ever losing eye contact. Angus then made his way to the Peacock Alley restaurant situated in the heart of the lobby. Nancy's admiring eyes never left Angus until he disappeared into the Peacock.

The maître d noticed Angus at the entrance and immediately made his way toward him.

"Good morning, Mr. Quin, the usual table?"

"Yes, Arno, thank you."

And again Angus discretely passed a one hundred dollar bill to the maître d. It's important in this rare air to keep the attention of a maître d. Angus hadn't even sipped his coffee and he was down $220.

"Coffee, Mr. Quin?"

"Yes, Arno."

"Phyllis will be serving you this morning, Mr. Quin," said Arno as he nonchalantly slipped the bill into his vest pocket without a look. You know they're going to look. They must look in order to assign an accurate level of service. It's just the way the system works. Conversely, no one throws a tip into a tip jar while the bartender has his back turned.

Angus then ordered his usual Eggs Benedict and a tall orange juice. He was eating alone this morning which encouraged the many competing subjects working on his mind. The one that kept dominating lately was the vision of a Cuban woman, a woman with skin the color of light brown tobacco leaves and an inseam that took it's time reaching her shoes.

These kinds of woman fixations were not unusual for Angus, especially since his divorce 3 years ago. Women came in and out of his life the way the circus came to town – competing visions of cotton-candy, tigers and clowns, but then he folded his tent and moved on.

Angus was a trim 42 years old. If he were standing before you you might describe him as eaten-up-with-average, certainly not ugly, but nor was he particularly handsome. However, Angus did have something – call it aura, charisma, that intangible ingredient that draws people in. He moved with a sense of grace and confidence that attracted women. There was sincerity and even a vulnerability that drew them near. Even in Angus' occasional dalliance he was sincerely superficial.

"Mr. Quin," came the greeting from a dark suited man with a crew-cut.

"Yes."

"My name is Fowler, Carl Fowler. Do you mind if I sit for a moment and have a word?"

"Please, have a seat," responded Angus.

"Mr. Quin, I work for the State Department, Bureau of Consular Affairs. Your office said that I might find you here."

"What's this about," inquired Angus.

"We show that you recently signed the charter documents for a yacht named The Vegetarian Coyote. Is this true?

"Yes, that's true. Oh, Phyllis, get Mr. Fowler some coffee. I'm having the eggs benedict, will you join me? I highly recommend it."

"Oh, no, I'm not allowed, I usually just catch something at McDonalds."

"C'mon, Carl, can I call you Carl? If someone rats you out you can tell them I forced you."

"Well, I don't want to cause a scene."

"Good, Phyllis, set Mr. Fowler up with eggs benedict, coffee and juice."

"It's just that I usually don't have the time to eat a proper breakfast."

"Believe me, Carl, this will be a proper breakfast. Now, what's on your mind?"

"Well, our Miami bureau indicates that this yacht: this Meatless Coyote, traveled into Cuban waters during the time of your charter. Do you acknowledge this?"

"Yes, I do."

"You are aware that government policy prohibits travel to and from Cuba?"

"Yes, not in a specific way, but I've heard the stories over the years."

"Can you explain why your yacht was anchored close to the Cuban shore for several hours while it was in your employ?"

"Yes, I can explain what happened …"

Angus then recited almost verbatim what they had agreed upon in the office the day before.

"You know, Mr. Quin, this may be the best breakfast I have ever eaten," as Angus continued his explanation.

"Please, call me Angus."

"Your story matches that of your partner, Mr. Fortney."

"Maybe you should also ask the captain of the yacht," suggested Angus.

"The Miami office tried, but it appears that Captain Rolf Jorgens has put to sea for an extended tour of the

Mediterranean. In my experience the Miami office will at some point pay him a visit."

"Do you get a lot of yachts carrying on nefariously off the coast of Cuba, Mr. Fowler?"

"We get all manner of attempts at nefariosity, Mr. Quin, from inner tube dinghy's to sleek jet boats, and even yachts with gyroscopic stabilizers."

"I suppose you do, Carl. How about that Castro? He's been around forever. Do you think he'll last much longer?"

"Word has it that he's been hospitalized and is in serious condition. He's given over control to his brother, Raul."

"Do you think he will recover, or is this the end of the Castro era?"

"We could be seeing the end of one Castro era and the beginnings of another. These guys are two peas in a pod."

"That doesn't sound encouraging for the people of Cuba."

"Communism, socialism, what did they expect?

"So true, Carl, so we could be seeing status quo in Cuba for some time to come. And by the way, that will be $92.50 for the breakfast. Ha, just kidding."

"The breakfast was delicious, thank you. And here's an FYI: your Vegetarian yacht that had navigation problems – it was the third in as many days. And those ugly black speed boats that were parked off your port side, they weren't Cuban. They were part of a private security detail that came off of a drilling rig in the Gulf of Mexico. Teams are being formed, Angus, players are being chosen. Proceed with caution."

"Port – that's he left side of the boat when you're facing the steering wheel, right?

"Have a good day and thanks again for breakfast. I'm going to save up and bring my wife here someday."

At this Mr. Carl Fowler walked away briskly.

What a revelation. You think you're something special and then you find out that you're just one of many. It's like the feeling you got from your high school girlfriend. Normally Angus would walk some portion of the way to the office before hailing a cab but not this morning.

"Willard, get me a cab would you please. I'm going to step into the men's facility for a moment."

"He'll be waiting, Mr. Quin.'

Angus stared at the wall behind the urinal. As if he didn't have enough to worry about with the collapse of the world's economy he now has to figure out this Cuban Rubik's cube. It was difficult enough when he thought they were the only players. Now he finds out they were one of at least three – *'Gulf of Mexico drilling rig, this is an obvious energy play, or is anything really obvious? Not to mention this Cuban seductress, Liliana.'* She's not something you want to be thinking about while standing at a urinal.

"You OK, Mr. Quin," said Willard shaking Angus from his extended meditative state of urination. "You're cab is ready."

"Yes, thank you Willard, I'm on my way."

"I thought you'd been hijacked by bandits, Mr. Quin."

"Mental bandits, Willard."

"Greenwich and Murray," were the directions Willard gave the cabbie.

Fortney, Quin and Hurst, Financial, occupied a single third floor in the financial district, a single floor that had become cramped with its 50 plus occupants dialing and sweating. Angus no longer had to dial for dollars or make a daily quota, and you would never see him sweat. However; lately, the cheese was beginning to bind.

This morning the news was no better for the financial markets. People in the office were gathered around the TV listening as the commentator read off the latest dribble of bad news:

> *'Freddie Mac was fined $3.8 million today by the Federal Election Commission as a result of illegal campaign contributions, much of it to members of the United States House Committee on Financial Services which oversees Freddie Mac.'*

"Philip, can I have a word? I just had an interesting conversation with a Mr. Fowler. I understand he spoke to you as well."

"Yes, he was waiting for me this morning as I opened the door."

"Well, thanks to your forethought at least we offered a consistent story. Apparently a similar story was given by at least two other yachts within days of our meeting. And did he tell you that the three "guard" boats were not Cuban? Maybe we should send the captain a full box of cigars."

"It's an interesting irony, don't you think, Angus? Cuba rising from the ashes as America goes down in flames."

"Philip, we need to stay focused on our own little island. Last night I studied the situation once again and I've come up with a course of action. Let's get Byron in here and I'll lay it out.

Byron, can you put a number on the firms total dollar exposure to the market. I mean exposure of any color or stripe?"

"I can have it within an hour, responded Byron."

"Byron, I want you to bring me the best trader you've got on the floor and have him bring a pad and a pencil."

"Sure, I'll be right back."

"Philip, this dribble of news we're hearing day by day is going to get worse and we need to establish a plan of protection as quickly as we can."

"Angus, I've always admired your ability to read the tea leaves, what do you suggest?"

"Angus, you remember Harold Schwartz?" said Byron as he returned. Harold is as close to the markets as you would ever want to be."

"Sure, Harold, this is what I want you to do – I want you to put together a package of diverse short plays equal to the firm's total exposure. Byron will give you that number when he gets it. I want you to put aside whatever it is you're doing and focus on this. Do you understand? I want you to have a list of potential shorts by the end of the day that we can all go over. Can you do that, Harold? I want shorts on housing stocks, financial firms with large exposure to subprime, and any other angle you might propose including futures and options. Do you get my drift, Harold?"

"I certainly do, Mr. Quin."

What Angus was proposing was a total hedge of the firm's entire financial risk going forward. A hedge is not just a row of bushes, you know. We've all heard the term: 'to hedge your bet.' Technically, in the world of finance, a hedge is established when you take an equal, yet opposite position to that which you already own. If you owned 100 shares of IBM you are said to be – *long* IBM. If you were to simultaneously hold a *short* position in an equal amount of IBM, that is to say: place a bet that its share price would fall, you would in fact be totally hedged against any market action up or down. You would be in neutral. That money that would be lost if the market fell on your *long*

IBM position would be made back equally on the *short* position – neutral, no market exposure.

The foundation was crumbling and Angus intuitively knew it. There are people who see minutia and there are those who see the big picture. It's just the way our brains come organized. Minutia people are very much necessary, but there also needs to be people who can see through the clutter. You wouldn't put a trim carpenter, a person who deals in sixteenths of an inch all day long, in charge of building your house. Their tendency is to focus too narrowly. You would end up with a failed house with beautiful trim carpentry.

"Philip, we've managed to run under the radar for all these years. We're a boutique player that stayed out of the spotlight. We're not a Bear Stearns or a Merrill Lynch. Maybe when it hits the fan there will be enough big players to keep the gendarmerie busy and we can survive. There are going to be trillions lost before this is over and Washington, with its failed social engineering polices, will not take the blame. Irony, indeed, the word doesn't begin to cover it. As Cuba tries to claw its way out of a failed socialist system, America is doing all it can to fill that void."

"Angus, this man, Fowler, what was your sense of him?"

"My sense is that he knew more than he told. First he was coy, then I was coy, then, just before he scurried away full of eggs benedict he suggested that there were two other boats there with similar purpose, and the three guard boats were not Cuban at all. But then he says: teams are being formed, players being picked, proceed with caution. What he didn't say was – stop what you're doing or we'll throw you in irons. No, he said – proceed with caution. Philip, it feels like we are being maneuvered into place from multiple angles, and I'm beginning to feel like an amateur that just stepped off the bus – and I don't like it.

I'm leaving in the morning to meet Robert's sister down in DC."

"Angus, let's play this out. Let's see where it leads leaving our options open as best we can. I have a feeling that events outside of our control are going to dictate our actions going forward. In the meantime it won't hurt to gather as much information as we can. I think your hedge strategy is appropriate. We'll review what Harold comes up with and we'll try and have it implemented by market close tomorrow."

By February of 2007 the subprime industry had collapsed with several major subprime lenders declaring bankruptcy. Central banks worldwide would coordinate efforts to increase liquidity for the first time since September 11, 2001. Central banks all over the globe were beginning to show panic. The United States Federal Reserve injected a combined 43 billion USD into the system in attempts to maintain liquidity. This followed by the European Central Bank with 156 billion euros. Later the Bank of Japan would toss in 1 trillion Yen adding to the offerings of the central banks of Australia and Canada. The subprime disease was spreading worldwide.

Not everyone read the leaves the same way. The leaders of Lehman Brothers would instead double down; they fired their internal critics and spent billions of dollars on real estate investments that would within a year become worthless.

Internal critics, how bothersome they can be. Your wife says: honey, better take out the trash before the rats take over, and you say: nag, nag.

~ANGUS and LILIANA~
Chapter VII
Cherry Blossoms

Angus caught a cab to Penn Station for the 11 AM train which would put him in DC at three o'clock. Another cab ride would put him at the mall in plenty of time for his 4 o'clock with Robert's sister. Naomi would be sporting a pastel pink dress, presumably to compete with the blooming cherry blossoms. In the spring – late March, early April, and only for a few days, some 1,700 cherry blossom trees lining the tidal basin burst forth in bloom. It's quite a display if you're into that sort of floral hyperbole.

Washington DC in the spring of 2007 was not, however, focused on the timing of the cherry blossoms, but instead on the blooming global financial meltdown. Elsewhere, in Florida, where the real estate excesses were the greatest, the bubble was about to burst. In a matter of months all construction would come to a complete halt in Florida and home prices there, and soon everywhere, would begin a precipitous fall to levels that would put many out on the ledge.

Everything looks so clear in hindsight, but in that moment when you're an average Joe sitting in front of the TV eating your key lime pie, it's just another Tuesday. Sarasota condo prices are increasing by $10,000 a month with people in Minnesota being put on waiting lists to purchase sight unseen. Isn't that normal? Then, on

Wednesday, you're laid off and it's years before you work again. Certainly no one in Cuba was looking north across the Florida straits and thinking: 'Pobrecito Gringo.' Ironically, Cuba would be effected least of all the countries of the world. How much more misery could be heaped onto this already beleaguered island.

Nobody wants this on their resume – not on their watch. President George Bush is taking preliminary steps to help ease the crisis while presidential wannabes are giving speeches and claiming to have all the answers. Certain members of congress whose finger prints are all over these subprime schemes are bobbing and weaving and trying to cover their political futures, all too smart by half.

And into this comes cherry blossoms. Mother Nature's way of saying: I'll see your global meltdown and I'll raise you – pink blossoms.

"Naomi," called Angus, "is that you?"

"No, not Naomi," said yet another woman wearing pastel pink.

Angus sat down on the bench closest to the point of their rendezvous. It wasn't quite 4 o'clock. Looking out over the falling petals and clamoring tourist, half wearing pastel pink, Angus almost got to a point of serenity, almost, in a multi-tasking sort of way. And so he sat.

At 4:05 a woman approached Angus as he sat on the bench.

"You must be Angus," said the woman, "I'm sorry I'm late. Robert described you perfectly."

"Please don't tell me how he did that," responded Angus.

"Oh, he was kind and accurate."

"I wonder sometimes if those two things can be compatible."

"They are compatible in your case, Angus. At any rate, Robert gave me a mission and although he did his best to downplay I see Agatha Christie all over this. However, I won't pump you for details."

"I'm sorry it was such a short notice, and Robert wanted to come but as you know he had to be on the left coast. So, here we are among the falling cherry blossom petals. There are worse places to be on a spring afternoon."

"Well, I don't mind so much. It gets me out of my usual boring work and into research which is what I enjoy. And, I have some contacts on the Caribbean desk. So, you want to get right into it?"

"I'm ready to accept your report giving it my full attention – let fly."

"Robert gave me a list of names starting with Ramon Nicolas Beltran. Sr. Beltran is well connected. He comes from old Cuban Sugar money. His father was part of the Central Hershey sugar mill that was constructed east of Havana around 1920 by Milton Hershey the chocolate bar magnate. Apparently Mr. Hershey had a life outside of Pennsylvania.

Ramon was a risk taker from an early age and was involved in Cuban auto racing – who knew there was such a thing. Apparently they used to race cars through the streets of Havana. Anyway, through personal insinuation and Fidel's need for moneyed connections Ramon became a fixture at the court of Fidel. There was a shared penchant for risk taking and apparently similar political ideologies, although his ideologies may have been held for expedience sake. One can easily adopt philosophy while in the presence of a dictator. He's never been a real player and has always kept a low profile."

"Is there any information about Ramon's relationship with Raul?"

"That relationship doesn't appear to be as warm, but there isn't a lot in the record in that regard."

"Is there an indication that Ramon has shifted his ideologies over the years?"

"No, nothing in the record."

"Do you have any indication that Ramon has a following in his own right?"

"There's no information in that regard. Of course people don't really seek a following above ground in Cuba. This has not been a healthy thing to do historically."

"How many children does Ramon have?"

"We have him with only one daughter and his wife is deceased."

"Good, who's next?"

"Well, next up is that very daughter – Liliana Beltran. Ms. Beltran is 36 years old, educated in Spain and oddly enough, Cornell University, with a degree in engineering. She holds a diplomatic passport and has worked in the past as an interpreter for visiting Cuban delegations at the UN."

"Is Ms. Beltran married?"

"Ms. Beltran is a widow. Her young husband was killed in Africa on one of Raul's military adventures. She has no children that we know of. There are a couple of bullets on Liliana's file. In recent years she has become more of a vocal force for normalization of trade. And there was a comment on a local Havana chat board which said: '*Cuba does not need nuclear weapons, we have Liliana!*' It was not clear whether this was a commentary on her political prowess or her striking good looks.

Ms. Beltran, like most Cubans I suppose, has a penchant for Salsa music and frequents the nightclubs of Havana including one called "The Cadillac." Salsa music at "The Cadillac" in Havana, it has a ring to it – it sounds better than league bowling Thursday nights, which is what I'm facing. We have to remember that she comes from a connected family and she has been connected her entire life, so her speech and her movements would be given more deference than the ordinary Cuban. We've never gone deep on Ms. Beltran. She never seemed to be a real player."

"Has Ms. Beltran worked as an engineer in Cuba?"

"She has spent time in various Central American countries studying their railway systems and bargaining for used rail equipment. She's been to Panama, Costa Rica, El Salvador and the like. As far as we know she's not sat in a cubical type engineering job; not that there are many opportunities like that in Cuba."

"Trains?"

"Yes, you know that Cuba operated the first railroad in Latin America way back in the early 1800's. It was from a grant from the queen of Spain. There is track running from one end of the country to the other, though now it's dilapidated and mostly unusable. It was part of the booming sugar industry that Milton Hershey brought along to deliver sugar cane to the mills. Trains in Latin America have always been about bringing the crop to market."

"OK, who's next on Robert's list?"

"Next we have General Roberto Fulgencio Cienfuegos, Army Airborne for the district of Havana. The General is just one of many of the type – old guard, been around since the beginning of the revolution. His loyalties to the Castro's have never been questioned. He was hospitalized last year with cancer treatment and appears to have recovered, probably the least interesting on the list."

"OK, who's up next?"

"Next is Enrique Maduro Fuente. Sr. Fuente is another, not unlike Ramon, that has been close to the Castro's for many years. Not military, not intelligence, per se, but more on the order of diplomat. Unlike Ramon, however, Enrique grew up on the peasant side of the tracks. He was part of Fidel's entourage from the early days of the revolution. It's said that it was Enrique that was the emissary between Fidel and Batista in the last days before Fidel rode into town. It was Enrique that convinced Batista that he should leave Cuba. He is another old player in the Cuban patchwork."

"Naomi, how is it that Robert has kept you under wraps all this time. You are a true secret weapon. Agatha Christie would be proud to have you on her team. Tell me about traveling to Cuba. I know we're not supposed to do it, but I hear about people going down there."

"You can get into Cuba if you have some official reason, or if it is a family visit, or for some journalistic reason, or if your activities are part of a foundation to benefit Cuba. The list continues."

"So if a private plane were to fly into Cuba, say from the Cayman Islands, would you be arrested at the airport?"

"No, but when you go through customs at the Cuban airport they are going to want to stamp your passport. And the problem will arise when you come back to the states with that stamp. Questions will be asked."

"Angus, I don't know what you guys are into, but I can tell you when it comes to Cuba – nothing is new, and everything is in motion. It's been that way since the lid was clamped on back in the sixties."

"Well, I'm going to see if I can get back to the city before midnight. I'm going to tell Robert that his sister was a real asset to our plans that don't exist. Thanks again, Naomi."

"You're welcome, Angus. You guys should proceed with caution."

As Angus made his way in the cab to the train station he couldn't help but hear again that now familiar phrase: *'proceed with caution.'* Not: *'stop what you're doing',* or, *'hey, you're punching above your weight',* or, *'what, are you guys nuts?'* But again – *'proceed with caution.'* It was probably just a coincidence of the turning of a phrase. Angus resisted the notion that this was some galactic conspiracy aimed at nudging them forward.

And then there was the train ride: a $300 first class ticket on the Acela, probably $150 without the mocha latte option. Almost four hours of trying to catch a wink or two. He could have chosen the Gulfstream option roundtrip at around about $1,700, gas only, but that wouldn't have saved any time, and anyway, it just didn't seem right. This wasn't exactly a Miami to NYC run. But mostly, Angus never passed up an opportunity to ride the train.

'Why did she have to mention trains?' thought Angus as he peered out the window into the passing darkness. *'Wasn't there enough to consider? Why couldn't it have been animal husbandry, or origami? I wonder if she knows that the Panama Railway is the oldest operating intercontinental railroad in the world.'*

The other thing that bothered Angus was what Philip had said: *"I have a feeling that events outside of our control are going to dictate our actions going forward."* This kind of passive wait-and-see attitude chaffed with Angus. Angus was more the type that liked to get out in front of events, create his own version of the future rather than being overrun by surprise. The wheels were turning – some logical, some not so much.

"No, Teterboro, it's an airport in the Meadowlands in New Jersey. Maybe three days. Just tell the cabbie to take you to the main terminal at Teterboro and I'll see you there at noon. OK? We'll have a great time and you can buy some things when we get there. OK? Good. See you soon.

Paul," said Angus on the phone to his Gulfstream pilot, "make a plan for Miami. Can you make that happen around noon today? Good. We'll be gone maybe three days. Bring charts for the Caribbean. And Paul, we won't need a stewardess."

This was Thursday morning and with the hedge in place Angus' mind was not so focused on the subprime crisis. Whether this was a good thing was yet to be determined. What had taken over Angus' mind was Liliana Beltran. According to her time frame she would be in NYC in ten days. What then? What questions would she have? What answers would Angus have? There was still too much unknown. From Angus' townhouse he continued his phone calls.

"Philip, I'm taking the G2 to Miami. I spent yesterday afternoon with Robert's sister in DC and I'm not sure I have much more to go on. Everything she came up with was guessable, nothing you could base an opinion on. I'll try and check back in, but I may be off the reservation for a few days."

"Angus, I do feel more at ease with our hedge in place, but our expenses don't stop. There will be a lid on any revenues as long as the hedge is in place."

"Philip, I would take 25% of the total hedge and double it as a naked short position. I'll call Harold and discuss it with him if you're OK with it. I feel strongly about this, Philip. Others on the street are reading this as a buying opportunity – they are wrong."

The news on the TV continues the dribble:

> *'According to CNN Money, states the commentator, business sources report lenders made $640 billion in subprime loans in 2006, nearly twice the level three years earlier; subprime loans amounted to about 20 percent of the nation's mortgage lending and about 17 percent of home purchases; financial firms and hedge funds likely own more than $1 trillion in securities backed by subprime mortgages; about 13 percent of subprime loans are now delinquent, more than five times the delinquency rate for home loans to borrowers with top credit; more than 2 percent of subprime loans had foreclosure proceedings started in the fourth quarter.'*

At 112 KIAS (knots indicated airspeed) the front wheel of the Gulfstream G280 came off the ground and the nose began to rise – it's a beautiful thing. Many people live their whole life and never ride in an airplane. Others will live their whole life without ever seeing an airplane. Few people in this world will ever ride in a private jet, let alone a Gulfstream G280. Gulfstream is to private jets what Cartier is to diamonds. The G280 can cruise at over 500 mph and can carry 10 passengers with berthing for 5, which should make it very comfortable for 3.

"Angus."

"Yes, Lilly."

"How long will it take to get to Miami on a plane like this?"

"About ten minutes."

"Really!"

"No, not really, it will be a few hours."

"Angus."

"Yes, Rose."

"Does the pilot always drive the plane?"

"Yes, he will always be flying the plane."

"For three hours?

"Yep, for three whole hours."

"You know, Angus," said Lilly, "it took a lot of scrubbing to get that zebra off my body. I'm not sure I got it out of all the cracks. Do you think you could do a spot check for me? You know I can't see everywhere."

"Me too, Angus," said Rose. "I feel like there is still some of that bobcat, or cheetah, still hiding in my cracks. What kind of animal was I, Angus? I think I can hear him growling sometimes, still."

"Well, you were certainly no cougar. You looked a little like a squirrel. I'll have to take an in-depth look; maybe my memory will be jogged. So far we've done trains, now planes – we'll have to work on automobiles."

"Don't forget boats, Angus," chimed Lily, "we haven't been on a boat with you have we Rose."
"As long as it's not like that Titanic boat," added Rose.
"And I don't feel like we finished that train thing, Angus," added Rose, "maybe we can get back to that someday. Would you tell us a train story on our way to Miami?"

Angus was looking for answers, and he wasn't going to wait around for random events to dictate his course. Nor was he going to let a potential petty State Dept. beef about a passport stamp slow him down. Why do you have lawyers on staff anyway?

To stumble around as a single gringo through the streets of little Havana didn't sound like a good idea, so, Lily and Rose would provide some additional cover, and, they were pretty good company.

After three hours of interesting flight the trio arrived at Miami International airport, gateway to the south. It was then on to South Beach and the Setai Hotel. At the Setai your reservation includes limo service from the airport. And for the Ocean Suite one bedroom you will pay $1,700 per night, and this is the low side for the Setai.

"Oooh, Angus, this is a nice hotel," Rose said, as she admired the view from their suite.

There was the Atlantic Ocean to the east, Biscayne Bay to the west, and Miami nightlife just beyond, including Little Havana, or *La Pequeña Habana*. Little Havana is famously the cultural and political capital of Cuban Americans, and the neighborhood is the center of the Cuban exile community. Not to mention the food, the music and hopefully – information. In Little Havana Angus would be as close to Cuba as a person can be without actually making the trip.

"Girls, it's four o'clock. I would like for you to go downstairs and buy a couple of party outfits. I mean the dresses the shoes, the, the, hair, whatever it takes. Tonight we are going to party like a Cuban."

"Oh, Angus, can we make it loud, can we make it Salsa?"

"Make it Salsa, but make it by nine, OK?"

"Girls, when you get to the lobby I want you to send the concierge up to the room, OK? Here's the key and here's my card. Call if you need something."

"OK, Angus," agreed Lilly and Rose, "we'll be back by nine and you be prepared."

"Don't worry about me, girls, just send the concierge up."

Angus was trying to plan for anything and everything. The one thing that is common to *anything* is cash.

When the concierge came to the room Angus wrote the Hotel a check for cash in the amount of three thousand dollars. Angus instructed the cash be in hundreds and fifties and that each thousand be placed in a small separate envelope. In addition to the cash Angus made out a personal check in the amount of $3,000 with the payee left blank and on the memo line he wrote: "Foundation for Cuba's Children." Maybe there was such a foundation. This check he placed in one of the envelopes containing ten $100 bills and on the outside of the envelope Angus marked an 'X.'

Angus used money like any other tool: a hammer, a saw. Like the cowboy that wore a two gun rig Angus didn't want to get shot for lack of shooting back.

"Give me room 523. Paul, the girls and I are going out tonight and could be out late. Things could get fluid so I'd like for you to have the plane ready to go at any time as we discussed. Right, so have it stocked with groceries and drink, you know the usual crap. Good. Have a nice dinner. We won't even leave the hotel until nine. Just don't turn your phone off. Thanks."

And the TV droned on:

> *Bear Stearns & Co informs investors in two of its CDO hedge funds, the High-Grade Structured Credit Strategies Enhanced Leverage Fund and the High-Grade Structured Credit Fund that it is halting redemptions.*

Maybe a nap would be appropriate ...

"Angus," called Lily and Rose has they burst into the room."

"What time is it, girls?"

"It's about 8:30. Well, how did we do?"

"Holy mother of Carmen Miranda! I had no idea. You look like toppings for a banana split. The dresses, the hair, and look at those shoes. Girls, I am overwhelmed."

At this the girls took a couple of laps around the suite in a conga line celebration.

"Girls, let's have a drink before we go. We need to have a talk about tonight. Mostly, what we are going to do is have a good time; however, there may be times when the truth gets lost between us and the rest of the world. What I mean is that there may be times when I come out with some thick bull shit. What I want you to do is go along with this BS as if it were the gospel truth. Also, it may be that we have to take on additional passengers for our journey, and this journey may even include leaving

Miami tonight. So, do we understand? This is going to be a fun night that could be full of surprises. Just follow my lead. If I say I am the king of Jamaica and you are my queen's just play along as if it were the gospel truth.

Also, I'd like for each of you to take 3 $100 bills and put one in each side of your bra and the other in your panties."

"Angus, we're not wearing bras, explained Rose."

"Well, put all 3 in your panties then. You are wearing panties aren't you?"

"Yes, technically. This is starting out to be a little kinky, Angus," thought Lily out loud.

"These are simply precautionary measures. Just remember what you've got and where you've got it."

"Jew got it, meng. Show him Lily."

Lily then pulls a hat out of a box.

"This is for you, Angus. We asked the clerk what a Cuban gangsta would wear and she brought this out."

"Cuban gangster? How do I look? I may need something to pull down over my eyes before the night is through."

"It's you, Angus," they responded in unison.

"Muy bueno, vamos chicas, vamos a bailar.

Angus knew just enough Spanish to get himself into trouble. And so out the door they went. To stand out on South Beach is not easy, but this trio was looking quite festive.

Angus said to the cabbie: "Sir, we are hungry. Will you please show us a restaurant that reflects all that is good in Little Havana? We want flavor, we want culture, we want kindness and understanding."

"I could maybe get you 3 out of 4, 2 for sure, will that do?"

"Do it," shouted Rose.

"And later we may need forgiveness," added Lily.

And so the party pulled up in front of La Carretas on SW 8th St., AKA Calle Ocho in Little Havana – this just down from the Woodlawn Park Cemetery.

"I like this place," said the cabbie.

"What's your name, amigo," asked Angus.

"I am Rejito at your service."

"Rejito, will you be working in the area tonight?"

"Yes, I'll be working all night tonight. Here's my card. You call me."

"Rejito, this is a down payment on the rest of the evening," and Angus gave him a crisp $100 bill. "You will hear from us again in an hour. In fact, be here in an hour."

"Gracias, I'll be here at 10:10."

The hungry part was no joke. It was late in the evening and they hadn't had a bite since snacking on the plane. The menu was pure Cuban comfort food. Angus ordered a Cuban sandwich and had it cut into thirds.

"So this is the famous Cuban sandwich, girls. It's a combination of ham, roast pork, Swiss cheese, mustard, and pickles on a Cuban roll. I've heard of these but this is my first."

"When in Rome," says Lily. "It's tasty, but I wouldn't call it great."

"It tastes like a ham and cheese," said Rose, "I'll take a Rueben over this any day."

Angus ordered a Calle Ocho Old Fashioned and the girls decided on a Canita:

Calle Ocho Old Fashioned

2 oz. aged Rum
.25 oz. demerara syrup
3 dashes tobacco bitters
garnish: tobacco leaf

Canita – in a bamboo cup

1 oz. fresh guarapo
.5 oz. fresh lime juice
.25 oz. honey syrup
1.5 oz. white rum
garnish: sugarcane stick

Then it was down to some serious eats that were shared by all:

Black bean soup
Tamale wrapped in corn husk
Shrimp Pineapple "tostones"- Fried Green Plantains
        filled with Shrimp in a Pineapple and
        Cilantro Creole Sauce
"Vaca Frita" – Shredded Beef Grilled with Onions
        and Cuban Mojo, served with Moros Rice
        and Sweet Plantains.
And for dessert it was Double Yolk Caramel Flan
        and Bread Pudding

As Angus paid the check he inquired of the waiter, who was now staring at another crisp $100 bill: "I am looking for a man but I don't remember his name. He frequents the Salsa clubs and he often goes back and forth to Havana. He's a really good dancer. Would you know who I'm talking about?"

"I think I do," responded the waiter. It might be Treenie. He hangs out at the Ball and Chain."

"Thank you so much," said Angus.

"Nice hat."

"Oh, thanks, my two sisters picked it out for me."

"Angus."

"Yes, Rose."

"Who is this Treenie?"

"I don't have a clue, I've never met him. I figured if I describe the kind of person that I need someone might come to mind that matched the description."

"You are a deliciously devious person, Angus Quin," said Lily.

"Please, call me Angus."

"OK, Angus, where to now?"

"Well, unless I miss my bet, we should find Rejito parked outside about now. Are you girls ready to Latin boogie down?"

"Angus," responded Lily, "my legs are full of such tension that if I don't boogie soon I'm going to take off like a rocket."

"You can put me down like that as well, Angus," agreed Rose. "And I'm so full I'm afraid my bread pudding will soon be soiling my $100 bills."

"Hey, Rejito, you remembered."

"Yes, I am here for you."

"Rejito, I am told there is a place called "The Ball and Chain," do you know it?"

"Yes, it's not far from here. It's a place for Cuban Salsa and Jazz music."

As they made their way to the "Ball and Chain" Rejito provided some history:

"This club is very famous with a long history. When the Jews lived here back in the 30's and 40's, before it became Little Havana, there were many great names that played at the "Ball and Chain": Billie Holiday, Count Basie, Chet Baker. It was shut down for years but now it's back. A lot of characters there now."

"Rejito, we are a lot of characters right here in your backseat. I am Angus and this is Lily and Rose. Rejito, do you know a person named Treenie?"

"Yes, I know Treenie. He's one of the characters I spoke of. You may find him there tonight."

"Would you say that this Treenie was a trustworthy individual?"

"As far as it goes, amigo. You know everyone has some larceny in them when you back them against the wall. We're all swimming in the same water, you know? I think that if you keep him away from the wall he's OK."

"Rejito, you just described every person working on Wall Street. One more question: are there many here that return to Cuba regularly?"

"They may go once a year to visit family if they are lucky, others more often if they have some purpose that they can explain to the authorities. Some even sneak back by various means. It's a mixed bag for sure."

"Do you go back, Rejito?"

"No, amigo, my mother is gone and my father died in prison in Cuba."

"Sorry, Rejito, do we still have some credit on that C-note?"

"Yes, you call me."

"Good, thanks for your help," as Angus passed him another $50. Angus believed in paying for information. It's a Wall Street tradition.

The music could be heard from the curb and the girls were beginning to jump. By 10:30 PM things were beginning to pop and Angus, Lily and Rose looked like they were going to fit right in – more so Lily and Rose. Whatever Angus lacked in Salsa style he could more than make up in bull shit.

"So let's get off the curb, Angus. Let's do this thing at the Ball and Chain," pleaded the girls.

"I feel like Janice Joplin," declared Lily.

The air was thick with all manner of scents, sounds, fragrances and substances. The music was loud with the constant back-beat that makes your hips want to move in an unfamiliar rotation. *Or should they be going side to side thought Angus?* Not to worry, no one would be focusing on Angus' hips while he was anywhere near Lily and Rose. The flowers were in their element, at least one of their elements.

"Girls, maybe you'd like to release some of that tension out there while I find us a table. Keep this in mind – I'm looking for a guy named Treenie. If you hear the name maybe you can steer him to me. I'll order us a few Mojitos."

"Gotcha, Angus, we're on the case," assured Lily, as she stood with one hand on her lean hip, her taut body was now in constant motion, even when standing still.

Among the many things that Angus liked about these girls was that they were savvy, they could take a role and play it with an intuitiveness that is rare. Angus didn't have to spend ten minutes giving specific directives with reasons and back story. He could throw it out there and they would run with it.

"Three Mojitos, por favor," shouted Angus over the horns and bongos.

"Coming right up," responded the server.

A Mojito is a traditional Cuban highball that consists of five ingredients: white rum, sugar, lime juice, sparkling water, and mint.

Angus settled in and surveyed the room. What a scene is this? *'What a man gotta come to when he loses five years.'* This he spoke to himself in his favorite Al Pacino movie voice from "Carlito's Way." *'Was that Pachanga walking up the stairs?'* Some of the scenes from "Scarface" were shot not far from here. Angus was getting close to Cuba.

'This – A chiropractor's dream,' thought Angus as he watched Lily and Rose dancing together. *'Women can do this,'* Angus thought; *'women can dance together with no worries.'* Anyway the girls would be years coming down off this trip. But then, just as he was getting comfortable in his seat …

"C'mon, Angus," chimed the girls, as they stood writhing with their hands outstretched toward him showing that sense of entitlement that women get when it comes to dancing. They always feel that they are entitled to have you out on the floor making a fool of yourself no matter how much you protest.

"No, really, I'm a professional dancer on vacation," he protested, but to no avail. They would not be denied. No woman will ever be denied, so a true man will just suck it up and expose himself for what he truly is – a hunk a hunk of burning love! When things become inevitable it's best to stand and bring it, and not in a subdued way, but instead in an Elvis at the Roxbury way. This is what Angus did. Damn the chiropractors, damn the taffy in the dentist's office, it was time to wear these girls down. When you're more than 50 miles from your primary residence you can act the fool.

After twenty minutes of competitive Salsa dancing Angus' mind began to drift toward Advil. Rose had been tapped away by another player and it was time to set Lily loose as well. It was a target rich environment for them for sure. Angus returned to the table and sucked down his Mojito and ordered another.

Ten minutes later Lily appeared at the table with a friend.

"Angus, this is Treenie, Treenie, this is Angus."

"Treenie, have a seat," said Angus, "how about a Mojito?"

"Sure, I'll have a Mojito."

Treenie then passes his business card to Angus.

Angus reads: 'Treenie – Professional Dancer – Call me when the music starts.'

"So, Treenie, you are a professional dancer."

 You're quite the dancer yourself, Sr. Angus," offered Treenie.

"Well, Treenie, as you could see, dancing is second nature to me. Or maybe third nature, could even be fourth nature."

"You're heading toward the right nature, Sr. Angus."

"Say, did you grow up on a cattle farm? Is that where you got this name, Angus?"

"Actually, Treenie, Angus is a traditional Irish, Scottish name. So you are a professional dancer, Treenie?"

"I have made some money dancing. But it's not an option with me, I have to dance whether I make money at it or not."

"Treenie just got back from Cuba, Angus," offered Lily, as Rose collapsed in her chair at the table.

"Really," wondered Angus. "I thought we weren't supposed to go to Cuba. How can you do that, Treenie?"

"I have my ways."

"Do you dance when you go to Cuba? Do they have places like this in Cuba?"

"They have clubs there. Wherever I am I dance. Hey, you guys with the government?"

"No, Treenie man," assured Angus. "When you were in Havana did you ever go to a club called "The Cadillac?"

"I never said I went to Havana, but I know of The Cadillac club. It's a well know club in Havana. You got a lot of questions, meng. I think I need to dance some more."

"Treenie, you can relax, we mean no harm, we're just tourists. However, I have been authorized to spend say $100 if you would answer a couple more questions."

"Who authorized you?" asked Treenie, still inching backward toward the dance floor.

"OK, Treenie, I'm going to level with you. I am the personal representative of Bill Clinton and I'm here to find out a few things regarding Cuba. I just have a few more questions."

"Who's Bill Clinton?"

"Bill Clinton, the former President of the United States?"

"I knew that. OK, Sr. Angus, you have caught me at a vulnerable moment in my financial history. Show me the money."

"Good, Lily, see if you can scramble up a few more Mojitos. You see, Treenie," as Angus pushed three $100 bills toward Treenie's side of the table, "President Clinton understands that information is a valuable commodity and when all that money started going to Haiti because of the earthquake he felt that Cuba too had suffered. Why not Cuba, he says."

"Haiti had an earthquake?"

"They will, Treenie, soon enough," as Lily and Rose look puzzlingly at each other.

"Treenie, when were you in Havana last?"

Treenie looked at the three bills and asked: "Are these three bills intended for me?"

"They are yours, Treenie, if you'll hang with us for a while."

Treenie slowly staked the bills then held one to the light.

"President Clinton needs your help, Treenie. Look at the faces of these two girls. Are these the sort of faces that could deceive? OK, that's a rhetorical question that you don't have to answer, but really you can relax. Lily, are the Mojitos coming?"

Treenie then pocketed the bills and said: "OK, what you need to know?"

"When were you last in Havana?"

"I was there three weeks ago."

"When you were there did you visit "The Cadillac" club?

"Yes, I was there. I go there and a couple of other clubs when I'm in Havana. Are you taping this conversation?"

"No, Treenie, have you ever heard the name: Liliana Beltran?"

"Sure, everyone in Havana has heard of Liliana."

"What do you know of her, Treenie?"

"She's got connections, she's beautiful, and she loves Salsa dancing."

"Have you ever danced with Liliana?"

"No."

"Treenie, I have a gift, and that gift is that I can look at a person and know whether I can trust that person. I believe that I can trust you, Treenie."

"And this gift has never failed you?"

"I trust that people, almost without exception, will act in their own best interest." Angus then pushed one of the envelopes toward Treenie that he had marked with an 'X.' "Look inside, Treenie."

Peering inside Treenie looked at the now seven one hundred dollar bills along with the check with the memo that read: "Foundation for Cuba's Children."

"Treenie, I need to get that check to Liliana Beltran on behalf of President Bill Clinton. Whatever else is in that envelope could be yours. Will you help me? That's a cool grand, Treenie, and it's just Thursday."

"How can I help?" asked Treenie, as he leaned forward while pulling the envelope closer. "I can be patriotic like the next guy."

"What are your plans over the next couple of days, Treenie? I want you to take the four of us to Havana and I want you to take me to this Cadillac club. I want you to be my eyes and ears in Havana. If you do this the envelope is yours plus what's already in your pocket. No joke, no tricks, that's it. And you will make a friend of Bill Clinton, the ex-President of the United States."

Treenie looked at Angus, and then he looked at Lily and Rose, with their beautiful wrist corsages and spikey heels, then back to Angus. "Nice hat, Sr. Angus. What a night, huh?" exclaimed Treenie. "You got a fast boat?"

"I have a very fast boat. All expenses are on me. When can you leave?"

"Do you know the Versailles?"

"No."

"It's just down the Calle Ocho. It's a famous place you can't miss it. I'll meet you at the outside window for coffee at ten in the morning."

"Treenie, all you need is a small bag with a change of BVD's, and whatever kind of deodorant dancers wear, all else is on me. You're doing a wonderful thing for the children of Cuba. I know that you will be there; however, I'm going to hold on to the envelope until that time. You keep the three bills."

"I like children," proclaimed Treenie, as he strolled out of the club, in time, turning on the beat.

"You think he'll get the hint about the deodorant?" asked Rose.

"We can only hope," said Lily.

"Girls, we're on the move again. I'm going to call Rejito; we have some more shopping to do, but first I should call Paul.

Paul, yeah, we're done for the night. Make a plan for the Cayman Islands in the morning then on to Havana. We could be at the plane by 10:30. Yeah, four passengers, we're done for the night, see you then.

Rejito, can you pick us up at the Ball and Chain, good, see you in a few."

Out on the curb it was pandemonium as every dancer in Miami jockeyed to get inside the Ball and Chain. The cab then pulled up across the Calle Ocho.

"Rejito, good man, we need for you to take us somewhere where these girls can shop for clothes. Do you know of any shops that are open this late?"

"Miami never sleeps, Sr. Angus. I know a place."

"And maybe some Advil, Rejito, take me to some Advil. Girls, I want you to dress again for a dance club, but this time we're dancing in Havana, so we want to dial it down a notch, not quite as uptown as tonight. You get my drift? We don't want to shine quite so bright."

"We understand, Angus," said Rose.

"You girls are the greatest. Have I said that yet tonight?"

"No, Angus, that was the first time," said Lily.

"You girls are the greatest. There, that's twice."

~ANGUS and LILIANA~
Chapter IX
The Yellow Cadillac

There was no assurance that Angus would find Liliana in Cuba, but it was Angus' nature to try. Angus couldn't stand the thought of standing around like sheep in a field waiting for the grass to grow, or worse, waiting to be sheared.

"Girls, we check out in ten minutes."

"Angus," asks Lily, "should I have taken out a life insurance policy before we left the city?"

"Probably," responded Angus.

"Great, now you tell us."

"What is life without a little adventure, a little drama, a sense of impending doom," said Angus. "We'll be fine, probably."

"And speaking of impending doom, how about this Treenie? Do you trust him, Angus?" wondered Rose.

"We need Treenie, without him we would be in the dark. Treenie is going to work out."

Per usual Angus and company show up at the Versailles 10 minutes early.

For decades the Versailles restaurant on Calle Ocho in Little Havana has been ground zero for the Cuban-American exiles in South Florida. The restaurant has been a gathering point for anti-Castro protesters and the press wanting to cover their opinions. This is where you meet to plot the demise of Fidel Castro.

"Three coffees please," called Angus at the walk-up window.

There was no sign of Treenie. Angus was right; things would be more difficult without a guide and interpreter. They could probably find the Cadillac club but Angus' Spanish wouldn't carry the day.

"And give me a dozen of those little fruit pies and a box of the Gallatecas de Montecado.

"Cafe, por favor," comes a voice from over Angus' shoulder.

It was Treenie. Treenie had his travel bag and looked ready to go.

"Treenie, my man, are you ready? You look ready," observed Angus.

"Yeah, I'm ready to go, but can we sit and talk for a minute."

"Sure we can, what's on your mind?"

"When we get to Havana there is a stop that I have to make. It's not far from the clubs and it won't take too much time."

"I think we can do that, Treenie."

"Also, when we get there I will need the envelope with the money."

"OK, Treenie, I understand. When we get to that place you will have the envelope and the seven hundred dollars inside. Do we have a deal?"

"You know, Angus, there is no guarantee that we will see Liliana tonight. We can try several places, but she may not show."

"I understand that, Treenie."

"Angus, even if we don't see her, the money is mine?"

"The money is yours either way. I just want you to guide us and translate for us when we need it. If you do that you will have completed your end of the bargain."

"Bueno then, to the boat!" declared Treenie with a smile.

"Treenie, my chariot waits…"

Treenie then stood up and began to sing: "La Cubana," with all the guests at the window of the Versailles joining in:

*Oye cubana, AU!! No seas tan mala, mira que te tengo
ganas,*
*Ponte bien bonita que vamos andar en la - 130 -ossib, ay
- 130 -ossi yay*
*Oye...vamos a bailar mi música cubana.... hasta mañana
por la mañana*

So into the limo they climbed and headed for the airport.

"Oye, Angus, I realize that I am Hispanic, but still I know
that they don't keep boats at the airport."

"Treenie, my boat has wings, mira, algo."

"Ay ya, ya, amigo. Is this your boat?"

"This is my boat. Welcome aboard."

"Paul, this is Treenie, he's going to make the trip with us.
You can set sail for the Cayman Islands."

"The Caymans?" questioned Treenie with surprise.

"We're going to first go to the Caymans then from there
we'll head for Havana. I think this indirect route will
serve us best. Paul, what will be your heading?

"We're going to first head due west and give Cuba a wide
berth. Actually, it may be a better plan to set down in
Cancun, and then go to Havana from there. The politics
are pretty much the same as from the Caymans and it
would be a shorter route."

"Paul, if you think that's best then we'll do that. Its 10:35 AM, I'd like to get to Havana just after dark.

The plane will be our safe house while we're there. Paul will be on board at all times and there's plenty of food and drink in the galley, so if someone gets separated you'll want to find your way back to the plane. We won't be checking into a hotel. If need be we'll sleep on the plane. Girls, I trust you have your money in its usual safe place?"

"You know, Angus, I think I'm beginning to get a green stain, maybe some kind of chemical reaction," said Lily.

"That's the least of your worries, Lily," which drew a groan from both girls.

"We'll investigate that stain on our way back to New York," offered Angus.

Paul, let's make this boat fly."

So it was west they flew in a straight line following alligator alley as it traverses the bottom of the state between Miami and Naples. Even now in some Florida precincts they were bracing for what would be one of the worst economic downturns in the state's history. For most workers the end would come swiftly and without a clear understanding of what lay before them.

At 600 plus mph it doesn't take long to lose sight of Florida. They would then make a sweeping left hand turn for Cancun, MX. In Cancun they would take on fuel and have lunch. The ride to Havana would be a brief.

Sitting on the tarmac at Jose Marti airport one could see only a couple of European commercial jets and the rest were old military planes mostly of the Russian variety. This was in contrast to the busy Cancun airport they had just left.

"At some point we are going to be confronted by someone in charge," said Angus, as the group prepared to leave the plane. "Treenie, here is $300, and here is our document for entry into Cuba. When we are confronted I want you to show this document and then use your judgement as to whether you need to spend the money. I would start with $100 and go from there. Hopefully the boss of this airport operation is home having dinner with his family."

The "document" that Angus spoke of was prepared by Angus at the Hotel with the help of the Spanish speaking concierge. It had all the buzz words that Angus could come up with including: The United States Department of State, President Bill Clinton, and "The Foundation for Cuba's Children."

"Treenie, if you have to get into explanations remind them that our mission here is brief and we will be gone by early morning so there is no need to stamp our passports. Then bless them for their participation on behalf of the foundation. Ask for his name and throw a $100 at him even if all goes well.

Lady's, Treenie, when we leave this plane we are a tight knit team. Our mission is to find Ms. Liliana Beltran. We are here on behalf of ex-President Bill Clinton and the Foundation for Cuban Children. Treenie, we will follow your lead. Oh, yeah, get that box of fruit pies. Put the pies down in front of them, Treenie."

"Jew got a lot of faith in me, meng," said Treenie.

"I know people Treenie and you were born to play this part."

The group walked from the plane to the building without a soul in sight. Inside there was one woman standing at the counter looking like she was only mildly interested in their arrival. The group sat on the bench as Treenie approached the counter. They spoke in Spanish and Treenie presented the paper and set the box of fruit pies down between them as they spoke. The lady picked up the phone and spoke momentarily. Two military guards then appeared from the room behind her. Treenie then returned to the group as the guards walked toward the plane.

"What's the trouble, Treenie" asked Angus worriedly.

"We're free to go," advised Treenie. "Those two guys will guard the plane until we return."

"You see, Treenie," smiled Lily.

"I didn't spend a dime. I think it was the pies," said Treenie as he returned the 3 bills to Angus.

"Good work, Treenie," said Angus, "let's find a cab."

"El Gato Tuerto," was Treenie's instructions to the cabbie.

"Where are you taking us, Treenie, what's this 'El Gato?'"

"It's 'El Gato Tuerto,' The One-Eyed Cat," advised Treenie. You want to go to The Cadillac, bueno, we will go there, but the night is young and I have seen this Liliana at a couple of other clubs. So, we'll make our way along, then, when the night is not so young we will be at The Cadillac. If we still haven't found her we'll reverse our tracks. If still no Liliana then you can make another plan."

"This is a good plan, Treenie," agreed Angus. "Vamos to this half blind cat. I hope it's not a black cat."

When they were near finished with their drink at El Gato Tuerto Treenie asked the bartender if he expected to see Liliana tonight.

"Yo no sé, es poossible," was the response.

So they finished their drinks and moved on to Treenie's second choice: "Club Salseando Chevere," but still there was no joy. Now it was on to Angus' first choice.

What a rousing place this was, The Cadillac club. There was a band stand that could hold a ten piece orchestra and a large dance floor that surrounded a yellow 1954 Cadillac Eldorado convertible with matching yellow leather interior. And for $10 American you could sit in this Cadillac with your girl, or girls, and have your picture taken.

"Please, Angus," pleaded the girls, "can we have our picture taken in this Cadillac?"

"Are you kidding? You couldn't drag me out of here without a picture."

The four posed in every conceivable combination. They posed in the backseat, the front seat, and even on the front bumper showing skin. What a hoot.

With this out of the way they settled into a booth. Angus put his hat to good use pulling it down over his eyes. It's not likely that Liliana would recognize him unless confronted up close. He was too far out of context and they were only together for a brief time. Still, Angus wanted to make his move on his own terms – if there was going to be a move.

Treenie couldn't be kept in his seat, nor could the girls. The rhythm was in them and the music too inviting. This left Angus alone in the booth to ponder his thoughts and clock the front door. For two hours they waited, danced, photographed and drank and still there was no Liliana.

"Angus," suggested Treenie, "lets backtrack to the El Gato Tuerto. We can stick our heads in and look around. This was the plan, no?"

"Yes, Treenie, that was the plan. Let's go girls"

And so they hailed another cab and pulled away from The Cadillac club and in the direction of the half blind cat. This time they decided to send Treenie in to survey the crowd while they waited in the cab.

"She's here," said Treenie upon returning to the cab. "She's here dancing." And so they all gathered up and walked in the door and found a booth.

There she was, dancing, sandwiched between two swarthy socialists. If this were a true socialist country these guys wouldn't have to share, each would have a similarly beautiful partner. Each would be paired with a woman with legs that took their time reaching the floor. Each would have a woman with lips that spoke without words, and skin the color of light brown tobacco leaves. Each would have a partner that moved around them with the grace of a leopard. But instead, in this messed up socialist, communist state, they had to share. From Liliana's side, however, it looked to be a fair transaction. In fact it looked like she could have taken on a third.

She was indeed beautiful. Angus kept his hat pulled down and he starred. She was as he imagined she would be – dancing in Havana, not a slow dance, but a dance with a Latin beat.

There are times when men become foolish and forget their purpose; this could be one of those times. Why was Angus here? Good question, surely not to chase after Cuban women. Angus probably could have rustled up a Cuban woman back home. But getting a grip was no easy matter for a man that loved women. Angus tolerated men, but he adored women. It's not just that he preferred women, he adored women. This can be a handicap, and in extraordinary situations such as this Angus would have a difficult time holding his ground. And then there was this train thing. Angus had never known a woman that knew anything about trains.

"Lily, when she stops dancing I want you to approach her and say this: 'The gentleman in the hat wonders if you still trust coyotes.' You got that, Lily?"

"Yeah, I got that."

"She will try and blow you off. Then I want you to say: 'a vegetarian coyote."

"A vegetarian coyote, this is what you want me to tell her?

"She will then approach the booth. When she does I want all of you to get up and dance.

"'Do you still trust coyotes?' Then, 'a vegetarian coyote.' Have I got it, Angus?"

"That's it, Lily."

"That's the weirdest pick-up line I've ever heard," added Rose, "you know, Angus, we're not leaving Cuba without you."

"No worries, Rose."

When Liliana had finished dancing she sat at the bar. Lily then made her move.

"Liliana?"

"Yes."

"The gentleman in the hat wonders if you still trust coyotes."

"What, that's the first time I ever heard that line," as she gave a glance in Angus' direction then turned away.

We are not likely to recognize people when they appear to us out of context. You see your co-worker at the grocery store and you can't quite place them, even though you see them at the office every day.

"A vegetarian coyote," added Lily.

At this Liliana held her position for a moment then turned and looked again at Angus under the hat. She then slowly moved in his direction.

"C'mon, Rose, let's make a Cuban sandwich out of this Treenie."

"So, Sr. Quin, what brings you to Havana?"

"Please, call me Angus. May I call you Liliana?"

"I think we can drop the last names, after all we've meant to each other. You've taken a risk coming here."

"Risk is what I do."

"I know you didn't come here to dance."

"You don't know that. I'm actually a very enthusiastic dancer, but no, I didn't come to dance. It is my nature to gather all the information I can on deals that are put before me."

"You are not like the frog sitting on the bank of the river, huh, Angus."

"I would have helped the scorpion build a raft and pushed him on his way."

"So, you have come here looking for answers."

This is where Angus has to hold it together – sitting close, his eyes darting between Liliana's eyes and lips.

"All we have is that you will be coming to New York City in a week looking for us to commit to the future of Cuba, a future that your father sees in a baseball stadium. This doesn't satisfy my need to make an informed judgement."

"Will you come with me now? I want to show you something."

"I've traveled 1,500 miles to get here of course I'll come with you, but first I have to gather my crew."

Angus then waved over the girls and Treenie.

"Ms. Liliana Beltran this is Lily, Rose, and Treenie."

"Treenie," said Liliana, "I've seen you before in the clubs around town. You're a good dancer, Treenie."

"Thank you and you are good as well. Maybe someday we can dance together."

Treenie passes Liliana his business card.

"'Call me when the music starts,' read Liliana. Maybe we will do that someday."

"Liliana and I are going to leave for a while. This may be a good time for you, Treenie, to make that stop that you mentioned. Girls, would you go with Treenie?"

"Treenie," said Liliana, "you will find us at the old sugar mill. Do you know it?'

"Yes, I know it."

"OK then," Angus said, "everyone has a mission."

"Sr. Angus, do you think I could have the envelope now?"

"Of course, Treenie, I'll see you later," as he passed Treenie the envelope.

"Angus, let's go out the back where my driver is parked."

~ANGUS and LILIANA~
Chapter X
The Sugar Mill

"Where are we going, Treenie," asks Lily.

"We are going to visit my girlfriend."

"So, Treenie, you got a girlfriend here in Cuba? That seems pretty inconvenient. Or maybe you got a girlfriend in every town, now that seems very convenient."

Rose was getting the run down in the back seat of a four door 1957 Chevrolet Bel Air as Treenie and the girls left the club.

"No, it's not like that," explained Treenie, "my girlfriend here is the only one I have. She's going through a tough time and this money will help."

"That's a nice gesture, Treenie," remarked Lily, "how far do we have to go? I'm a little uneasy being away from Angus. I don't know if I trust that Liliana woman. You know Angus will fold like a cheap suit next to that. Next thing we know he'll be joining the Peace Corps in Cuba."

"And what's all that about with that woman," asks Rose.

"I don't know, Rose. I'm not going to ask him. I think he's putting together a deal here in Cuba and this woman is part of the scheme."

"It's not far now," advises Treenie.

The cab pulled up to the end of an alleyway. On either side of the alley were single story tenement style apartments, some with bright colored fronts and all looked run down and not your first choice for housing.

"I'll go in by myself," said Treenie, "please, give me fifteen minutes inside."

Treenie got out of the cab and made his way through the clutter to the third door on the right. The girls waited in the cab.

"Fifteen minutes," thought Lily out loud, "talk about a quickie. Maybe he makes love the way he dances – in a hurry."

Ten minutes later Treenie came back to the cab sobbing.

"What is it, Treenie," asked Lily, "what's wrong?"

"Isla, she is sick, she's going to have a baby and she is sick. I'm going to have to stay."

"Treenie, we're going back in there with you. Rose and I are nurses, this is what we do, we know these things. Take us back in there."

"You, amigo," said Rose to the cabbie, in a voice that was now stern and nurse like. She lifted her dress and reached down into her panties and pulled out a hundred dollar bill. She then tore it giving one third of the bill to the cabbie. "You see this? You get the other part if you stay right in this spot. Don't move, comprende?"

"Yes, I will stay," said the cabbie.

"And don't smell it, I've been dancing all night."

The girls with Treenie left the cab and moved down the alleyway for the third door on the right. A nurse can turn on a dime. Take them outside of their medical surroundings and they can become easy and compliant, however, when a situation arises that brings them back to their training they instantly transform into a full bird colonel. The girls were again in their element, yet another element.

Angus and Liliana had just arrived at the long abandoned Central Hershey Sugar Mill. The driver was directed by Liliana when they finally stopped and began to walk, a walk that would have been difficult were it not for the full moon that lit their way.

"You see this, Angus" began Liliana as they approached the building, "I want to show you what's on the other side. This is one of the Central Hershey sugar mills that were built almost a hundred years ago by the American Milton Hershey. You know the chocolate candy maker from Pennsylvania?

And look at this – this is a …"

"This is a steam locomotive built in the U. S. at the beginning of the twentieth century," Angus says, stepping on Liliana's description.

"Yes, you do know your trains. It's a beautiful thing, no?"

"I know a little about trains. It sounds like you have been checking up on me."

"Should I be upset that you have checked up on me?" asks Liliana. "You check on me I check on you. It's what cautious people do.

This sugar mill, this train, sitting here broke, collapsing, this is Cuba to me. My father was part of this when everything worked. We lived nearby and I would play around the tracks. Jaime and I would run on the tracks in front of the train. The closer it got the more the whistle would blow. Then we would jump from the tracks at the last minute. Sometimes the chickens would run with us. Then they took my Jaime away."

"This Jaime, you married him?"

"Yes, we were married for a short time. Raul then took him with his army to Africa. Jaime a soldier, ha, that's a laugh. Jaime couldn't kill a bug. I never saw him again. He must be buried in Africa somewhere."

"This sounds personal between you and Raul."

"There are two 1200 hp locomotives like this in Argentina. I went there and looked at them."

"Liliana, these things that your father envisions: the stadium, the new Cuba, these things have been dreamed for years, for decades. How can we know when Cuba will be free?"

"Next week I will be in New York City. At that time Cuba's future will be revealed to you and your friends. There is a BBC film crew here this coming week. They will be filming for a documentary about Cuba. You will see a new Cuba emerge at that time."

"And the other boats, why were there other boats besides the Coyote?"

"Those other boats are not your competition, Angus. Look, your country is going into the baño as we stand here. Your famed capitalist system is turning on itself. If you want to become socialist, fine, personally, I wouldn't recommend it. The people on those boats were not socialists they were people who control products, products that we will need in the near future."

"Why me, Liliana, why my firm?"

"Look at you, Angus, look at where you're at, look what you are doing. You've traveled 3,000 miles to a country that forbids it. You have gathered together an improvised, specialized crew to assist you – all this one week after our meeting on your coyote boat. And why? Por qué? Because you are the right man for the job. We could have approached a hundred Wall Street hot shots, but I would gamble that none would be talking with me here now, here, at a sugar mill with my broke steam engine – Mal Tiempo # 1355. The reasons you are here are the reasons you were picked.

Stay with me Angus. Be a part of what's to come. You won't regret it."

Back in the cab, waiting for Rose and Lily, the cabbie was getting impatient – he leaves his cab and knocks on the third door on the right – Treenie opens the door and the cabbie looks in the room and says:

"Madre mia!"

The room was dimly lit and Rose and Lily were examining Isla as she lay on the bed in view of the door. Her large belly and below was nude. Quietly, in the corner, sat an old woman – it was Treenie's mother.

"Treenie, we need to get this woman to a hospital," Rose said, again in a voice that was authoritative."

"Rose," answered Treenie, "they won't take her anymore; they tell her to go home because they can't fix her."

Lily pulls Rose aside: "Rose, we need to get this woman some help or she's not going to make it. I say we go find Angus and this fancy woman and see if they can throw their weight to get her some help. One of us should stay here. I'll stay if you don't want to."

"No, I'll stay," said Rose, "Cabbie, como te llamas?"

"Rogilio," said the cabbie looking like a deer in the headlights.

"Rogilio," then she turned away and dug into her panties once again.

"Rogilio, here is the other part of the hundred. And here is part of a second hundred. I want you to take Lily to meet our friends at the sugar mill. Do you know this place?"

"Yes, I know it."

"If you do this and you bring Lily back here with them I'll give you this part of the second hundred. Do you understand, Rogilio?"

"Yes, I understand." This was turning out to be a very good night for Rogilio.

Angus and Liliana were now giving locomotive; 'Mal Tiempo' # 1322 a thorough inspection. They were dancing, like men and women do – a waltz, close, but not so close as to touch completely. Angus was trying hard not to show his amazement at the depth of knowledge Liliana showed regarding the train.

"I would sit just off the track and watch the train go by. And then one day it stopped. I asked my father if there was something we could do to fix the train. He said go to school and become an engineer, you will then know how to fix it. So, I did, I went to school and now I understand that instead of being fixed it should be replaced with the very best. My father is passionate about baseball, Angus; I am on a different track."

A horn was heard as the cab pulled up next to Liliana's car.

"That must be the girls," figured Angus.

Again the horn sounds.

"What's all the honking," as Angus sees that it is just Lily. "Where is Rose?"

"Angus, we have a situation. Rose is still with Treenie and Isla. Isla was Treenie's stop and she is pregnant and in need of medical help right away. Treenie says that she has been to the local clinic but apparently they don't have the skills needed. She needs a hospital Angus. Treenie is beside himself. Will the two of you come and help?'

Liliana spoke first: "You lead the way and we will follow."

Liliana then instructed her driver to follow the cab.

As they arrived and entered the room it was the same scene: Lily kneeling over Isla with Treenie standing near her bed, his mother sitting silent in the corner with her hands in her lap.

"Angus," said Lily, after taking him to the corner of the room, "Treenie won't leave her and she's not going to make it. If we don't get her some help she won't make it. What about this woman you're with, does she have a better place to go than this local clinic?"

"I'll ask."

Angus then took Liliana outside to see what could be done.

"Liliana, Lily says that this girl won't make it if she doesn't get help. These girls are nurses, they would know. This girl has been to the clinic and apparently they need more specialized help for whatever it is that's wrong."

"Angus, I can take her myself and I can try and bully our way in, but if its special treatment that she needs then she may be out of luck. I can try, but it may not turn out well."

Angus thought for a moment then returned to the room.

"Lily, Treenie, everyone, gather this girl up and put her in Liliana's car. Treenie, pack her a bag, pack everything that she owns in a bag. We're going to Miami. Liliana, do you mind if we use your car to go to the airport. We'll also need the cab.

Rose, look around and see what you think she would want to take. We'll put her in the backseat of Liliana's car and you and Lily can ride with her. The rest of us will follow in the cab.

I better call Paul…

Paul, turn the key, start the engines, we're on our way back and we'll be heading for Miami. I want you to call ahead and have an ambulance waiting for us at the airport. We have a sick pregnant woman. Yeah, we'll be there in just a few, OK. Treenie, are you OK with this plan?"

Treenie could not stop sobbing and nodding – yes.

"And my mother?"

"Everyone, Treenie, everyone that wants to go should decide."

Treenie then went to his mother and explained that they were all going to America and she could go as well. No, she said, she would stay behind. All Treenie could do was shake his head – "I understand," he sobbed, and he hugged his mother and said goodbye.

The two cars then headed for the airport. When they arrived they found that the two guards were asleep in the waiting room where they first arrived. It was a straight shot to the plane without interference. Rogilio and Treenie managed to get Isla up the stairs and into the plane where Paul had made a berth for her.

On the tarmac Angus and Liliana said goodbye.

"Angus, this is a decent thing that you are doing. I know this girl will have a better chance with you in Miami."

"We'll see. I'm probably breaking a dozen laws and will end up in somebody's prison."

"I hope for your sake it is an American prison and not a Cuban prison. Either way I will visit you when I can."

"I recognize that twisted sense of humor; I see it in the mirror in the morning when I shave. Liliana, I have arranged for your accommodations in New York. I hope you will allow me this. Can I help with the transportation?"

"No, Angus, I'm set, I'll see you next Thursday in your office at one o'clock sharp."

With this she leaned forward, pressed herself against him and kissed him on both cheeks. She kissed him with those lips and touched him with skin the color of light brown tobacco leaves.

"I guess we should get this ambulance off the ground. I'll see you Thursday."

"Yes, see you then, Angus."

Angus stumbled on the first and third step as he boarded the plane while looking back over his shoulder.

"There are people approaching, Liliana."

"I'll take care of these people, you take off."

And they did.

The ride to Miami was brief. The girls and Treenie hovered over the poor pregnant girl while Angus stared out at the reflection of the moon on the water below.

Business, romance – it's hard to fight these two battles simultaneously. Invariably you end up screwing up one or both. Angus tortured these two competing forces around in his brain:

'How did she know that I would be the type to get on a plane and go to Cuba? Who would be able to give her these insights?'

Angus was developing theories as to who might be playing double in this game of chess.

'Is she taller than me? If she is it's not by much. Her eyes seem neither high nor low. Cuba doesn't need the nuclear bomb, they have Liliana. Geez, I'm beginning to get a sense of what that's all about.'

Paul then advised over the intercom that they would be landing in a few minutes.

"Treenie, come sit with me. Treenie, I never knew your last name."

"It's Obregon."

"Is Treenie your real name?"

"No, it's Trinidad. I was born in a little town in central Cuba called Trinidad."

"Do you have a driver's license or something with your proper name on it?"

"Yes, I have a driver's license and it has Trinidad Obregon on it."

"Treenie, in all the confusion I never got to give this check to Liliana. I'm going to write your name on it and maybe you and Isla and the baby can use it to get started."

"I don't know what to say, Angus. You have changed our lives around." Treenie then began to sob again.

"What's the trouble, Treenie?" asked Rose.

All he could do was shake his head and sob: "Gracias, gracias, Rose, and Lily, and Angus, gracias," as he stared at the check.

"I can see the EMS vehicle on the tarmac," Lily said.

"What's the plan, girls?" Angus asks.

"We are going to follow behind in a cab and help them get admitted at the hospital. We'll get them lined out and then we'll come back."

"Lily, here, take this card and use it to get them in if you have to."

"Angus, I'm going to think of something special that I can do for you, or to you, or both."

"That's ditto for me," says Rose."

"Girls, don't hurt me. You know I can't stand pain. Have I told you today that you're wonderful?"

"No, Angus, and I think you skipped yesterday as well," Rose said with a smile as she kissed Angus on the top of his head.

"Girls, you are the greatest. I'm considering bigotry."

"Goodbye, Angus, and I think you mean bigamy."

Paul then opened the door and the EMS staff came on board. There was plenty of help getting Isla down the stairs and into the EMS unit.

"Lily, call me when you're finished. I'll be somewhere near the plane. We'll meet back here."

"OK, Angus, we'll be in touch."

"Paul, how are you for sleep? Should we hold up here in Miami for the night before we head north?"

"Angus, the girls should be gone for a few hours. Maybe we could catch a few here on the plane and then I'd be good to go."

"Good call. My eyes are getting heavy so I'm going to grab a blanket and sign off."

~ANGUS and LILIANA~
Chapter XI
Donuts at the 7-11

In the hospital, Treenie, Lily, and Rose were sitting in the waiting room when the doctor approached.

"Are you Treenie?"

"Yes, I'm Treenie."

"Isla is not yet ready to deliver. Her condition has improved and I anticipate that we could now have a normal delivery, but we think it's best to have her rest and build up her strength for a while. We'll keep her here for a few days more. You're lucky you got her here when you did."

"Thank you, doctor."

"Well, Treenie," said Rose, "I guess we'll be taking off."

Treenie's phone rings …

"If that's Angus tell him we're on our way back."

"Hello."

The voice on the other end says: "The music is starting."

"Who is this?" asks Treenie.

"Your card says 'Call me when the music starts,' so I'm calling to tell you that the music is starting. Maybe you recognize my voice, Treenie? I found your card in the back pocket of a woman that is here with me. I'm here at the jail and I have your mother. She's sitting the way she always does – in the corner of the cell, hands folded on her lap."

"Why have you taken my mother?"

"I also have this woman, Liliana, which aided you in your escape with your whore girlfriend. This woman, Liliana, she only stands and curses me. How do you make such friends, Treenie?"

Treenie waves at Lily and Rose for them to stay.

"My mother is innocent. You have no use for her."

"Innocent? No one is innocent, Treenie? You abandon your country and then you sneak back in when you want. I want you to stay. I want you to stay with me, Treenie. You should come back and check on your mother and this fiery woman, Liliana."

"I will come back and I will dance on your grave if you harm my mother."

"Ha, Treenie, just come back and we will discuss this mano a mano. The music has started, Treenie," he then hangs up.

"Who was that, Treenie," asked Lily.

"He has my mother and Liliana."

"Who, Treenie, who has them?" asks Rose.

"Guillermo the butcher – the butcher of Los Pinos. He was one of the prison guards at Isla de Pinos and now he is at the Havana jail holding my mother and Liliana. He wants me to come back and he's holding them hostage. He is a murderer and is capable of anything. He has murdered many people in the prison. He is a very dangerous man."

"Oy ve, Treenie," sighs Lily, "Angus is going to want to hear about this."

"Treenie," says Rose, "go kiss your Isla and tell her you will see her soon. We need to get back to the plane."

Ah, Cuba, the land of Miracles. When those at the top are butchers it's easy for those beneath to follow suit. In the prisons throughout Cuba these "butcher" psychopath types flourish. It doesn't take much to get thrown into prison in Cuba. If you look wrong at a dog, or sneeze at a passing taxi you can be thrown into prison and wait years to plead your case. While in prison you can easily run afoul of guards like Guillermo. The sound of a firing squad is common in a Cuban prison. Or even mock firing squads where prisoners are lined up with the guards just pretending to shoot, and then laughing.

"You have done so much for me I can't ask you to get involved in this."

"Treenie, come with us back to the plane," says Lily, "this involves that woman and Angus will want to know."

"Soon I will watch you swing naked from a Sycamore tree in the town square," proclaimed Liliana. "The days are numbered for you and those like you. If you were smart you would bash your own head in with a rock.

Personally, I hope you don't do that. I want to see you swing in the breeze like a chicken without his feathers. The people will leave you there for days while children throw rocks at your stinking corpse."

"You got a big mouth, Liliana Beltran, and your father might come for you if he only knew you were here. So, I would be careful talking about Sycamore trees because you might find yourself lying beside one with many of my friends lined up taking their turn with you."

Sr. Guillermo knew that all he could do at this point was trade jabs with Liliana and take her insults. If word were to get out that he had her locked up there would be hell to pay if she were harmed. Otherwise, he could just plead ignorance as to who she was and get off with a scolding. However, taking verbal abuse from a woman was not something that The Butcher of Los Pinos was accustomed to. Liliana was dancing on thin ice.

"You are a pig," says Liliana once more, as she spit on the cell floor.

"Angus, wake up, Angus," pleaded Lily.

"What's the trouble," asks Paul, as he wakes.

"OK, I'm awake," responds Angus, "what's up? Is everything alright?"

"Well, not completely," responded Rose. "There is a situation back in Cuba. Liliana and Treenie's mother are in jail. Here, Treenie, you tell him."

"My mother and Liliana are in jail in Havana. There is a man, a man that was a guard at a prison that has taken them. He wants me and he is holding them hostage."

"Why does he want you, Treenie?" Angus asks.

"This man has been put in charge of stopping people from slipping back and forth into Cuba. I have done it many times and he has promised to catch me. This is a very dangerous man. He is called Guillermo the butcher. He has tortured and murdered many people in prison and he is capable of anything."

"Well," says Angus, "Just when I thought I was out... they pull me back in."

"This is my fight, Angus. You've done enough already."

"Treenie, you've created this mess for your mother, but I'm responsible for Liliana. We have the same responsibilities and the same goal. Now we need a plan. All we need to do is sneak back into Cuba, break two women out of jail while a man known as "The Butcher" is guarding them and expecting us. Do I understand the problem, Treenie?"

"Yes, Angus, this is the problem."

"Treenie," said Lily, "I don't mean to complicate your thoughts, but you've got a woman, and soon a baby, in the hospital here and both will be lost if something happens to you. I'm just saying …"

Paul calls to Angus from the door of the cockpit.

"Angus, could you join me for a moment?"

Angus leaves the group and pulls the door to the cockpit closed behind him.

Rose wonders: "Treenie, have you ever come face to face with this butcher?"

"I came close once. He screamed at me from across the dance floor, but I managed to escape. I know what he looks like. His eyes have the look of the devil. I was scared for days."

"You don't scare me, pig," declared Liliana. "Soon Cuba will be free and there will be no need for butchers like you."

"Ha, Cuba, free, you've been reading too many comic books Señora Beltran. All countries need men like me to do their dirty work."

"In the past you were protected, in the future you will run like a squealing pig."

"It could be that Treenie decides not to come. Maybe he and your rich friends have parted and he thinks he has everything he needs in America. Maybe he will just forget about his mother. In a few days we will know and when that time comes you too will be forgotten and I will not listen to your insults anymore. Then, I think I might enjoy you for a short time."

And still Treenie's mother sat silent with her hands folded in her lap.

Angus returned from the cockpit and said:

"It pays to have a marine pilot on your team. Treenie, how were you able to sneak into Cuba?"

"I travel on a small slow boat when I go to Cuba, but I know of a man down in the Keys, Marathon, and he has a very fast boat. If you have the money he will get you to Cuba quickly."

"Can you get in touch with this man and tell him to get ready for another trip?"

"Yes, I can do that."

"Call him now and tell him that we will meet him at 9:00 PM tonight."
"Paul, see if we have enough runway in Marathon and if so let's set sail, it should be a short hop from here. I'm going to close my eyes again and I suggest the rest of you do the same. Paul, when we get there set your alarm for eight. I'll fill everyone in on the plan at that time.

What an interesting life we lead, girls. I was hoping for eggs benedict in the morning. Now it looks like 7-11 donuts – if we're lucky."

"Angus," said Rose, "I'm running out of money in my shorts. And see if you have some older bills. I think I got a paper cut down there."

"That's the least of your worries, Rose. Have I told you girls today that you're wonderful?"

"Yeah, you already said that today, Angus," said Lily as she slugged her pillow and adjusted her blanket.

Treenie did indeed have a contact in Marathon and all had gathered on the dock at 9:00 to get a look at his means of transport. Angus asks:

"What kind of boat is this, Mr. Smith?"

"This is a 38' Cigarette with twin Teague 900 SCI's and NXT drives, and it comes to you by the hour. And each hour that I'm away from this dock it will cost you $500. That's a minimum of $1200 if you only touch the shore and step back in."

"So, as I do the math," figures Angus, "we will be traveling at 75 mph?"

"We have fair seas and we will be traveling at 85 mph, and unless someone is meeting you there on the shore there is a $2,000 deposit that you will leave here with this lady before we take off."

"You seem to have this all worked out, Mr. Smith. What time do you recommend we leave?"

"We will leave at 1:00 AM."

"Here is a $1000 deposit, little lady. You'll get the other grand when we get back. And we will leave in 30 minutes, Mr. Smith."

"To leave that soon it will be another $500."

"Don't push it, Mr. Smith. We'll be back in 30 minutes, you be ready to go. If you hold up your end I'll kick in another $500."

"Little lady what is your name?"

"Mrs. Smith."

"Of course, would you mind running us up to the 7-11?"

There they sat on the curb of the 7-11 eating donuts and drinking coffee. To the casual observer they looked to be a crew that was down on their luck.

"Paul, if we leave at 10:00 o'clock we should be there at maybe 11:15, and let's say that it takes us 30 minutes to find transport to this jail. That's 11:45. With luck we could be at the jail at 12:15. What does that suggest for your take off time?"

"I'll take off at 11:30 and be on the ground waiting by 12:30. Like before I'll swing wide and come in from the west like we did from Cancun."

"Treenie, you've given the directions to the jail to Lily. This butcher fella won't sleep at the jail, he'll go home. He won't expect Treenie to respond so soon so he won't have his guard up just yet. We should be dealing with some night watchman at the jail. We'll be in and out before they know what hit them.

And Treenie you will call Rejito and have him waiting at the airport in Miami with his cab. With any luck he'll have a fare before 2:00 AM."

"Yes, but I think that I should go with you."

"No way you're going, Treenie. You've got too many responsibilities back in Miami."

"And girls, I can see this operation happening with only one of you. Would you like to flip a coin to see who stays behind with Treenie?"

"Ha," says Lily, "you can't keep me out of this operation. Rose and I are a hand full individually, but together we are invincible. Don't you see it that way, Rose?"

"I'm not staying here, Angus. Paper cut or not you ain't keeping me off that boat. What one of us can do, two of us can do better."

"Well, I'll have to agree with that, but you've heard what we're up against here."

"I know," said Lily, "and it's not fair to them, but sometimes life isn't fair."

"Girls, when we get back, its eggs benedict all around. Let's do this. Treenie, we'll be back hopefully before morning, so don't stray too far away from that dock."

"Sr. Angus, I just want to say that President Clinton made a wise choice when he picked you."

"Well, if we pull this off I would say that you are right, Treenie. This operation needs to be quick in and out. If we get tripped up and things drag out our chances for success diminish, so that's it. Let's get back to the boat."

~ANGUS and LILIANA~
Chapter XII
Guillermo the Butcher

"And so, Liliana Beltran, how does it feel to be locked up? All those people in prison … you knew it, no? While they were starving and being beaten you were eating chicken and rice. I bet you never thought you'd end up like them. I'm going home for my supper. Maybe Treenie will come tomorrow, maybe not. You should hope that he does. We will see what he thinks of his mother."

"At least I won't have to smell you through the night, Mr. Butcher. After you beat your wife have her scrub you with soap and water."

"You can try your jabs on young Fidelo when I'm gone. Fidelo, you call me if she rips these bars open with her big mouth. It's no wonder your husband left for Africa."

Well, that one hurt, and it brought a glare from Liliana that sent Guillermo the butcher home to his supper.

"Fidelo, do you like this man, Guillermo?"

"Please, Señora."

"You know that someday he will turn on you."

"Why would he do that, Señora?"

"Do you know the story of the scorpion and the frog, Fidelo?"

"No, Señora."

"I will tell you. One day there was a frog sitting on the bank of the river when a scorpion came to him and asked:

'Would you ride me on your back to the other side of the river? The frog said: If I put you on my back you will sting me and I will drown.'"

'But if I sting you we both would drown," said the scorpion, "I wouldn't do that.'

"After further discussion the frog agreed to ride the scorpion across the river on his back. When they got to the middle of the river the scorpion stung the frog and they both drowned."

"But why did he do this?" asked Fidelo.

"Because it is the scorpion's nature to sting, Fidelo, and he could not deny his nature. Be careful of this man, Guillermo the butcher.

Fidelo, why don't you let us go? You know we have done nothing wrong. We are only here as hostages and when my family finds out that you kept us locked up there will be hell to pay for you. If you open the door now I will see to it that Guillermo cannot harm you."

"I can't do that, Señora."

"Fidelo, word is going to get out and soon there is going to be hell to pay."

After being jolted up and down in their seats for what seemed like forever Angus comments:

"I thought you said we would have fair seas."

"Oh, this is not bad. When it's bad it will rattle your kidneys and you'll pee blood for a couple of days."

"How much farther?" asks Angus.

"You can see the lights of Havana in the distance there. We're going to pull up just east of the city where I've arranged for a car."

"Nice going with the car. I was worried about that."

"Hey, you would have gotten sandwiches if you'd waited till 1:00 o'clock."

At a secluded broken down dock the passengers were off loaded.

"Mr. Smith, we don't plan on staying any longer that we have to. If things go according to plan we could be back here in less than two hours. I want to see you at this dock when we return."

"I'll be here, Angus. You might throw a little something at the driver on your way in."

"I'll take care of the driver, you just hug this dock."

So far so good. Angus, Lily, and Rose now sat in an old Buick just outside the jail.

"Girls, you're up. You're going to have to wing it going in. I'll give you 5 minutes then I'll be in behind you. If it all looks wrong one of you come out and let me know."

"Angus," Lily said, "would you tell us now, one more time, that we are wonderful? I would like to hear it one more time before we go in there."

"Girls, as we stand here words cannot convey my admiration for the two of you."

"Say it anyway, Angus, don't give me that 'words cannot convey' bullshit. Sometimes a girl needs to hear it."

"Girls, you are wonderful in so many ways. You have a bright future in espionage if the nursing thing doesn't work out. Now, show me some attitude and get in there."

At this moment Paul is only a few minutes from touchdown.

"We're going to have to ring the bell, Lily."

"OK, here goes nothing."

"Yes, who is it," came a voice from within on a speaker at the door.

"Is Guillermo here now," said Lily into the speaker.

"No, he is home."

"Actually, he sent us here for you," Rose said, "could you come to the door and see us?"

"OK, I'll be there in a minute," said Fidelo

Fidelo's desk was near Liliana and Treenie's mother's cell. Liliana's ears perked up to the sound of the girl's voices. As Fidelo answered the door to the jail …

"Hello, what's your name?"

"My name is Fidelo."

"Yes, Rose, that's the name we have," said Lily as she put her hand on Fidelo's chest and her foot inside the door.

"Fidelo, what time do you have? Because the time we can spend with you is limited."

"Do you have an office where we could go, Fidelo?"

When Fidelo smiled they knew they were in. When Lily saw Liliana in the cell next to Fidelo's desk she winked.

At the Havana airport Paul was just landing. He pulled up to the same spot where they had parked just hours before. From the plane he made his way to the terminal office.

Once the girls had their hands on Fidelo, Lily said:

"Fidelo, you are about to receive a phone call from the airport. You should take that call. Also, in a couple of minutes a man is going to show up here. He is the special representative of the United Nations and envoy to President Bill Clinton. When he arrives you should pay close attention to what he has to say. For your own future and the future of your family you need to pay close attention to what this man tells you. Do you understand me, Fidelo?"

The front door buzzer then rang.

"Fidelo, let's you and I go to the front door," said Rose, "and please, Fidelo, listen to this man very carefully."

When they had left Lily assured Liliana and Treenie's mother that they would be out soon and to just play along.

The phone began to ring and Fidelo came running back to answer. Rose took this opportunity to let Angus in.

"Hello," answered Fidelo.

"This is Maria at the airport. There is a plane here with a man named Treenie aboard. Guillermo asked that I call you if he showed up."

When Marie had hung up Paul laid three crisp one hundred dollar bills on the desk in front of her and walked back to the plane.

"Fidelo," said Angus in his best U. N. representative, presidential envoy voice.

"Yes, I am Fidelo."

"Fidelo, you are now safe. The call from the airport has been arranged for your protection. You need do only one more thing to ensure your safety and that of your family. I want you to call the man named Guillermo and tell him what the caller told you. Tell Guillermo that Treenie has just arrived and is at the airport. If you do that, Fidelo, you will be safe and under the protection of the United Nations. Will you do this Fidelo? Will you call Guillermo and tell him that Treenie has arrived?"

"Is that true? Is Treenie at the airport?"

"This is what the caller said, isn't it, Fidelo? All you have to do is what Guillermo would want you to do and that is to relay the message that the airport gave you. If you do this there will be no need to fear this man ever again and no one will question your actions. All you are doing is following orders. Do it now, Fidelo, call Guillermo and give him the message."

Lily then picked up the phone and handed it to Fidelo.

"Do the right thing, Fidelo, dial the number and relay the message that you got from the airport."

Fidelo took the receiver and thought for a moment.

"He would want me to give him the message," Fidelo thought out loud.

"He would be very angry if you did not," said Angus.

"It was Guillermo that kept the girl from being treated at the clinic," Fidelo said, apologetically.

Fidelo then dialed Guillermo's number and waited.

"Señor, I just received a call from the airport. Treenie has just arrived on a plane."

"Bastard," said Guillermo, and he hung up.

"You did the right thing, Fidelo," Angus said, "and now we only need to wait for a short time.

Guillermo pulled in front of the Terminal office and went inside. Soon he reappeared and headed for the plane.

From the tarmac Guillermo yelled at the plane and Paul lowered the stairs and answered:

"Yes, what can we do for you, sir?"

"I want you to send Treenie out right away."

"We don't have a Treenie, here," said Paul as he looked toward the back of the plane.

"I'm coming up to look," said Guillermo.

"Are you sure you have the right to do this?" asked Paul.

"Oh, I have the right, sir, get out of my way," as he topped the steps and headed for the back of the plane.

Paul then entered the cockpit and threw the switch that automatically raised the steps and locked the door. He then locked the cockpit door and turned the key. In seconds the Gulfstream G280 was flying down the runway.

For the few who have ever flown on a private jet there are fewer still that have ever experienced what is called a "high performance" take off. Pilots reserve this maneuver for airports that are surrounded by tall mountains where they have to gain altitude very quickly. It's not a vertical takeoff, but its close. For the unfamiliar it can be a frightening experience. And as for the only passenger, Guillermo, he was plastered to the rear bulkhead trying to claw his way to a seat as he screamed:

"What's happening? What's happening?"

After Paul had gained all the altitude he dare he then began a steep decent back into Miami International. This was no less frightening for the passenger. Paul then sent the following text to Angus:

'The butcher is cooked."

Angus opened his phone and gave a sigh:

"We're home, girls. Fidelo, you can now set these women free. You will never see this Guillermo the butcher again."

"Angus," said Liliana with a smile, "should we all spend the night in jail, or should we get out of this place? Fidelo, call Treenie's mother a cab so she can return home and forget this night."

"Liliana, we'd love to stay and dance with you but we have a man waiting in a boat. Would you like to come with us and show us off?"

"I would," said Liliana, "I would also like to say that I am a great admirer of these two women that you seem to always be with. Cuba will need women like you. If you ever come to Cuba you look me up."

"That's something to think about," Rose said with a smile from ear to ear.

"Girls, I want you to empty your panties out on Fidelo's desk. And we need to get going; I'm spending $500 an hour on this bloody boat."

Back at the Miami airport the Gulfstream was coming to a stop on the tarmac. Paul hit the door switch and the stairs began to drop. When Guillermo reached the top of the stairs he saw a smiling Rejito at the bottom.

"Buenos dias, Señior Guillermo, welcome to Miami. I'm here to take you to your hotel."

Slowly Guillermo descended the stairs and got into the cab.

"First, after such a long day we'll stop for some refreshment at my favorite place: The Versailles. I think you will like this place."

Guillermo appeared to be in shock in the back of the cab as Paul turned the plane around and headed for Marathon.

The group was now approaching the Cigarette boat still tied up at the rickety dock.

"I'm going to see these girls back home," Angus said to Liliana, "they actually have jobs to return to. They've had a lot of excitement in the last few days, as have I. If you have any pull with the folks that might question our activities over the last couple of days we would appreciate any help you could give - starting with this speed boat ride back to the Keys."

"I'll see what I can do, Angus. You are a brave and interesting man, Angus Calumet Quin. By the way, what is this name Calumet?"

"It's a long Indian peace pipe. It was also the name of my father train back in Chicago."

"Peace pipe, hmmm, I'll see you Thursday, Angus."

"Girls, Mr. Smith, avante!" exhorted Angus, "and Mr. Smith, try and go easy on the kidneys on the way back."

Back in Miami Rejito's cab had just reached The Versailles. Waiting for Rejito and Guillermo was an angry mob of Cuban expatriates who dragged Guillermo from the cab and beat him to death.

~ANGUS and LILIANA~
Chapter XIII
Back in the City

Sitting in the conference room at FQH was Angus, Robert and Byron. Paul was conspicuously absent as Robert remembers:

"You know someone we didn't talk about was this general, the one who's name I won't remember – the one that was on the coyote boat with us. He was head of the air force for the Havana district."

"It's true," Angus says, "this must be a plum position within the military and apparently they have this guy in their pocket."

On the TV in the conference room the reporter states:

> *"In market news today the Dow Jones Industrial Average closes above 14,000 for the first time in history. This as a worldwide 'credit crunch' hits and subprime mortgage backed securities are discovered in portfolios of banks and hedge funds around the world, from BNP Paribas to the Bank of China. Many lenders have now stopped offering home equity loans and 'stated income' loans."*

"Robert," Angus observes, "the market is going to tank. I can feel it in my bones. Have you taken any measures to protect yourself?"

"We don't hold equity in the firm's name. As for myself I'm split between crude oil futures and treasuries. You know, I think we should start a futures contract based on the Cuban peso."

"Crude oil futures?" questions Angus, "You're a mad man, Robert Starr. That's an interesting idea about the Cuban currency contract."

Rosemary enters the conference room to announce: "There is a Liliana Beltran at the front desk; she says she has an appointment."

"Thanks, Rosemary, I'll retrieve her," says Angus.

"Greetings, gentlemen," said Liliana as she entered the room.

"Rosemary, call Nancy at the Waldorf and have them pick up Ms. Beltran's bags and take them to her room. The room will be under our account in the name of Liliana Beltran.

So, you've come direct from the airport."

"Yes, it's been a hectic morning. I would like some water or juice if you have it."

"Well, you are among friends here," assured Angus, "you can relax and if you'd like we have a lounge were you could freshen up."

"Just something to drink, please, then we can get started if you don't mind.

Gentlemen, in Cuba our plans have progressed and are on schedule. Fidel is now in a coma and out of the picture and Raul has been in charge since Fidel's surgery. My father, along with other hand-picked associates, has been planning our moves for the last couple of years and we are now strategically placed throughout the government and the military. With Fidel out of the picture there will never be a better time to act.

As to Raul – it has been arranged that he will retire, exile, if you will, to a designated place in Spain."

"This is agreeable with Raul," wonders Robert.

"This retirement will be presented to Raul while on vacation on a certain coyote yacht. Raul will board the yacht in Lisbon, Portugal and it will then sail for Marbella, Spain. While on board it will be explained to him, in terms that he will understand. I leave for Marbella on Saturday morning to make the final arrangements. We have gone to great lengths to put together an attractive package not only for him but for his family. I am assured by General Cienfuegos that it is an offer he will not refuse.

Please, can you turn the TV up? I was following this at the airport in Miami this morning:"

> "This just in from Miami – the body found yesterday morning in the parking lot of The Versailles restaurant in Little Havana has been identified simply as Guillermo, and more specifically: Guillermo – the butcher of Los Pinos, a notorious prison in Cuba. It's unclear at this time how this Guillermo got to Miami, or who is responsible for his death."

"Good riddance to Mr. Guillermo," offered Liliana, "this is justice."

"Probably a professional hit man," thought Angus out loud.

"The purpose of my visit today, gentlemen, is to inform you of our progress and of our plans for Cuba's future.

Soon we will implement a plan that will encompass the transformation of the following: Energy self-sufficiency, information technology, and transportation. These will be joined shortly by education, health care and controlled tourism. In each instance we will join with selected partners outside of Cuba, partners that have demonstrated not just excellence in their field, but a flexibility to act without undue bureaucracy.

It's true, yours was not the only boat that visited Cuba, there were others. One belonged to an energy company located in San Antonio, Texas, called Avante-Primero Energy. This is a privately owned company involved in drilling and exploration in the Gulf of Mexico. Its management is nimble and lacks the bureaucracy of the major energy companies.

Cuba has in its waters an abundance of oil and gas reserves. The Russians and the Chinese have tried and failed to exploit these reserves. In the short term we will seek to extract these reserves for export and for our own domestic needs. As our cash position improves we will begin to transition to cleaner energy options.

Secondly, in regards to transportation, there is a man in California who has designed a train. We have been in discussions with this man to implement his design in Cuba. Also, this same man is on the cutting edge of the design and manufacture of electric cars. It is our goal to establish a plant in Cuba for the purpose of manufacturing a vehicle that runs on batteries.

Thirdly, as our cash flow position improves, and with the equity input from partners we would like to begin construction of a state of the art sports stadium and hotel complex on the outskirts of Havana.

What we need from you, gentlemen, is one: the architecture of the agreements between partners, investors, and the Cuban government, two: a list of potential investment partners, and three: recommendations as to an equitable sharing of revenue between these partners and the Cuban government. For your part you will receive some negotiated percentage of each partnership established.

I leave Saturday morning for Spain to solidify the arrangements for Raul and his family. When I return I will visit San Antonio to confer with Avante-Primero, then on to California for similar discussions.

Gentlemen, I am out of breath, do you have any questions?"

Byron spoke first: "I have a question – these entities: energy, transportation, tourism and others, each of these are significant undertakings with specific skill sets. Do you plan to administer these entities yourself?"

"As I mentioned before, my father has been planning within the government for at least two years; however, I have been planning for much longer. My own education and training is suited to the transportation segment of our plan. There are Cubans with other specific skills that are designated to head the other disciplines. They too have been planning their future for a long time."

"Next came Robert: "From your explanation, you are going to surprise Raul with this exile plan. What if Raul decides that he would rather keep the status quo and live out his life in Cuba?"

"This will not be an option for Raul."

It was becoming clear that this woman that sat before them was extraordinary on many levels. Not only was she calculating, but she appeared to be shrewd and even ruthless.

"Liliana," began Angus, "you must be tired. Why don't you let us digest all that you have said while you get yourself settled into your room at the Waldorf? Unless you have more to give us I'll get you a cab? If we come up with more questions there will be time for further discussion."

"I would like that," responded Liliana.

"Good, then, I'll see you out."

As Liliana entered the cab Angus suggested: "Liliana, it's just now two o'clock, will you allow me to take you to dinner tonight? Say seven at the clock in the lobby?"

"OK, Angus, I'll see you at seven."

Angus gave the fare to the cabbie then watched as it drove away. It was a good idea to get her out of the room. While Angus was not staring at those lips his mind could focus more on business. Angus could more easily plot a course outside of her presence, even if he melted into his loafers over dinner.

"This sounds like a capitalist coup," said Robert as Angus rejoined the group, "has there ever been a capitalist coup?"

"This will be one for the history books," added Byron.

"It's all pretty ambitious, but wouldn't it have to be?" asks Angus. "I can understand that when you're selling yourself to the people you wouldn't want to nibble around the edges and appear weak kneed. The galaxy abhors a vacuum and where weakness is perceived others will rush in.

And still, it all seems to ride on how they manage Raul. If they can get him out of the picture, and if they truly do have their ducks lined up, then what's to stop them?

I'm going to have dinner with her tonight. If other questions creep into your minds let me know."

"You know, her approach seems very reasonable," offers Byron, "staying away from the conglomerates and going with lean organizations. Even FQH fits this mold to a tee. Does anyone else get the impression that this entire parade is the brain child of one woman?"

This was an interesting posit. If true would it be less legitimate? Would it be less remarkable if it were a man? Liliana would not be the first woman in history to rise through the use of her charms, then backed up with brains: notably there was María Eva Duarte de Perón, AKA Evita, of Argentina. And surely there would be a few hundred million other less notable examples.

"Willard, it's a beautiful evening on Park Avenue. Don't you ever go home?"

"No, Sir, Mr. Quin, I sleep right here on my feet."

"Willard, were you on board this afternoon around two o'clock when a Latina lady arrived by cab."

"Yes I was, Mr. Quin."

"Did you notice anything remarkable about her arrival?"

"The only thing remarkable about it was her, if you don't mind me saying so, Mr. Quin."

"No, not at all, Willard, she is a head turner that's for sure."

"She did leave shortly after she arrived and returned with some shopping bags."

Angus then slipped Willard a twenty and entered the hotel lobby. In the middle of the lobby, standing nine feet tall is the famed, ornately carved, bronze Waldorf Astoria clock, set on an octagonal base made from marble and mahogany and topped with the Statue of Liberty.

Could there be a more elegant pair? Standing alongside the clock was Liliana, naked, with both hands gripping a small black clutch purse and wearing only a broad smile. As Angus approached he acknowledged the smile then forced himself to include the dress:

It was a simply cut black dress that clung to her every curve. It was short in length with small teal colored stones placed on the inch. The stones descended from the top of the broad straps and swerved down and out to cover her hips and continue to the bottom hem, leaving the plain black dress through the center. It would appear that Liliana had not spent the entire afternoon resting in her room.

On any street corner in the free world Angus' $2,500 custom made suite with coordinated $300 silk tie would be a stand out, but here, under the clock, approaching *this*, Angus would strain to be adequate.

"You look lovely, Ms. Beltran."

"Please, Angus, when a man has sprung a woman from jail in a foreign country he has earned the right to call her by her first name."

"Well, Liliana, if this is the only rights you give up I'd say you bargained well. Shall we have a drink before dinner?"

"Of course, let's have a drink."

And in to the famed "Sir Harry's" bar they strode. Angus had covered these steps many times before but none of his companions eclipsed the stunning Liliana Beltran.

"Purvis, set this lady up with whatever she desires."

"Angus, what do you suggest?

"Well, the "Rob Roy" was invented here. Personally, I find it a bit heavy handed. Would you like a glass of wine?"

"I'll have a Dr. Pepper, do they have this?"

"Purvis, do you have Dr. Pepper? I'll have a vodka tonic to calm my nerves."

"Of course, one Pepper, one vodka tonic, coming up."

"When I leave home there are certain things that I like to catch up on, things from my college days. One of them is Dr. Pepper."

"That's understandable. Tell me another thing you like to catch up on."

 You're going to think I'm silly, but – hamburgers, also pizza."

"Really, I warn you that I was prepared to spend as much as $50 in the hotel restaurant. But if you're serious, I know a hamburger near my home in Connecticut that will get you thinking about defecting. It's a bit of a drive, but well worth it."

"Take me to this hamburger, Angus. I can see the headlines in the Granma newspaper: 'Liliana defects for hamburger.'"

"'Granma' seems an odd name for a newspaper."

"'Granma' is a boat, not a person. Fidel, with his brother Raul, Che Guevara, and others sailed this boat named 'Granma' from the port of Tuxpan, Mexico to Cuba to begin their revolution. Now everything is named after this boat.

"If you are trying to impress me with a cheap hamburger date you are succeeding. No one wants a cheap date from Angus, peace pipe, Quin. We'll have to take a cab to my apartment up the street to pick up my car. We could be there in no time the way you drive."

"The way I drive?"

"Have you ever driven an Aston Martin at night on a windy road through Connecticut? I highly recommend it."

"Oooh, a hamburger and a windy road, you're sweeping me off my feet, Angus, peace pipe, Quin."

"Convertible, Peace Pipe, Quin!"

Liliana was screaming as she repeatedly crossed the center line.

"What's the speed limit, Angus? I want to keep driving all the way to Boston."

"Just try and keep it on our side of the road. Actually, just pick a side, the other cars will adjust. There, just up ahead on the right, this is your hamburger joint.

Two cheeseburgers with fries, oh, and two Dr. Peppers," was Angus' order, "and give us a pepperoni pizza as well."

"You are smothering me in luxury, Angus. I will waddle back to Cuba."

"I'm only vouching for the burger, not the pizza."

As they settled in for their multi-national fest Liliana asks: "Angus, you said that your father was a train conductor, did you ever ride on the train with your father?"

"Oh yes, when I was a young boy he would wake me in the middle of the night and I would ride with him on one of his trips out of the Chicago yard. I developed a real knack for blowing the whistle. At least my father said I did.

Unless you'd like another hamburger I'd like to show you something."

"Just one more bite of pizza and I'm done. Where will we go now, Angus?"

"I'd like to show you my train."

"You're train! Will I get to drive this train through Connecticut in the dark?"

"We could turn the lights off. I'll drive this time, it's not far."

Angus switched the lights on in the basement to reveal his masterpiece of railroad miniaturization."

"Oh my God, Angus, look at this! I want this!" and she ran to touch the trains. "You have old and new trains, and this one, it has 'The Calumet' written on the side of the locomotive. Is this your father's train, Angus?"

"It is, it's an exact replica of my father's train. And that's him hanging out of the cab with the calumet pipe hanging out of his mouth. I had it custom built."

"Someday I will have a train and on the side will be written: #1355, 'Mal Tiempo,' and I will run in front of it again with the chickens, and sparks will fly from under the wheels as the black smoke rises.

Angus, I could use that drink now. Do you have something stronger than Dr. Pepper?"

Angus and Liliana sipped cognac while Angus explained all the different types of trains and the mountains and lakes and tall grass prairies that stretched throughout his basement. All this as Angus stood in front of the skirted opening that once hid naked African animals from children's view.

It was inevitable when finally Liliana looked at Angus with those lips, and suddenly, in a spring like motion, she pushed Angus backward onto the tracks as they crossed the tall grass prairie. Like a spring that had been coiled too long with worry she began to release on Angus.

There are women whose nature it is to take charge and there are men with the good sense not to get in the way – that is to say: Angus was holding steady. Like the gyroscopic stabilizers on the coyote yacht Angus did all he could to hold his position. But the spring that was Liliana began to uncoil, even as the Manitoba Express of the Canadian Pacific Railway made its way through the tall grass prairie and slammed into Angus' thigh – then backed up, gave a disapproving whistle and slammed him again, Angus held firm, and was getting firmer.

Finally, in a single encounter, Angus had managed to marry together the two things he loved most: women and trains, one pressing him down from above while the other bruised his thigh from the side. The locale was different; Angus had seen himself in a gentleman's private car making passage through the Canadian Rockies, but this would serve.

Mercifully, Liliana stood up freeing the train to pass. The two now standing Liliana backed away and began to disrobe. With her eyes focused unwaveringly upon Angus she began to slowly unbutton, unzip, and furthermore release all manner of restraint. Piece by piece she revealed her bare skin, skin that was, with a few notable exceptions of pink, the color of light brown tobacco leaves.

Angus was trying to take in all that was before him and simultaneously not have a heart attack. He had heard of men, young men dropping dead in their forties. And surely a man's last vision on earth could be worse than that of a naked Liliana Beltran, but Angus prayed to be spared until tomorrow. As Angus removed his shirt the pounding of his heart was so loud that he was certain the neighbors could hear. The truth be known, as Liliana's bejeweled dress hit the carpet, her heart was also about to leap from her chest. Again she came at Angus.

This time there was no tall grass prairie, no Manitoba Express to interrupt, only the perils of a plush carpet decorated with choo-choo trains. Again it was Liliana who maneuvered Angus. Even as her bare knees chaffed against the carpet and her teal stoned dress lay in a heap nearby. Liliana began to release the burdens of the oppressed, she moved for all those that had been wrongly held back or imprisoned. All were liberated at this moment. With variable intensity she threw her head back then bounced her forehead off of Angus' chest as she spoke Spanish words.

A less experienced man would try to match Liliana's intensity. Even so, the train was speeding up for Angus, the mountain tunnel was just ahead and the whistle was about to blow. Men have limitations when faced with the unfamiliar.

As she finally laid her head still on Angus' chest she wondered: "Would the Indians considered us to have smoked a piece pipe, Angus?"

"You mean between brave and squaw? I can see that it could have happened like that. However, technically, the pipe has yet to be smoked."

"Details," said Liana, as she began to remove this remaining technicality. And off they went once more.

Their relationship was now, as they say: *advanced* to the next level, and it would never be the same again – it never is the same again. It's like when you spit in the ocean, or fire a gun, you can't get it back, you can't catch up to that bullet and say never mind – let's forget I pulled the trigger. As Angus drove them back to the city Liliana asked:

"Angus, why don't you come with me to Spain?"

"Can you promise me that you will stay out of jail?"

"I can't make a promise like that."

"So I'll have to take my extraction crew along as well."

"OK, I'll be good and stay out of jail."

"Here, call this number and tell Paul that you want to go to Spain. Paul is my pilot and you should thank him because it was his plan that got you out of jail."

Liliana hits Paul's number on Angus' phone …

"Is this Paul? Paul, I want to go to Marbella, Spain, and we may have to take Angus with us. Ha, he says we don't have to take you. I also want to thank you for getting me out of jail in Havana.

Paul wants to know if he will need a similar plan for Spain. He says he has a different plan for each country. I can stay out of jail, I hope. Angus and I want to go to Marbella at the south tip of Spain Saturday morning, can we do that? Here, he wants to talk to you."

"Paul, do you know this place, Marbella?" asks Angus.

"I've not been there," says Paul, "I think we have to fly in to Gibraltar. This is one of the trickiest runways in the world."

"So you're too scared to go?"

"I'll gather my strength. When do you want to arrive in Marbella? It's seven hours to Madrid so it would be something similar to Gibraltar, then there's the time difference."

"Liliana, when do you need to be in Marbella?"

"I have a meeting there Monday morning."

"Let's take off at 8 AM Saturday morning, Paul."

~ANGUS and LILIANA~
Chapter XIV
Marbella

The Rock of Gibraltar jets up from the landscape at the southernmost point in Spain and looks south across the Straits of Gibraltar toward Tunisia, Morocco and the north coast of Africa. Adjacent to the rock is the Gibraltar Airport which has been described as one of the scariest in the world. It's not enough that the runway dumps into the sea at both ends, almost unprecedented is that the runway intersects with a major pedestrian road that must be shut down during takeoffs and landings.

Nevertheless, Angus and Liliana safely landed and made their way to the four star Hotel Fuerte Marbella on the Costa del Sol. This luxury hotel lies a short distance up the eastern coast from Gibraltar and has historically been a hot spot for the rich and famous of the world.

The news never stops coming, even while staring out at the Mediterranean from your beach side suite. Angus sat on the bed late Sunday morning and read:

> *Treasury Secretary Henry Paulson and Fed Chairman Ben Bernanke meet with key legislators to propose a $700 billion emergency bailout through the purchase of toxic assets. Bernanke tells them: "If we don't do this, we may not have an economy on Monday."*

From her shower, Liliana, dressed in a towel, landed on the bed belly first.

"Angus."

"Yes, my Cuban peppercorn."

"Could we have a stock market in Cuba?"

"Of course you could."

"What about a bond market?"

"You could have that as well."

"I think I understand what a stock is but could you explain bonds?"

Angus put his newspaper down and laid his head across the back of Liliana's knees, and like a Spanish thief he looked north up under her towel.

"Sure," said Angus as his hand lay between Liliana's thighs. "Unlike a stock a bond is a debt owed by the issuing entity." Angus' hand began to inch further north as he spoke.

"Imagine your assets were held, say right about here."

"No, not there, Angus, a little bit further up."

"You mean here, or here, or maybe up higher?"

"I mean up more, then over to the middle, and then down. This is where I keep my assets."

"Now imagine that someone wanted to use your assets for a short time."

"Not too short a time, Angus, now a little down from there. Yes, there. That's it, use them right there for a while longer. I don't think I'm learning just yet. Keep, keep ... teach me more about bonds!"

"Education can be a lengthy process, but I feel my commitment is growing."

"I like your bonds, Angus. I want to understand more. Yes, yes, I'm getting it now ..., keep teaching me, Angus."

And for a while longer, as the breezes off the Mediterranean lifted the sheer Moroccan linen drapes, Liliana took in the lessons of finance.

"I'm a slow learner, Angus; we may need to go over this again."

"You know the mind is a terrible thing to waste," replied Angus as he surveyed the topography of Liliana's backside. "Clearly you are a gifted learner"

"Seriously, Angus, what is a bond?"

"So soon, you want to go over it again?"

"No, really, Angus, that wasn't my fault."

"OK, now focus this time and I'll repeat: A bond is an instrument of debt, and unlike stock it bestows no ownership rights to the holder. Governments, municipalities, even corporations issue bonds instead of going to a bank to borrow money."

"Why would someone buy a bond?"

"Some like the predictable steady interest that a bond offers. Stocks are at risk to daily market ups and downs, but in most cases a bond's principle, usually $1,000, will be re-paid in full at maturity. The holder of the bond would expect to receive regular interest payments throughout the life of the bond. The amount of interest is determined by the market at the time of issuance. When the bond matures the principle is repaid and the relationship ends unlike a stock which in theory never ends."

"Is this what you said before?" as she flipped over onto her back.

"This is exactly what I said before."

"So when I see that a bond is AAA what does this mean?"

"These letters represent the bond issuers credit worthiness, and correspondingly, how much interest would have to be paid to the bond purchaser. A company whose finances are questionable would have to pay more interest than say the US government who can raise money through taxes to satisfy bond debt. The more risk the purchaser assumes the more interest they will expect to receive."

"And who decides if you are AAA or ZZZ?"

"These ratings are assigned by independent rating agencies like Standard and Poor's, or Moody's. The bond issuer has to pay for these services."

"If I have a bond could I sell it to you if I don't want it anymore?"

"Yes, this would be a sale in the secondary market, not unlike the stock market. After the initial issuance the bond could change hands many times in the secondary market before it matures. This is one of the risks the bond holder must face. When you sell your bond before it matures your $1000 may have to be adjusted up or down so that the interest payment that it provides matches the current interest rate market.

"So in Cuba we could issue bonds to raise money within our bond market?"

"Well, remember, you have to find people with money to purchase your bonds. You won't be able to sell them to the citizens of Cuba alone, they don't have any money. You would have to sell your bonds on other exchanges around the world. This is a common practice."

"You are a smart man, Angus."

"It's just what I do. I suppose you would be good at calculating the size of a beam needed to hold up a building."

"And, I can tell you exactly where to find my assets." And she kissed Angus and suggested: "Let's go see if we can see Africa from the beach."

As Liliana and Angus sat in beach chairs and peered south across the Mediterranean toward Africa Liliana asks:

"What ever happened to the dancer in Havana, the one with the pregnant girlfriend?"

"You mean Treenie. We left him and the girl in Miami. She was in good hands at the hospital. I assume that all went well, but I don't know."

"He was a really good dancer, one of the best in the clubs in Havana. Maybe I'll see him there again. I'd like to dance with him someday."

"What kind of engineer are you, Liliana?"

"I studied transportation engineering which is a component of civil engineering."

"So you would be good at building roads and bridges?"

"And railway systems."

"Do you have a busy schedule tomorrow?"

"There is a large estate here in Marbella that was once owned by a man named Adnan Khashoggi, a rich Arab magnate sombitch. The estate has changed hands over the years and has been split into smaller parcels. I will be attempting to close on one these parcels tomorrow."

"I remember this Khashoggi character; he was once a heavy hitter. He was one of the richest men in the world at one time. Donald Trump bought his yacht."

"That's the one. It seems that years ago he did some arms deals with Fidel and Raul. Back in the late 80's Raul came here to one of Adnan's famous parties and that's all he talked about for months afterward. Ironically, this is the very place where Batista died in exile in 1973. Over the years it has become a purely artificial place built by the nouveau riche, Ferraris and yachts all over the place. Even so, it's more than Raul deserves. The Coyote sets sail from Lisbon tomorrow."

"Careful with that nouveau riche talk, I'll take nouveau riche over church mouse poor any day."

"Somewhere in the middle there is a balance, Angus."

"No one stops in the middle, not on purpose anyway.

So the plan is to bring Raul here to Marbella to live in exile, then your father, along with others will take control of the government. And the drama will occur when the plan is laid out for Raul on board the boat as it sails toward Marbella. Is that it?"

"That's the plan, Angus."

"I get the impression that it would be in Raul's best health to accept this proposal."

"Again, you are right. There are people on this boat that will not take no for an answer. And Angus, I am taking you into my confidence. The last chapter has not been written. The next few days will be crucial."

"Liliana, I am here only to plunder your assets to the best of my abilities. I have no interest in getting in the way of history."

"Do you know what I would like right now, Angus?"

"More bond education?"

"No, paella, I would like some paella for lunch. I looked at the menu and they have it here in the restaurant."

"Let's go find some of this paella."

As they walked from the beach to the restaurant Liliana explained:

"Paella is considered the national dish of Spain and when I studied at the university in Madrid I ate paella all the time. We have our own versions in Cuba, but it was born here in Valencia on the eastern coast of Spain."

"It says here that they have paella Valencia, seafood paella, or hamburgers, which do you prefer?"

"When in Rome, Angus. Actually, paella is a mixture of Roman, Moor and Spanish influences. We should get the Valenciana since we are so close to the region."

As the paella arrives Angus gets a phone call from Robert back in NYC.

"Robert, how's every little thing?"

"Angus, I don't know how close you've been to the rumor mill here in the city, but word is that the FBI is about to round up hundreds and it's conceivable that you could be in their sights. Where are you now, Angus?"

"I'm here in Vancouver, BC dining with a friend."

"They've been talking to Byron; no one has seen Philip for a while. I doubt they would take Philip in because of his age and that leaves you, Angus, next in line."

"You're a good man, Robert. I'm in the middle of that thing we were discussing down Florida way. Thanks for the heads up and watch your back, Robert."

"I think I'll be OK, Angus. Is that Florida thing still a go?"

"It could be a go, the next few days will tell the tale."

"Maybe you should hang out there for a while longer, Angus."

"Interesting times, huh, Robert, I'll talk to you soon."

"Everything OK, Angus," said Liliana after Angus hangs up, "you know that we are in Spain, right?"

"The paella is hitting the fan back home."

"Do you need to return to New York?"

"Actually, it may be best if I stay away for a while."

"Don't they need the plane?"

"No, the plane belongs to me; I lease it to the firm from time to time. How's the paella? It looks delicious."

"It is delicious, here, do you like artichokes? And try the crusty rice at the bottom that's the best part.

It's hitting the fan for both of us, Angus."

"It may be best if we use your credit card for a while."

"I don't have a credit card, Angus. We don't have Visa in Cuba; I use American Express travelers Checks."

"We'll use Paul's credit card. What time is your meeting tomorrow?"

"I have to make a phone call at nine in the morning, and then be ready to go to a place that is not yet known to me."

"Do you want to go alone?"

"Yes, its best I go alone."

"Have you ever wanted to see Montenegro? We could be there tomorrow and we could leave all this business behind us."

"Someday, but I've got a lot of people depending on me."

"I knew that."

The next morning Liliana was dressed and ready to leave with her game face on.

"I don't know how long I will be," said Liliana."

"I'll be somewhere around the hotel if not in the room. Good luck. Take deep breaths."

"Yes, good luck would help … no pressure here."

The day passed slowly for Angus as he busied himself trying to read the local newspapers and puttering through the hotel shops. By 4 PM Angus was lying in the sun on the beach.

"I could use a Dr. Pepper," came a voice from behind, "maybe something stronger. Is this what history looks like when you are living it?"

"Did you have a historical day?"

Angus flagged down one of the waiters.

"Amigo, bring us a vodka tonic and whatever the lady wants."

"Chablis, you're not going to believe my story."

"I'm prepared to listen."

"The Coyote left this morning as planned. On board was my father, Enrique, General Cienfuegos, your partner, Philip Fortney along with others that I don't know. I think that we will change the name of the newspaper from 'Granma' to 'Coyote'."

"Philip is on board? This is remarkable."

"Apparently it was Philip that arranged for the yacht. All this, however, is secondary to the events of the day. When the plan was unveiled to Raul he proclaimed that he would not live out his life at a place of "whores and pimps" such as Marbella. It's just as well because the people I talked to today said that they would not welcome a murderous dictator into their community. This has opened the door for a new nonviolent resolution, which was always my preference. I believe that there are those on this boat that would rather push Raul overboard than see him living the good life, but I know that that would complicate our ultimate goal. I don't care what he's doing as long as he does it away from Cuba."

"So where does this leave you?"

"I now come to the most remarkable part of my story. Raul apparently has developed some trust in the aforementioned Adnan Khashoggi who presently lives somewhere around Monte Carlo. It would appear that this Khashoggi character is still the deal maker. Raul now says that he would consider a life in Monte Carlo if it can be arranged through Señor Khashoggi. And here's the best part: I have a meeting with Khashoggi Wednesday in Monte Carlo. I am to check into the Hotel de Paris then arrive at the casino no later than ten. Someone will contact me at the Baccarat table. Do you know this Baccarat?"

"Well, I've watched "Casino Royale" several times and James Bond makes it look easy. I think you could come up to speed pretty quickly. That is an amazing tale."

"We have casinos in Havana but I don't go. You don't have to follow me all around Europe, Angus. You must have business of your own to attend to."

"Actually, I don't have any business to attend to anymore. It seems that the industry that I worked in has now collapsed onto itself. Paul and I would tag along if you don't mind the company?"

"Angus, you're welcome to come along. After all, I'll need someone to check on my assets from time to time."

"I have always wanted to walk into the casino in Monte Carlo with a beautiful woman on my arm – like James Bond. We'll need some wardrobe enhancement and Paul can help.

"Paul, we are going to break wind for Monte Carlo tomorrow just as soon as you can make ready. And I'm going to need you to pay for our room here with your credit card. Book us into the Hotel de Paris. Also, look into our book of statistics and order each of us a tuxedo and have them delivered to the rooms. That's right, when you have a plan for exit give me a shout."

"Angus, I'll need a dress."

"But in my dream I'm in a tuxedo and you're wearing nothing."

"You got the dream part right, Mr."

"Can I use your phone? I need to call the office."

"I'm starting to worry about you, Angus. No credit cards, no phone, you sound like a man that's trying to hide his whereabouts."

"These are just precautions. I'm a carful man."

"Fortney, Quin and Hurst," answered the receptionist.

"Marie, put me through to Stan. Stan, this is Angus, I want you to go get Byron and bring him to your phone, and don't mention my name."

"This is Byron Hurst."

"Byron, how's it going there?"

"Well, things are falling apart very quickly. The FBI was in the office yesterday quizzing me about the business, which has completely dried up by the way."

"Byron we're going to have to start laying people off. As you go through your list I want you to identify your best sales people – not necessarily traders but people who know where the money is. The plans we spoke of down Florida way will either be realized or not in the next couple of days. Keep your list close until that time keeping in mind what we may need going forward. If this all falls apart then we may have to let everyone go.

Has the FBI inquired about me?"

"Oh, yes, they've inquired, and they've taken notes on all of us as we spoke. Wherever you are you may want to stay put."

"Byron, get yourself one of those throw away phones and give the number to Robert. He can call me and tell me the number. Thanks for being there and taking the heat, Byron. We'll land on our feet."

"Understood, Angus, take care."

~ANGUS and LILIANA~
Chapter XV
Monte Carlo

All that money - it was the English playwright and novelist Somerset Maugham that said of Monaco: "it is a sunny place for shady people." Such a concentration of wealth will no doubt attract the occasional scoundrel. There have been reports of such scoundrels insinuating themselves into the lives of the rich and famous with tragic results. Millions have been bilked from the naïve, well healed patron – even murder! And then there are the petty thieves and pick-pockets that will snatch your purse right off your arm, or better yet, lift your wallet without as much as a *merci beaucoup*.

It's hard to imagine where Raul Castro might fit in with this crowd, except perhaps on the side of the petty thief, a smash-and-grab artist.

Angus and Liliana were flying in to the Cote d'Azur Airport at Nice, France, eleven miles east of Monaco. From there they would take a taxi to the famed five star: Hotel de Paris.

"Liliana, I'm going down to the lobby and speak with Paul. I'll be back in a few."

"How's the room, Angus? Did you find your tux?" asked Paul as Angus approached in the lobby.

"It was hanging in the closet, perfect. It even had a carnation in the lapel.

Paul, I need to borrow your phone. Believe it or not Philip is on the same Coyote yacht with Raul heading for Monaco. I'm going to try and get in touch with him.

Philip, it's Angus, how are you holding up out there on the high seas?"

"How did you find out?"

"There are no secrets in the world anymore, Philip. I'm in Monaco with Liliana awaiting your arrival. How's the mood on the boat?"

"Angus, the mood is murderous. We'll be lucky if we make it to Monaco before Raul is made to walk the plank. I keep my distance but there are people on this boat that hold deep hatred and don't like the idea of him living out his days in comfort. They feel that change is now within their grasp and they're not going to let anything stand in their way. Are you assisting Liliana in her efforts?"

"Well, I'm not doing a lot of assisting, more like facilitating. She has a meeting with this Khashoggi character in an attempt to find a place for Raul. We'll see how that goes. Try and keep a safe distance from the weapons.

I spoke to Byron and things are heating up back in the city. This may be our only gig going forward."

"I've got to go now, Angus. I guess I'll see you soon, take care," and with this the phone went dead.

"Paul, Liliana and I are going to get dressed and look for some pizza then head over to the casino. I think I'll look around the hotel for a few minutes."

"What time will you leave the hotel, Angus?"

"Let's say seven. We'll catch a cab out front."

Back in the room Angus asks: "Did you know that this hotel is 150 years old? And it has a wine cellar under the flower garden that holds thousands of bottles of wine?"

"I didn't know that. Did you know that the Principality of Monaco is the second-smallest independent state in the world?"

"I didn't know that. What's the smallest?"

"Vatican City. Is it time for pizza? I think I will just wear the dress I bought in New York. I don't have the budget for an evening gown. You could probably spend a fortune in this town on an evening gown."

It's easy to get spun around in an unfamiliar place. Liliana's request: "Bonne pizza s'il vous plaît" to the cabbie, put them on a course back to Nice before they realized. They were now dressed to the nine's and standing in front of a cheesy out of the way pizza joint. The cab abruptly drove away and left them in front of: "C'est Magnifique – Chez Sophie - Bistro & Pizzaria" as it was painted on the window.

"Shall we? I think we will be the only guests," gestured Angus, as he peered through the glass.

As they waited for their pizza Angus asked: "When you are home what do you eat?"

"First of all, I probably eat better than most Cubans, but generally we all eat the same things. There is a lot of fish, we eat a lot of rice and beans either prepared separate or together. There are stews of pork with a mojo sauce made with oil, garlic, onion, lime juice, and various spices such as oregano. We have all the tropical fruits as well. Our food is influenced mainly by Spain, Africa, Puerto Rico, and the other Caribbean islands."

"Do you have access to American movies?"

"It is very limited. There is a state run TV that carries a few American programs, but it is limited."

"I want to open a movie house and show all John Wayne movies."

"The trouble is the people don't have money to spend on anything other than necessities. We have to put money into the hands of the people. They must have jobs that pay a good wage. Then they will come to your movie house and see John Wayne."

"So you have never seen 'The Godfather,' or 'Star Wars,' or 'Butch Cassidy and the Sundance Kid?'

"No, I haven't seen those movies."

"I envy you in a way. I've seen them so many times that they are no good to me anymore. Maybe someday we can fill a bowl with popcorn and catch you up on these movies."

"I'd like that."

"Mademoiselle, that is a beautiful dress," said the lady from behind the counter.

"Merci," responded Liliana.

"Would you like to trade the dress for the pizza?" said the lady in perfect English, yet with a heavy French accent.

"No, merci," responded Liliana, "I think we'll just pay for the pizza and keep the dress."

"Claude," was the response from the now grim faced lady, and the cab driver that drove them walked through the door of the kitchen. He then approached the table where Angus and Liliana were sitting.

"Stand up," said Claude, in a threatening tone and he grabbed Liliana from behind and pressed a knife against her throat. "To the kitchen," he gestured to Angus.

"Are you sure you want to do this, Claude?" asked Angus.

"Bring them to the kitchen, Claude," said the lady. Everyone then began walking toward the entrance to the kitchen and the back of the building.

"We'll come peacefully, you don't need the knife, Claude," Angus said calmly.

As they reached the kitchen the lady said: "Take off the dress, and you, take off the tuxedo."

"Liliana, stay calm, we are not alone, just do what they say.

Do you have a good hospital here in Nice, Claude?" asked Angus.

"You're hospital is at the bottom of the Mediterranean," answered the woman coldly.

To this Angus responded: "You have only a short time to do what's right. We can put our clothes back on and you can send us on our way. Of course you would have to pay for the pizza for causing us this inconvenience, but this would be much better that a trip to the hosp ..."

Before Angus could finish his sentence Paul came quickly through the kitchen door, grabbed Claude and threw him head first into the pizza oven, which sent Claude screaming and holding his face and bumping into walls. Paul then made for the woman.

"No, Paul, she is mine," said Liliana.

With nothing on but her panties and bra Liliana executed a perfect left cross to the side of Sophie's jaw, followed by a straight right to her chest. As the woman began to fall Liliana laid a side kick up against her head.

"I warned you, Sophie. The next time you try this this man is going to put your head in the oven. Paul, let's get out of here and leave this mess to these French pizza makers."

Liliana was just getting warmed up: "You would kill me for my dress? You piece of French shit."

Angus then had to pull Liliana off the woman again.

"Here, Liliana put your dress on and let's get out of here. Paul thanks for the help. I think these people were going to kill us for our clothes and our purse. Take us to find a cab. We'll go back to the hotel then on to the casino. Grab yourself a pizza."

"Angus," said Paul over Claude's howling, "I think Liliana could have taken them both out."

"You do handle yourself pretty well, Ms. Beltran," suggested Angus.

"My friends call me Liliana," as she gestured to Paul to zip up her dress.

Before they left Paul says to Angus discretely: "Angus, I can't rule out the possibility that there was a third person involved in this little rodeo. Stay on your toes; this may have been more than a random criminal act."

"Understood," replies Angus, "Always the intrigue with these Cubans. You watch yourself as well. If you are right they could have made your involvement. Let's not leave together out the front door. You take the back and we'll find our own way back to Monaco."

Able to hail a cab, Liliana and Angus headed back to Monaco. As they travel Liliana asks Angus: "So, is Paul always there for you?"

"I pay Paul for more than being a Pilot. He's always in my shadow when I travel."

"This is a good concept. All it takes is one evening like tonight and you feel like your money is well spent."

"When you arrive in a private plane, when you stay in the best hotels, you are a constant target. It's more effective when he's not with me but instead nearby. And where did you learn those moves?"

"I've had to take some training. There are a lot of creeps out there."

"Have you considered that there could be people here trying to thwart your efforts, maybe do you harm?"

"This is always a possibility. Raul has many resources and he has hated me for a long time. Ever since he sent my Jaime to Africa to die I have tried to be a thorn in his foot. Doing me harm in Cuba would be difficult, but here in Europe there would be less explaining to do. And now he knows that I am here in Monaco putting this together. I know that whatever he says on that boat cannot be trusted. He will say what he has to to survive then he will betray the agreement when he first gets the opportunity."

"Well, you've managed to stay a step ahead of him so far."

"Treachery is something you learn early on if you want to survive in Cuba."

"We have an hour to get to the Baccarat table. How's your hand? You gave that woman a good beating."

"I've been injured worse; maybe a Band-Aid would be good. I don't like bullies, Angus, they make me very angry."

"You may not have time to become an expert Baccarat player. The good news is that this is probably just a convenient place to meet and not a Baccarat challenge. Do you know if your meeting will be at the casino or will you have to travel to another location?"

"I don't know. Hopefully it will be at the casino. I don't like the idea of leaving with strangers."

"Well, if you like I can have Paul watch your back. He seemed to enjoy looking at your back when he zipped up your dress."

"Oh, Angus, would you do that. That would give me a lot of comfort."

"Done."

"Do you know what else would give me comfort?"

"What, pray tell?"

"Give me your hand."

"I think I can do this without looking," said Angus.

Driving a cab can be a very entertaining endeavor. People will lose themselves in a cab. Maybe its nostalgia – the memories of those teenage years when a backseat was all you had. Backseat memories in Cuba are probably no different than backseat memories elsewhere; it's just that the cars are older.

And on they drove toward Monaco, with Angus' hand solidly up Liliana's dress and Liliana solidly gripping Angus' wrist, as she entertained the driver with the kinds of sounds that suggest: I know you're there, I just can't help myself.

As they pulled up in front of the casino Angus said: "Your assets are holding up just fine under the pressure."

"You are a good steward of my assets, Angus. I'm now ready for this Baccarat, whatever Baccarat is."

The approach to the Casino de Monte-Carlo is one of a kind – the iconic facade at night is a rush – the history in movies, literature, and behind is the Port of Hercule with the Med beyond. This visage would stir even the hardest of hearts. The inside of the casino, however, is not unlike other great casinos around the world: Las Vegas, Macau, Singapore. A sea of machines await along with roulette, craps, and all the other games designed to rid you of the lunch money your mother gave you.

Like many other casinos Baccarat is played in a more secluded area of the room and is roped off from those that would get too close. If you wish to play you would signal your intention to one of the croupier who runs the game.

Angus phones Paul to ask: "What's your location?"

"I'm just outside the entrance on the right as you go in."

"It may be that her meeting will be here inside the casino, but she's not sure. She could be taken to some other location. If she leaves I'll let you know."

"Roger that."

"It's rude to be late, don't you think, Angus? What time do you have now?"

"It's almost ten thirty. When, if, they show, get them to tell you where you are meeting, then before you leave ask to use the restroom and take your time."

"I've watched them play this Baccarat all I want. I think they could find me easy enough."

As Liliana finished her sentence a middle aged, swarthy looking, well-dressed man approached.

"Ms. Beltran?"

"Yes, I am Liliana Beltran, who are you?"

"I am the emissary of Adnan Khashoggi. Do you wish to come with me and meet Mr. Khashoggi?"

"Where is this meeting to be held," asks Liliana with Angus nearby.

"You will meet on a yacht just outside the harbor."

"And what is the name of this yacht?"

"It, it is the... Star."

"I would first like to visit the ladies room. If you will wait here you can then take me to this yacht and Mr. Khashoggi."

"Very well, Ms. Beltran, I will wait for you here."

Liliana returned then walked away with the so-called emissary of Adnan Khashoggi, once the richest man in the world and now relegated to making deals for petty dictators.

"Paul, she's leaving with a man and heading for the harbor. They're meeting on a yacht called 'The Star' just outside the harbor. Go quickly and see if you can arrange a boat. I'll try and contact the Port Authority and see if there is a yacht in port with this name."

"Understood,"

Paul moved quickly toward the harbor which is only a couple hundred yards away.

"Do you know the yacht – 'Star,'" he asks one of the dockhands.

"No, Monsieur, I don't know that yacht."

"Merci, do you know of a boat for rent."

"Try down the quay, maybe there."

"Merci beaucoup."

As Paul made his way down the quay he was approached by a man who asked for a light of his cigarette. As Paul explained that he did not smoke another man came up from behind and put a knife to his back.

"Don't turn around, Amigo," was the voice of the man in front.

Paul could then see Liliana boarding a boat 100 yards ahead.

"We have a boat waiting for you. Tell me, Amigo, do you like fish?"

"Oh, yeah, love fish," said Paul as they walked a few feet to a speed boat.

"That's good, Amigo, soon you will spend all your time with them. Get on board."

Paul could see that Liliana's boat was pulling away from the dock. And as one of the men started the boat a voice shouted from the dock:

"Hey, did one of you drop this wallet? I think it fell out of your pocket as you walked toward your boat. It's got 300 Euros in it shall we split it up, or is it yours?"

"It's mine," said one of the men and he reached out to get the wallet."

With his hand reached out Angus grabbed his arm and threw him into the water. Simultaneously, Paul took on the man starting the boat. As they fought Angus joined the fray and the two managed to overcome the second man.

"Paul, get his gun," and the two then threw the second man into the water.

The boat now started, Angus hit the throttle and off they went into the night after Liliana's boat.

 "Paul, the harbor master does not have a boat named Star in the harbor. We need to catch that boat as quickly as we can."

Two men, with carnations in their lapels, were now giving chase across port Hercule - and were in fact gaining.

"Paul, sell them the wallet. I'll hide my face."

As they pulled alongside the tender Paul yelled out to the two men on the boat: "Hey, you there, you dropped this on the dock."

Liliana, seeing Paul, moved quickly to his side of the boat. And as she did one of the men grabbed her arm.

"You dropped your wallet on the dock as you boarded your boat. It has a lot of money in it. Here, come closer and I'll hand it to you."

When the two boats touched Liliana elbowed her captor in the throat and tried to jump to the other boat. She was then caught and held by the other man as the boat began to pull away and again put distance between them. With one of the men still gasping from the blow to the throat, Liliana threw one more punch and jumped into the sea and began to swim toward Angus and Paul.

With Liliana now in the water the boat turned back toward her as if to run her down. Angus then squared his boat up against the other boat and rammed it amidships while Paul fired a shot into the engine and held the gun on the two men.

Angus then pulled Liliana into the boat while Paul pushed off from the bow holding the gun on the Cuban assassins. As the boats separated Angus pulled away and made distance between them as the other boat began to sink.

The three then made their way back to port with their boat listing and wanting to take on water.

"Angus, they were going to kill me and dump me out in the sea. Two times in one night someone has tried to kill me. This is a record. This is Raul's work. I'm lucky; his men were never that smart. I'm cold, Angus, hold me."

And so he did as the boat limped its way back to the dock.

"Angus."

"Yes, Liliana."

"Make proper love to me tonight. No cab drivers will be watching."

"I could probably find some cab drivers and bring them up to the room if you like."

"I wouldn't like, Angus. Are cabbies the only option?"

"What else would satisfy you, Liliana?"

"A pony, could we have a pony? I never had a pony as a child."

"You'd like me to bring a pony up to the room to join our love making? I think you need a blanket and a cup of hot cocoa. And besides, the closest thing I have to a pony is Paul."

Looking up at Paul driving the boat Angus notices that blood is covering the back of Paul's tuxedo coat.

"Paul," calls Angus, "you're hurt," as he rushes to Paul at the wheel.

"It was the guy that we jumped for the boat. He put his Knife in my back to get my attention. We can look at it when we get in."

Making their way through the lobby Angus covered Liliana with his jacket as the two of them walked close behind Paul to block his blood stained jacket from view. Once in the room they stripped Paul's shirt off to reveal a knife puncture wound.

"Well, Paul, you've screwed up any chance we had of getting our deposit back on this tux.

Liliana, do you feel well enough to find us some alcohol and some bandages? It may be that the hotel carries a first aid kit."

"Of course, let me get out of this dress and I'll go and find what you need."

As Liliana leaves the room Angus says: "Well, Paul, we really stepped in it this time. We need to stay away from the authorities. We don't want to get involved in this mess. We've been lucky so far."

"We have been lucky," says Paul, as he lay on the bed face down, "I'll be ready to go as soon as you get me patched up."

"I have a first aid kit," Liliana said as she entered the room. Does it hurt, Paul?"

"Careful, Paul, she wanted me to bring a pony up to the room. What can you do with a woman after she's been with a pony?"

"What are you talking about, Angus?"

"I think you were in shock and the kinky side of your brain took over."

"I once made love to a pack of wild hyenas," said Paul. They looked fine just before I passed out, but the next morning … whew. A pony would be a new experience for me."

"OK, you guys, we don't need any ponies, or hyenas in the room."

"What's your next move, Liliana?" asks Angus.

Liliana sat on the bed and watched as Angus dressed Paul's stab wound.

"It's clear that Raul is not going to cooperate. He will now try to eliminate everyone that has tipped their hand. As long as they are on the boat he will say whatever is necessary to survive, but once the boat arrives everyone will be in danger.

I'd like to tell both of you something: this is the third time you have saved me. I owe you my life and I will never forget it. I want you to know that whatever you want, whatever I have, is yours. Whenever you call I will come.

I know all three of Angus' names, but I only have one for you, Paul. What is your last name?"

"Paul is like 'Cher' and 'Madonna' he only has one name."

"My last name is Nelson."

Angus spoke first: "I know what I want – popcorn and a movie of my choice. That would put us even."

"You are a simple man, Angus," said Paul, "I can't get that donkey out of my mind. I think I'll see if they will let me in the casino with a hole in my back. Maybe I can replace this donkey vision with something more reasonable. I'm assuming you guys won't be getting into any more trouble tonight."

"There was never a donkey, or a pony, no ducks or geese" complained Liliana, "and the only one that will need saving tonight will be Angus."

"Yikes! Paul, take two aspirin and call me in the morning. And you might check yourself in the restroom from time to time to make sure that bandage isn't leaking."

"Now she's bringing in the whole barnyard. These Cuban women scare me, Angus. I'm heading out."

"She gets like this after there's been an attempt on her life. We've now established a pattern. We'll see you in the morning, Paul.

When does the Coyote get to port tomorrow, Liliana?"

"Early in the morning. I don't know if the events of this evening will reach the boat. Whether I am dead or alive wouldn't alter Raul's plans, but it could alter the plans of the others on the boat. My father would not wish to hear that Raul's assassins were here trying to kill me.

Angus, there are contingency plans that I won't share with you. History is getting in the way of you and me. Angus, I want you to know that I have enjoyed these last few days very much and no matter what happens we will see each other again someday.

Now I have to think."

Liliana then rolled over on her back, closed her eyes and went sound asleep - so much for the safety of Angus.

When Angus woke it was seven AM and Liliana was not in the room. He picked up the phone and called Paul.

"Paul, are you awake, how's your back?"

"My back hurts a little and it itches where I can't scratch. I think you may need to change the bandage."

"Come on over, Liliana has disappeared. I'll change your bandage then we'll have some breakfast."

As they sat down in the restaurant the waiter said:

"Have you heard? One of the Castro's is dead right here in Monte Carlo. It's been on the news this morning. They pulled him off of a yacht this morning. Here, I'll turn the volume up on the TV. Would you like some coffee, gentlemen?"

"What happened to him?" asked Angus.

"I don't know, maybe they will tell us. There's going to be a press conference soon."

"Oh my, Angus, you don't think Liliana killed Raul?"

"I hope not, Paul. She said there were contingency plans. Look, this must be the press conference."

As they watched it was Liliana that stepped to the microphone.

"My name is Liliana Beltran and I am part of the Cuban delegation visiting here in Monaco. Last night at approximately 11:25 PM the President of Cuba, Raúl Modesto Castro Ruz, suffered a fatal heart attack while traveling to Monte Carlo. This was to be the first stop of a long anticipated Mediterranean tour. We appreciate the assistance of the Monaco authorities in expediting the transport of President Castro back to Cuba.

Thank You"

"Waiter," called Angus, "where is this press conference being held?"

"It looks like it's here on the docks."

"Let's go Paul," and they rushed out of the hotel in the direction of the docks only a short distance away.

"Ms. Beltran, will there be an autopsy performed here in Monaco, asked a reporter?"

"President Castro died in international waters and therefore Monaco has no authority over his body. All necessary procedures will be conducted upon our arrival in Cuba."

"Who was President Castro meeting with here in Monaco?"

"This was an unofficial visit, there were no planned meetings."

"Ms. Beltran, has President Castro been in poor health recently?"

"President Castro appeared to be in the best of health when he left Cuba.

Thank You."

Liliana then pushed through the small crowd that had gathered and found Angus waiting.

"It was the frog, Angus, that lured the scorpion into the river. I am leaving now with my father. We are flying back to Havana. Remember what I told you."

With this Liliana walked away and got into a waiting car.

"Amazing," said Paul.

Angus and Paul were then approached by Philip.

"Angus, I'm going to travel with them as far as Madrid then I'll be heading back to the city. What are your plans?"

"I'm not sure, Philip. It's a scary place back in the city you should be careful."

"I think I will have to close down the office.

These events confirm what they've always said: nothing is going to get in the way of their plans. The next few weeks will be the test. Managing events back home may prove more difficult than simply getting rid of a dictator. Check in when you can, Angus."

"I'll do that," said Angus as Philip walked to the car.

Angus could only stand and watch as the car drove away.

"Paul, I'm going to go back to the room and lay down for a while. This is not a woman that can be easily forgotten."

As Angus crossed the lobby of the hotel a voice called his name from a chair. From behind a newspaper the voice called:

"Mr. Quin."

It was a familiar face – Carl Fowler, the man who loved eggs benedict.

"Mr. Fowler, you do get around."

"Have a seat, Angus, chat with me."

"Sure, always happy to see a fellow countryman when I'm abroad."

"That was a handy piece of work out in the bay last night."

"Thanks, I have good help."

"And now Raul is dead. If we needed further assurance that these people are all in we now have it. You see, we've gone through these dramas before, and even though people are well meaning and appear serious, well, history has proven that getting rid of a Castro is no simple matter. Without you and your friend this beautiful Cuban woman may not have made it through the night.

Things will move quickly from here on, I suspect. There are still dangers in the near term back in Cuba, but this group has impressed so far."

"Are you guys everywhere, Carl?"

"Everywhere that matters, Angus. I want you to consider me your friend going forward. We like where you're positioned and if we can help give a jingle. For obvious historical reasons we don't want to appear to be proactive in events in Cuba, but a healthier Cuba will benefit everyone.

And another thing, you really need to be in the cockpit during takeoff and landings. I may not be able to hold these FAA guys off much longer."

"What about these FBI guys that have been hanging around my office back in the city? Do you hold any sway in these matters?"

"They have to go through certain motions, but you're office, what's left of it, will survive."

"Well that's something worth shouting about. I'll admit I was more than a little concerned about that. Tell me this, Carl, from a purely business, capitalistic point of view; would you say that it's still too early for me and my friends to start gearing up an office of Cuban affairs?"

"Ask yourself this, Angus, would you rather do that or continue to sell mortgage backed securities? Which do you see as the greater risk?"

"Good point, Carl."

"Take care, Angus. I must admit, I've enjoying your case: the eggs benedict, travel to exotic locals, I've had worse assignments. I'm now off to Puerto Rico."

"Are you dropping us, Carl?"

"No, same case, different players, take care, Angus."

"Yeah, you too, Carl. And by the way, you still owe me $92.50."

Carl smiled and walked away briskly.

~ANGUS and LILIANA~
Chapter XVI
Train Dreams

Angus lay on the bed with his eyes wide open. He began to think about Margret, a woman he had dated seriously for over a year. And then one day she announced that she was moving to Baltimore. Her company offered her a better job and she decided to take it. Things were going great then poof, she was gone. There were a couple of visits back and forth but it finally died of its own weight. It's difficult to give yourself over to someone when there are so many Baltimore's out there. Angus closed his eyes.

"Angus, wake up," then the knocking on the door, *"wake up, it's 4:30 and we have miles of track in front of us."*

"OK, dad, I'm coming."

"Your mother made you this sack lunch. Here, take my lunch pail too and let's get a move on. We'll have some breakfast at the diner in the train yard.

Its nine degrees, burr, we'll warm up when we get in the cab and get the old girl started.

"It's really cold, dad," agreed Angus, *"this must be the coldest time of the day."*

"Here, wrap that scarf around your head and just leave your eyes to see, there, now pull your flaps down."

As they arrived at the diner it was Chuck who said: *"Who ya got with ya there, Roy?"* Chuck was a round man with greasy overalls and a cigar that was so short it must have been started yesterday.

"This is Angus, my number one engineer," replied Roy proudly.

"Angus, are you going to man the throttle today?" asked Chuck.

"I've done it before," replied Angus assuredly.

+++

The plane ride from Nice to Madrid was short, but the next leg was six hours plus - plenty of time to reflect, too much time to reflect.

Liliana wondered: *'When was the last time I went to confession? Father Louis will soil his robe when he hears of what I've done. He will tell me that being involved in the taking of a life is a terrible sin – then he will be happy. As a priest he will condemn, as a man he will turn away and smile. This is such a long flight.'*

> (In Greek mythology, Atropos was one of the three Moirae, the Fates, the female deities who supervised fate rather than determine it. It was she that chose the means of death and ended the life of each mortal by cutting their thread with her shears.)

And she begins the dream she always dreams:

> *"Someday I will dance at the Copa and be rich, and then I will marry you, Liliana."*
>
> *"Someday you will marry me even if you are not rich and dancing at the Copa. Someday everyone will be rich and dance at the Copa.*
>
> *Here comes the train! C'mon, Jaime, run. C'mon or the chickens will beat you."*
>
> *"I'm coming, Liliana, don't be so bossy, I'm coming and I will beat you and the chickens."*

"Jump, Liliana, jump! You always wait too long. Someday the train will swallow you up and you will be no more."

"Jaime," shouted Liliana as she continued to dare the train, "what's the point of running in front of the train if you jump 100 meters in front?"

"You're waiting too long, Liliana," then, she stumbles and falls onto the tracks only a few meters in front of the oncoming train. The whistle blaring, Jaime goes back onto the tracks and pulls her away with only seconds to spare. The conductor shouts curses as the train passes.

"You see, Liliana, you were almost killed, don't ever do that again. Your legs are too long they get tangled up."

"Kiss me, Jaime, kiss me now."

"What are you talking about? You were almost killed, Liliana."

"You saved my life, Jaime." The twelve year old Liliana Beltran then grabbed Jaime and kissed him on the mouth.

"Would you like a beverage, Miss?" asks the flight attendant.

"No, thank you. Do you have a pillow?"

+++

"Dad, how far is Council Bluffs?"

"It's 450 miles, Calumet will get us there about five o'clock."

"Do you remember where you got that pipe, dad?"

"Oh sure, I took this pipe off of Chief Sitting Bull just before the battle of Little Bighorn. If Custer had smoked this peace pipe he might not have gotten his ass kicked."

"C'mon, dad, that was a long time ago.

How fast can we go?"

"We can go 50, but we're going to hold it at around 42 for this trip. Here, Angus, we're coming up on a crossing. I want you to signal our coming with a whistle. Do you remember the proper whistle when the train is approaching a public crossing?"

"I think I do. It starts not less than 15 seconds but not more than 20 seconds before reaching the crossing, and it's two longs a short and a long. The signal is prolonged or repeated until the engine completely occupies the crossing."

"You got it, now we're getting close... OK, let her go."

"Angus, you got a real touch with that whistle. You play it like Satchmo blows his horn."

"Who is Satchmo, dad?"

"Louis Satchmo Armstrong is a great trumpet player down in New Orleans. You sounded just like him when you blew that whistle."

"Did Satchmo know Chief Sitting Bull, dad?"

"Are you saying that your dad is full of bull?"

"Maybe a little."

+++

"Please don't go Jaime. I can hide you here and they will never find you."

"I have to go, Liliana, they will find me and it will be worse for both of us."

"We could get a boat and go to America. We could leave tonight I know of a boat."

"You know I will come back to you, Liliana. The memory of you will make me strong. You are not a woman that can be easily forgotten."

+++

"Answer the phone, Angus. Go on answer the phone."

"Hello," answers Angus from his sleep.

"Angus, its checkout time," advised Paul, "you want to stay another day?"

"Come on over, Paul, and we'll discuss it."

As Paul arrives in the room Angus asks:

"Paul, let me borrow your phone. I've got to call Robert."

"Hey, Robert, how's every little thing?"

"Well, if it's not Angus. I heard that you're traveling with those legs, I mean with that Cuban woman."

"It's true, I was. Have things loosened up any around the city?"

"You know, I think they have. If you're talking about the heat coming down on you guys. I think the FBI and other agencies are being overrun by events. There have been riots in several cities in the last few days. The cops shot an unarmed black guy in Cleveland and also somewhere in Missouri and all hell's breaking loose. I think they're out-manned and overwhelmed. The cops are getting scared to make arrests for fear of getting into a scrape. This thing could get out of control quickly."

"Did Byron give you a phone number to use?"

"Yeah, he did. Tell you the truth; I don't think you're going to have to worry about it. My sources tell me that they just don't have the man power to chase these matters. Will you be coming back to the city?"

"Raul is dead. They took him off the Coyote yacht this morning. There loading him up and taking him back to

Cuba as we speak. Robert, these people mean what they say. This Cuba thing is happening. Philip is returning to the city to close down the office and presumably gear up for what's coming down south. Are you still in?"

"I'm still in, Angus; I'll get in touch with Philip and discuss these developments. With all this turmoil life on the Coyote is sounding better and better. I may out bid you for those shares. Will we see you soon?"

"I'll be back soon. Shall I place a bet for you at the Roulette table?"

"Put a hundred down on green, Angus, see you soon."

"Will do, see ya."

"Well, Paul, there's rioting in the streets back home. The economy is going into the crapper and social unrest is boiling over. What kind of times are these?

"Maybe times of opportunity."

"Maybe so, down where the water is warm. You know with capitalism there have always been losers, but now the ratio between winners and losers has grown to such an extent that it may never come back. In fact, if we get into a prolonged recession, and I think we are heading for that, it will put even more pressure on those at the bottom."

"I see it like this," said Paul, "technology is the enemy of the unprepared. Technology is starting to displace all those that were just getting by. If you are uneducated then you better be able to run like a deer or sing like Etta James. There will be a point in time, maybe now, when things will begin to accelerate against the have-nots; when that point is reached – anarchy will follow."

"And there is no predicting what will be the spark that sets it off. Maybe a cop shoots an unarmed man; maybe a sparrow flies into a window pane.

You know this Cuba thing is heating up and we've been invited to join. It would be an interesting adventure. How's your back? Let's have a look."

"It seems to me that Cuba has always been set at polar opposite to the US. In the fifties when we were surging ahead Cuba was taking a left turn and headed down. Now, they could be on the upswing and it's us that are taking the left turn and heading south.

I think that if you can get stabbed in Monaco you can get stabbed anywhere. I've been shot at by anti-aircraft, but this is my first stabbing. I was always too high to be stabbed."

"You're lucky he didn't drop you on the spot."

"Could you do it, could you fly the plane back home if he had dropped me?"

"I think I could but I don't want to think about that. With any luck you'll survive."

"When we leave you need to be in the cockpit, Angus. I don't want to get a call from the authorities. We've pushed our luck lately. Anyway, you need to sharpen your skills. I'll take the right seat and you can take me home."

"We may have had an angel on our wing in this regard, Paul.

I suppose we should get back to the city. It's too late today. Let's stay the night. We'll break the bank at the casino, and then leave in the morning."

"Ha, how many a wayward traveler has said just what you said?"

~ANGUS and LILIANA~
Chapter XVII
Arranging Visits

Merrill Lynch is sold to Bank of America amidst fears of a liquidity crisis and a Lehman Brothers collapse. The next day Lehman Brothers files for bankruptcy protection. The following day Moody's and Standard and Poor's downgrade ratings on AIG's credit on concerns over continuing losses to mortgage-backed securities sending the company into fears of insolvency. This is then followed by a run on money market funds - 140 billion is withdrawn this week.

"It's a shame, Philip," said Robert, "shutting down the office after 45 years in the business."

"It's not a terrible thing for me, Robert; I don't have that many more years. I am sorry for the people that we had to let go."

Byron adds: "The Fed just loaned $85 billion to AIG to keep them afloat. I doubt they will make an offer to us."

"Should we open a small office in Havana," asks Angus, "or would that just be a fun thing to do?"

"We might wait just a bit," counseled Philip. "I think they will make some kind of public declaration soon. They declared Raul dead in Monaco, but I think they are going to officially declare a new government in some manner before too long. If things don't go against them, and when that declaration is made we will then be free to travel and do as we wish. I think we will have a great deal of access to whatever we need in Cuba."

"How was it on the boat, Philip?" asks Angus.

"It was terrible. What we never understood in the US is that these people have been in a war inside Cuba for decades. Finally there comes a group, not with guns or slogans, not with outside interference, but with brains and organization. Once Raul walked onto that boat the battle was over. They believe that they have the organization in place to carry this through.

The details of what happened on the boat are not important. I can tell you that they now have in their possession the numbered Swiss accounts belonging to both Raul and Fidel. There are billions in these accounts and it should provide them a bit of seed money going forward. In his last act Raul signed over to Enrique the power of attorney over these accounts. He did this to save his family. I really think they were going to let him choose exile but Raul's belligerence was continuous. I don't think he fully understood the situation he was in, even though it was explained to him over and over again."

"What an amazing piece of history that you were part of," Robert said.

"Yes, and it won't be my name that goes down in the history books. I was staying close to Captain Jorgens as best I could; trying to keep his attention away from the activities on the rest of the boat."

"History is written by the winners," reminds Byron.

"So Enrique is your main contact?" wondered Angus. "It occurs to me that they should test that power of attorney as soon as they can. It would not be wise to go racking up debt only to discover some flaw in the document."

"That's good advice, Angus, I'll pass that along. Enrique and Ramon Beltran now have our contact numbers. I took the liberty of sharing them as they are eager to start.

We should talk about the kind of staff that we will need. I suggest that we take on legal counsel right away. We could start by throwing some names out for consideration. Would anyone like to offer a name?"

+++

"He tried to kill me twice, father. This is why he offered Monaco – they were waiting for us there. If it had not been for Angus and Paul I would be dead now. I want you to know that I owe them my life not once, but twice. Not to mention that they got me out of that disgusting jail and in the process rid the world of that pig Guillermo.

How are you feeling, father? Are you ready to make your announcement to the UN? Shall I make arrangements for the trip to New York?"

"I want to talk to you about this trip, Liliana. I think it would be best if you gave the speech to the UN."

"Me? Father, this is your moment, your time to tell the world how things are now."

"The words are the same and people will hear them more clearly if they are spoken by you, Liliana. I am old and tired and you are young and passionate. This is what the world needs to see. You've been to the UN, you know the players. Speak to them from your heart and Cuba will be well served. I'll take care of things back home."

"Are you sure this is what you want, father?"

"I'm sure this will be best for Cuba. Go, make your arrangements. And Liliana, stay away for a while, things might get rough here and I don't want you mixed up in it. Someone must stay clean."

"I had always planned to go with you to New York. I have some ideas about the presentation to the UN."

+++

"Hello," answered Angus.

"Hola, is this Peace Pipe Quin?"

"Peace Pipe Quin speaking, how may I assist you?"

"What are you doing, Angus?"

"Actually, I'm busy putting together a little surprise for you. This is how sure I was that we would see each other again."

"I love surprises. Can I eat it?

"No, it's much too hard."

"Is it always hard?"

"Yes, it will be hard always, it's also black, and it's not a pony, before you go off on one of your sexual fantasies."

"Well, I'm only slightly disappointed. I'm coming to the city soon; will I have to take a taxi from the airport?"

"When will you arrive?"

"I'm addressing the General Assembly at the UN on Friday so I'll be arriving on Thursday mid-day."

"You have advanced to Head-of-State already, Liliana, congratulations."

"My father was going to do it but he's exhausted from recent events, so he asked if I would give the speech."

"Let's see, today is Monday, of course I will pick you up and make arrangements at the Waldorf if that's OK. How long will you be in the city?"

"I will be leaving Saturday morning for San Antonio to meet with Avante-Primero Energy, then on to California for another meeting. Would you like to join me on my trip, Angus?"

"I would like to. Let me confirm that when you are here."

"Ok, Angus. There's just one thing. I'm going to need two rooms. The Waldorf is good, but I would also like a room at a Holiday Inn. I'm bringing someone with me."

"OK, I'll arrange for one room at the Waldorf and one at a Holiday Inn."

"I have a request to make of you before we say goodbye."

"Good, I love fulfilling requests."

"I'd like for you to find the very best salsa music in the city and take me there Thursday night."

"You've heard that I am a salsa machine. I will put my agents to work on it."

"Thanks, Angus, I'll see you soon."

"Yes, soon, goodbye."

Salsa dancing brought back memories of Little Havana, of Lily and Rose, and of Treenie.

'This might be a good time to settle some neglected scores,' thought Angus. 'I should get over to the hospital.'

"Lily, are you and Rose on duty this morning?"

"Angus! How are you? Yes, we are here saving lives and balling doctors on break."

"Good, so you're staying in shape. How about I come over and we can have some of that good hospital food for lunch? This will give the doctor's time to rest."

"Sure, Angus, we break for lunch at 11:45, can you make that?"

"I'll see you in the cafeteria."

Angus caught a cab to The Presbyterian University Hospital, which is only a few blocks east of Angus' apartment.

"Lily, Rose, my two sweethearts of medicine. You both look completely professional in spite of some of my most cherished memories."

"Yeah, good to see you too, Angus," responded Lily, "we also have visions of you that are best kept in that jar on the mantle."

"How are you feeling, Angus?" said Rose, "Shall we prep you for any special procedures while you're here?"

"I bet you've got a special room where you could do just that," laughed Angus.

"You can believe it, Angus. We have all contingencies covered," said Lily.

"I was thinking, girls, about the special ops mission that the two of you accomplished for your government down in Cuba. Your government would like to pay you properly for your service in the face of danger. How would you girls like to go shopping for shoes when you get off work? We may even look at boots. What do you think, girls, can you break away?"

"You being our government – are you kidding, shop for shoes and boots!" squealed Rose, "I want boots!"

"You'll need to dress festive because I want you to use all your skills and contacts to find the very best salsa dance music in the city."

"We should get in touch with Treenie," thought Lily.

"Meet me at the clock in the lobby of the Waldorf at what time?"

"How about six?" offered Rose; we'll take you to the "Green Tangerine" up in Spanish Harlem. It's upscale with the best bands in the city, and a stout cover."

"Six it is," agreed Angus, "Hmm, the "Green Tangerine," I assume you girls also know where the best shoes can be found."

"Oh, yes we do, Angus. You are the best," agreed both Lily and Rose.

"Well, let's say I'm one of the best. I don't want get too high up the ladder. I don't want a bunch of crazed love sick doctors running after me with a syringe full of something ugly.

See you at six. We'll find some boots, have dinner, and then we'll do salsa."

"You got it, Angus, see you at six," said Lily with a very broad smile on her face.

When Angus got back to his apartment he looked up the "Green Tangerine." The web site said:

"FRIDAY – Salsa dance contest – Intermediate to Professional.

This brought another thought to mind. After digging around in his wallet he found the card which said: 'Call me when the music starts.'

"Hola, this is Treenie."

"Treenie, the music is starting."

"Angus, my man in the city, how are you my friend?"

"Treenie how's the family?"

"The family is great thanks to you. My baby is growing every day thanks to you, Angus. And do you know what is his name? It's Angus."

"Oh, Treenie, are you sure you want to hang that handle on an innocent baby?"

"Yes, I am sure, Angus, I am very sure."

"Well, that's great news and I'm honored. Say, the reason I'm calling is this: I'd like to bring you to the city for the weekend coming up. I have need for a salsa dancer and as I recall – you fit the bill very well."

"Don't joke with me, Angus. You know that I am predispossessed to this kind of activity."

"It's no joke, Treenie, I'll pick up the tab and if you want you can bring the familia."

"Angus, just tell me what to do and when to do it. I would show up only if you wanted me to move furniture, but salsa dancing … this is what I live for – to dance in New York City."

"Treenie, I'm going to text you a number to call. Ask for Rosemary, she will arrange for your flight and hotel. Treenie, bring your dancing clothes and polish your shoes, people will be watching."

"I don't breathe until it's time. Thank you again, Angus. All I do is thank you."

"What you are doing is a favor to me, Treenie, no need for thanks. I'll see you in the city. I need you here Wednesday night and you can stay through Sunday. Just get your instructions from Rosemary."

"OK, Angus, I may have to leave Isla and Angus here. Angus is still pretty small, but you can count on me."

"I knew I could, Treenie, see you Wednesday."

~ANGUS and LILIANA~
Chapter XVIII
United Nations

Those that are new to money, real money, often have problems. Life is simple when *choice* isn't there to blur your mind. Big money moves in on the simple life and provides choice in the extreme. Many people are incapable of making decisions when there are so many options. For them it's like picking out the perfect wallpaper ten times a day, day after day – it makes them crazy. Others, however, slide right in and pull the trigger.

"Let's do Greek," Angus said with clear authority.

"Right here you want to do Greek?" asks Lily.

"No, over on W. 58th I want to do Greek. It's called ah, ah, I can't pronounce the name. It's a new Greek joint."

"Sure, OK," agreed Rose, "how does Greek feel to you, Lily?"

"It can be uncomfortable at times, but I roll with …"

"You girls kill me."

In the cab on the way to the Greek joint Angus explains:

"I have parallel motives for finding salsa dancing tonight. The woman that you sprung from jail in Havana – and changed the course of history – is coming to the city in a few days and she asked me to find the best salsa dancing."

"Really, is she coming after you, Angus?" wondered Rose.

"Well, actually, she's coming to give a speech at the United Nations."

"Really, who is this woman, Angus?" asks Lily.

"Lately I've been involved with Cuba. Cuba is on the verge of change and this woman is knee deep in the process. And, I have another announcement: Treenie will be here as well. I talked to him this afternoon and he's coming to dance. He also told me that he named his new son Angus."

"That's a nice touch; will we be able to see this baby Angus? Is he bringing Isla as well?" asks Lily.

"He was a little apprehensive about bringing the baby and Isla, but he was floating on a cloud with the thought of coming to the city to dance.

Here is what I'm thinking – I looked up this "Green Tangerine" and their web site said that they are having a salsa dance contest Friday night. What I'd like to do is enter Treenie and Liliana in this contest. We'll check this place out tonight, then when Treenie gets here Wednesday the four of us will go back and you two can give Treenie a good tune-up. Maybe Treenie can get noticed."

"Of course I'm in."

"Me too," added Lily, "you know that these contests are frequented by Broadway scouts."

"Great, then Friday night," continued Angus, "Treenie and Liliana will enter the contest and the two of you will enter as well."

"Are you saying that Rose and I will dance as partners in this contest?"

"Who would stop you?" wondered Angus,

"Well, the one person that would stop us is our boss," advised Rose, "we both work Friday night and we can't get out of it. Angus, your mind runs wide and deep."

"Three dimensional, wide and deep," agreed Rose.

With the aroma of Barbounia, AKA Grecian Red Mullet, mixing with the smell of new leather boots (over the calf), Angus, Lily and Rose sat and sipped Moschofilero, a Greek rosé.

"Ladies you know that women lead me around by the nose, I have no control over my actions. I'm a puppet to the desires of women."

"It's not just you, Angus, men are the simplest creatures on earth."

"You are right about that," agrees Lily, "give them food, sex and a warm place to sleep and they won't bother you.

Deny them any of these things and they become a danger to themselves and to others. They will leap from a bridge in despair, or worse, proclaim you to be their enemy and kill you.

At least you have a kind heart, Angus, even if you are a simple creature."

"Yes, but what if my heart gets broken and I leap from the Brooklyn Bridge in despair?"

"Then Rose and I will leap after you. We will drag you from the murky waters of despair."

"That's nice, girls. I may do that just for the experience. You know when you save me you are then obligated to provide me with food, sex, and a warm place to sleep."

"Would you settle for 2 out of 3?" asks Rose, as they all laughed.

"We love you Angus. We won't let anything happen to you."

"How are those boots feeling, girls?"

"It's not about the boots, Angus," insisted Lily, who was a bit miffed at the question's suggestion. Do you think that we love you because you are generous?" She then reached down and unzipped her boots. Holding one in her hand she proclaimed: "I love my new boots." She then removed the other boot, walked outside to the curb and threw them both into the traffic. Upon her return she said to Angus: "I loved those boots, but it's not about that, Rose and I love you without the boots, Angus."

"I feel the same, Angus, but since Lily made the point so well with *her* boots there's really no need for me to sacrifice mine, do you think? I would, you know I would … but these are the finest boots I've ever owned." And with her eyes tearing up Rose reached down, unzipped her boots, and walked barefoot to the curb and threw her boots into the traffic.

"Girls, you nourish my soul. I'm speechless. I feel like I should throw something into the street. What a scene is this? - Three grownups sobbing in public. We should retire to some private place before we get hauled away."

Rose continued, "Angus, you had me when after 3 days in my hospital bed in Italy, you woke, smiled and said: 'I guess a blow job would be out of the question.' You'd been under for three days and these are your first words?"

"Obviously I was delirious with fever. And three days without a blow job, well…"

"You are still delirious with fever, Angus Quin – money, no money; you will always have the fever."

Lily then rose from her Lavraki (a lean white fish with a mild, moist flake), and screamed to the room: "Its salsa time!"

+++

As Angus greets Liliana at the airport he sees that she has brought two friends with her.

"Angus, I'd like you to meet Lydia Rosales and Yolanda Cruz. Lydia is one of our national treasures and Yolanda is a friend of the family and will be assisting Lydia while she is away from home. Lydia will go with me to the UN; she too has something to say.

Señoras, éste es el Señor Angus Quin."

"Welcome to New York, ladies."

Both ladies nodded and shook Angus' hand.

As Angus drives the three ladies from the airport he asks Liliana: "How do you feel? Are you still up for dancing? Please don't say no because I've arrange a surprise."

"Of course I want to dance. This was my wish."

"Good. And to better serve you in this regard I have brought in a ringer."

"What is a ringer?

"There is a club here in Spanish Harlem called "The Green Tangerine" and we are going there tonight. The surprise is that we will be meeting Treenie there. Do you remember Treenie from Havana?"

"Yes, I remember Treenie. Have you brought Treenie all the way from Havana just so you wouldn't have to dance with me?"

"Not precisely. There is another leg of my story. Tomorrow night the two of you will be competing in a salsa dance competition at this same club."

"What? You have entered me into a contest?"

"I thought that if the two of you were able to practice some moves tonight that you might have fun with this. You said that you would like to dance with Treenie someday."

"Madre mia! Angus, I'm no professional dancer."

"C'mon, I've seen you dance and you're pretty good, you've got a lot of soul. And besides, the contest was billed as 'intermediate'."

"Will I be punished if I do poorly?"

"Of course you will be punished."

"What will you do to me, Angus?"

"I will rip your dancing clothes from your body, lay you across my bed and punish you repeatedly. Well, maybe not repeatedly, but at least a couple of times."

"You shouldn't give me incentives to fail, Angus. While I'm being punished will I be on top or bottom?"

"You will definitely be on the bottom until you show contrition."

"Angus, what is my contrition? Won't it be showing already if you have ripped off my clothes? I only ask that you wait until after we leave the club to rip off my clothes."

There were whispers and giggles from the ladies in the back seat. It seems that Yolanda knew more English than she would admit to. Liliana turns to them and winks.

"You could shoot for Miss Congeniality."

"Thanks, I don't think I'm the type. If we win what will be our prize?"

"You will win the respect and admiration of all of Spanish Harlem and I will sing the song: 'Spanish Harlem' on the steps of the Cuban Embassy."

"There is no Cuban Embassy in the US, Angus. Would you sing this song for me now?"

"*There is a rose in Spanish Harlem. A red rose up in Spanish Harlem. It is a special one it's never seen the sun ...*"

"That's enough, Angus, and this is if I win?"

"OK, so I can't sing. We're meeting Treenie at the club at eight. Are you nervous about your speech tomorrow?"

"I want to do well for Cuba. I've been there several times before so that will help. I'm not going to give a long speech the way Fidel did years ago. I have just a few points that I want to make and it won't take long. Anyway, it will be Lydia that steals their hearts.

Angus, I need your help with something. I am going to San Antonio to meet with this petroleum co., Avante-Primero Energy; I want to discuss with them the exploration of our offshore oil and gas. Do you have someone in the field of energy that you could contact? I want to know the standard split between the driller and the owner. I know these deals are done all the time and I want to have some knowledge going in of what would be a starting point for negotiation."

"Usually there is a lease arrangement between the driller and the property owner. The property owner, the Cuban government, collects a percentage of the revenues and the driller operates the well. I'm not up to speed on what these percentages are, but I know that all things are negotiable. This driller may be willing to sweeten the deal if they are given an exclusive.

When we get to my apartment I'll look through my book. There are a couple of names that come to mind. First we'll get them checked in at the Holiday Inn.?"

"Angus, I'm the one that will stay at the Holiday Inn. Lydia and Yolanda will be staying at the Waldorf. This is not the time for me to stay in such a hotel."

"That's a good idea, Liliana. I understand completely. We'll set them up right. I'll put Willard and Nancy on the job. Then we'll go to the Holiday Inn and get you checked in; however, no one will know if you don't actually wrinkle the sheets."

"So where will I be punished?"

"You can stay with me at my apartment."

"That would be nice. This venture into offshore oil worries me, but we are going to need cash flow to do what we need to do. In the future I'd like to move away from the oil."

"Would you like to bring along another player to Texas, someone with this specific knowledge?"

"No, I want to limit the number of players to as few as possible. All I need is a general idea of what these people usually get on these deals as far as percentages. I don't expect them to do this for nothing, but I don't want to appear foolish either. People smell your ignorance and then they take advantage."

"We'll make some calls when we get in, there is a guy that worked a desk in our office that will be a good source – then its salsa dancing at the "Green Tangerine. This is what I love – multi-tasking. Have you ladies had anything to eat? Let me guess – hamburgers or pizza?"

"Yes, that will be fine. I'm wondering if we should refine the crude right there in Cuba. The greatest profit comes when you refine the crude and add value."

Liliana was obviously in a state of flowing consciousness and had a lot on her mind.

"We'll bring Stan over to my apartment before we leave for Texas and pick his brain. Stan just got laid off so we'll throw him a consulting fee. If he shows good knowledge we may use him going forward."

"So you are coming along? I'm happy. And Paul will drive us?"

"And Paul will drive us."

"Angus, can you also make a meeting with Robert? I need to talk baseball with him."

+++

Is there anyone who really likes Cuba the way it is? The old Soviet Union perhaps, but their patronage has faded. Perhaps a few other despots in the region feel a sense of comradery with Fidel, but these are weak players in the overall mix. The only ones left that want to perpetuate the present Cuban condition are the handful of would be dictators that are inside Cuba - men who dream about the day that Fidel and Raul are no more. These men, with their sense of entitlement and desire for succession to the throne of Havana, would be the challenge.

Estado Libre Asociado de Puerto Rico, officially The Commonwealth of Puerto Rico, is a United States territory. Puerto Rico was claimed by Christopher Columbus for Spain in 1493, and like Cuba, Puerto Rico remained a Spanish colony until 1898 when Spain ceded its control of the island to United States following the Spanish-American war.

"I demand that my family be allowed to return to Cuba immediately," said Sr. Albelardo Rosales Hernández, head of the National Assembly of People's Power of Cuba.

"As I have said Sr. Hernández, your papers are not in order."

"Are we prisoners here in Puerto Rico?"

"Certainly not."

"Then why can't we leave, I continue to ask?"

"You can leave anytime you wish, although you cannot return to Cuba at this time."

"And what of my requests to speak to someone in your State Department?"

"Actually, we now have a person here from the State Department. Would you like to speak to him now?"

"Of course I would, this is what I have been asking for days."

"Yes, then, I will arrange a meeting for you tomorrow. Is two o'clock good for you?"

"I want to speak to him now, not tomorrow."

"Let me make a call. If you would like to wait here I'll see what can be done. I trust your family is comfortable at the hotel?"

"Yes they are comfortable, but that's not the point."

"I'll see what I can do, please relax here in the lounge or maybe you would prefer to return to the hotel. I could call you when I know something more."

"I will remain here for your answer."

The immigration office clerk then retreated to an adjacent office.

"He's getting very angry, Sr. Fowler."

"Good, tell him that there is a chance that I can meet with him today at three o'clock," said Carl as he shuffled the deck for another round of solitaire.

"This is maddening," said Sr. Hernández, "it is now only ten. There will be consequences for this outrage."

Three o'clock comes and Sr. Hernández again approaches the desk where a different person greets him.

"I am here for a three o'clock meeting," announces Sr. Hernández.

"Meeting?"

"Yes, I am meeting with someone from the U. S. State Department at three o'clock."

"Please have a seat and I'll see what I can find out."

With this he leaves his post and finds Carl watching a cooking show on TV.

"I love this Giada. I could watch her all day long."

"Sr. Hernández is back. He says he has a three o'clock meeting."

"Yes, tell him I am tied up and I'll be available at four. At that time come back to me and I'll let you know if I'm ready."

"Mr. Fowler has been detained and he will see you at four, please make yourself comfortable."

"You are joking with me?"

"No, Sr., please have a seat, Mr. Fowler is a very busy man."

At four o'clock Carl emerges from the office and greets Sr. Hernández.

"Sr. Hernández, please come, this is the best we can do for an office. Tell me," asks Carl, "what's on your mind?"

"I will take this to the streets, Sr. Fowler."

"Exactly what is it that you want to take to the streets, Sr. Hernández?

"My family is being detained illegally here in Puerto Rico. I must return to Cuba immediately. I will take this to the streets and shout until I am heard."

"You could do that, this is mostly a free country. But consider your argument, Albelardo: Cuba is now on the verge of meaningful change, a change from poverty, isolation and political oppression that you and your friends have engineered for decades. What will you shout in the street? 'Oh please, send me back to Cuba so that I may continue the policies of Fidel for another half a century. I've held you off so that you would have the opportunity to witness your opposition. Just now, at the UN, there is a lady about to give a speech. This is what you're up against, Albelardo."

And there in the office of immigration, Carl Fowler and Sr. Albelardo Rosales Hernández, ex head of the National Assembly of People's Power in Cuba, watched on TV as Liliana was about to be introduced to the General Assembly at the UN.

Liliana's father had alerted the media, not just in Cuba, but in most Central and South American countries, and a few in Europe. And he made personal phone calls to contacts in Miami and Little Havana. As best he could he made sure the entire world would be watching Liliana give her speech. All of Cuba would be gathered around whatever TV's were available.

"It's the whore, Liliana Beltran," offered Sr. Hernández, as he and Carl watched as Liliana is introduced.

Speech to the UN General Assembly

"Ladies and Gentlemen, this assembly now recognizes Liliana Beltran, representative of New Cuba."

"Thank you, muchas gracias.

In September of 1960 Fidel Castro stood where I am standing today. On that day Fidel spoke for over four hours. Today Fidel Castro lies in a hospital bed unable to speak, and Raul Castro is dead.

My name is Liliana Beltran and my time before you will be brief.

Living in fear for such a long time numbs the mind. For 50 years the people of Cuba have been afraid to speak, to think, afraid to act with determination and purpose. Today Cuba is free of that past. Now, like prisoners rubbing our eyes, we stumble into the light.

The good news for the people of Cuba is that recent events have not caught us off guard. There are those in Cuba that have been planning for this day. Systems are in place, people are aware and plans are being executed.

Even as we look to the future we will never forget those that have lived the nightmare of the past. There are many people in Cuba whose stories should be told. And in the months and years ahead we will make their stories known. One such person is here with me today. Better than I ever could, Lydia Rosales speaks for the New Cuba.

And now I would like to introduce to you Señora Lydia Rosales."

With Liliana's help Lydia makes her way to the podium.

Finally, Lydia stood alone at the podium. She raised herself up as straight as she could and looked out at the imposing scene. All the countries of the world stared back. Hundreds of people, some with plaques in front of them showing the names of the countries they represented. Lydia gripped the sides of the podium with her gnarled, arthritic hands and she made them wait. This frail mulatto woman, with her weathered, leather face, made them wait. Then, finally, with a voice that was stronger than expected, she spoke:

"My name is Lydia Rosales. For 49 years I have sold newspapers on the street corner in Havana. My first paper was called *'Hoy,'* then it was *'Revolución.'* Now, for a long time it is called *'Granma.'*

For my first 24 years there was Batista. Everything was corrupted. The nightclubs were filled with criminals from the Unites States: Lucky Luciano, Frank Costello, Vito Genovese and others. I knew these men, they would buy my papers. With their money and their guns they made whores of everyone.

Then, in 1959 there came Fidel, and Raul, and Che Guevara. This was a very exciting time. I cheered from my street corner like everyone when they came into the city.

We waived flags of the revolution; we honked our horns and banged on our cooking pots. Batista ran away and we were happy.

For a long time there was excitement, but the years went by, and more years, and slowly we realized that Fidel was just a different kind of Batista. In 1965 I was asked to place a sheet of paper in all my newspapers. This paper was from an opposing view from Fidel. I was arrested and put in prison where I stayed for five years. When I was close to death they showed me the door. There were many people like me in prison and many are there still. Soon I was again selling my newspapers on the corner.

Except for my time in prison I have read every word in my newspaper. These words are written mostly by scared men. They are scared that someday the people will understand that they are only scared little boys. I think it must be like this all over the world.

To all you little boys in front of me today I say – your days are numbered. Go home, do something good for the world and for your people before it's too late for you.

I see in front of me the name of Russia. We have had many Russians come to Cuba. You were like the Cosa Nostra only your guns were bigger. And even though the Russians have now gone, and Fidel is no more, men like these are still here. These men will always be with us, watching and waiting for their opportunity.

The people of Cuba want to be left alone. We are a good, hard working people and we want to make our own way. I see them ever day passing my corner. They struggle to feed their children, to teach their children, even for the right to speak their minds. We want to do our business without the government, or our neighbor, looking over our shoulder.

And now, again, change is promised. Only this will be a different kind of change. To you in front of me today – Cuba won't ask for your missiles, or your bankers, or your criminals. Today the change will not ride into town with guns and flags. Our change will come from within our hearts and our minds, and when our minds are set free Cuba will be free. This kind of change will take time for some. For old people like me change does not come easy and this is the way it will be. For old people even an injustice that is understood will be preferred to the uncertainty of change. But for the nimble mind of the child – computers will bring information and knowledge and their minds will quickly run free.

I have witnessed much change in my life and even the sound of the word makes me tired. But until I am dead I will have hope. I say to my many friends in Cuba that you should now, right now, put down what you are doing and go to the street. Take your cooking pots and bang them together. Go to your cars and your taxis and honk your horns. Everyone go to the streets and shout to the world that a good change is coming for Cuba. Do this now and when I return to Cuba I will join you from my street corner with a newspaper that is new and filled with words that are not scared but full of hope. This I believe.

Muchas Gracias.

And if I'm still alive after this, another day I will tell more.

Muchas Gracias. Viva Cuba!"

Lydia then repeated her words in Spanish:

"Ahora, para mis amigos de habla hispana:

Mi nombre es Lydia Rosales. Por 49 años he vendido periódicos en una esquina de La Habana. El primer periódico que vendí se llamaba Hoy, luego vendí Revolución. Ahora, desde hace mucho se llama Granma.

Durante mis primeros 24 años estaba Batista. Todo era corrupto. Las discotecas estaba llenas de criminales estadounidenses; criminales como: Lucky Luciano, Frank Costello, Vito Genovese y otros. Yo conocí a estos hombres, ellos solían comprar mis periódicos. Con su dinero y sus pistolas convertían a todo el mundo en rameras.

Entonces, en el 1959 llegó Fidel, y Raúl, y el Che Guevara. Fue una época muy emocionante. Desde mi esquina aplaudí y grité, igual como hicieron todos los demás cuando ellos llegaron a la ciudad. Agitamos las banderas de la revolución, tocamos bocinas y golpeamos cazuelas con cucharas. Batista huyó y nosotros nos alegramos.

Por mucho tiempo hubo un ambiente de emoción, pero al pasar los años, poco a poco nos dimos cuenta de que Fidel era otro tipo de Batista. En el 1965 me pidieron que colocara una hoja en todos mis periódicos. Esta hoja expresaba un punto de vista opuesto al de Fidel. Me arrestaron y me pusieron en prisión, lugar donde estuve durante unos 5 años. Cuando estaba a punto de morir me echaron a la calle. Hubieron muchas personas como yo encarceladas y muchas todavía están allí. Pronto regresé a mi esquina a vender mis periódicos.

Con la excepción del tiempo que duré en la prisión, he leído cada palabra del periódico. Estas palabras en su mayoría fueron redactadas por hombres asustados, temerosos de que un día las personas se den cuenta de que solo son niños miedosos. Me imagino que será así igual por todo el mundo.

A todos los niños miedosos que están frente a mí hoy, les digo: 'Sus días están contados. Váyanse a casa, hagan algo bueno, algo que valga la pena para el mundo y para su pueblo, antes de que sea demasiado tarde.'

Veo en frente de mí a Rusia. Hubo muchos rusos que vinieron a Cuba. Eran como la Cosa Nostra, solo que sus pistolas eran más grandes. Y aunque ya se han ido los rusos, y Fidel ha dejado de ser, todavía hay hombres como ellos aquí. Estos hombres siempre estarán con nosotros, al acecho, esperando su oportunidad.

El pueblo cubano quiere ser dejado en paz. Somos un pueblo bueno y trabajador; y queremos allanar nuestro propio camino. Veo al pueblo cubano pasar por mi esquina todos los días. Están luchando para darle de comer a sus hijos, para enseñar a sus hijos, hasta para darles el derecho de expresarse libremente.

Queremos atender a nuestros negocios sin que el gobierno, ni el vecino nos esté vigilando.

Ahora, una vez más, se nos está prometiendo un cambio. Solo que este cambio será diferente. A ustedes que se encuentran frente a mí hoy, les digo: "Cuba no les va a pedir sus misiles, ni sus banqueros, ni sus criminales." Hoy el cambio no entrará a la ciudad con pistolas y banderas. El cambio ocurrirá en nuestros corazones y mentes, y cuando nuestras mentes sean puestas en libertad, Cuba será puesta en libertad. Este tipo de cambio tomara tiempo para algunos. Para las personas viejas como yo, el cambio no es nada fácil y así será. Los viejos prefieren una injusticia que comprenden, a la incertidumbre del cambio. Sin embargo, para la mente ágil de un niño, las computadoras traerán información y conocimiento, y sus mentes rápidamente se echarán a volar.

He sido testigo de muchos cambios en mi vida y hasta de solo escuchar la palabra me siento cansada. Pero mientras que esté viva tengo esperanza. Les digo a mis amigos en Cuba que ustedes deberían dejar lo que están haciendo y ahora mismo deben salir a las calles. Cojan sus cazuelas y golpéenlas con cucharas. Salgan a sus carros y a sus taxis y toquen bocina. Todos, salgan a las calles y griten a voz en cuello al mundo que un cambio bueno viene a Cuba. Háganlo ahora y cuando yo regrese, me uniré a ustedes desde mi esquina con un periódico nuevo que tendrá palabras llanas de esperanza en vez de llenas de temor. Yo creo en esto.

Muchas Gracias.

Si todavía estoy viva después de esto, otro día les contaré más.

Muchas Gracias. ¡Viva Cuba!"

Liliana then joined Lydia at the podium. Liliana raised Lydia's hand to the cheers of most of the assembly.

+++

CNN news with Wolf Blitzer:

"The world is suddenly intrigued by this woman from Cuba, Liliana Beltran. Last night she was seen dancing to salsa music here in the city escorted by Wall St. executive Angus Quin. And today she speaks before the UN General Assembly.

For over half a century Cuba has been under the thumb of the Castro's. Cuba now appears to be under the spell of Liliana Beltran.

Will Cuba be able to keep to itself? It will be difficult. No doubt the island nation will be seen as a beautiful oyster lying fresh in the Caribbean Sea – brimming with possibilities. It will be difficult to keep the carpetbaggers out.

And what genius it was to bring the newspaper lady, Lydia Rosales, from the street corner of Havana. She spoke to this assembly with courage and wisdom as only an elderly, time weathered woman can.

The world will be watching with great interest as Cuba immerges from its Castro era.

We now have footage of what is happening in the streets of Havana. This appears to be in response to Lydia's plea. The cars are stopped with horns honking and people coming out of their houses with pots and pans and clanging them together. This may indeed be the start of something good for Cuba. I am being told in my ear-piece that similar scenes are being played out in Miami, Caracas, and even in Moscow."

+++

"So, this is what you're up against, Albelardo. And who do you think the world is rooting for – you, ex head of the National Assembly of People's Power, or these two women? To tell you the truth I want to go into the street myself and honk my horn."

"I will tell my story and I will use your own words," threatens Sr. Hernández as he pulls from his pocket a tape recorder.

Carl then points to the corner of the ceiling and says: "You see that little gadget there in the ceiling, Albelardo? This gadget has two purposes: with the flip of a switch it can either turn on my recorder, or it can disable yours. Which way do you think the switch was set?

Here's the plain speak, Albelardo – you're fucked! You have pitiful few options, and none of them include returning to Cuba. They don't want you there. They don't want you or the others like you that have been lured away to various partner locals by various means.

If you accept your new condition you may find me helpful in landing you a reasonable life outside of Cuba. I suggest you return to your socialist villa on the beach and talk this over with the familia. Be persuasive, Albelardo, I'll be here for only a couple more days and after that you will truly be fucked. Now, if you don't mind I will return to my cooking show. I am committed to learning how to make eggs benedict."

~ANGUS and LILIANA~
Chapter XIX
The Green Tangerine

The plan was that Liliana would take a cab from the UN to the Holiday Inn. She and Angus thought it best if they didn't give the press any extraneous information that might distract from her message. The fact is that Liliana was causing quite a stir and reporters, parasitic creatures that they are, had latched on to her like a flea on the back of a Bichon Havanese.

"Angus, when will you come for me? This press will not go away. I think they may follow us where ever we go."

"This may not be a terrible thing," surmised Angus, "Talk to them, win them over. This may give more momentum to your message. You may want to take a cab from the Holiday Inn to the club instead of having me pick you up. They may well follow you but once they have their story they will fall away and we'll be free to do as we wish. It's your call, Liliana. In fact, I could have Treenie pick you up. The press won't know what to think of him."

"Yes, Angus, that might be best. This will all fade quickly enough, but for now let's play the game. Let's have Treenie pick me up and we'll meet you at the club. After that I'm yours and I don't care."

At seven o'clock Treenie's cab pulled up in front of the Holiday Inn on 45th just off 5th Ave. As Liliana emerged from the elevator the crowd of fleas was waiting for her.

"Ms. Beltran, will Cuban's now be free to travel to the U. S.?"

Liliana stopped and addressed the reporters.

"There are many details that must be worked out between your government and the government of New Cuba. In the coming weeks and months there will be announcements made in this regard."

"Ms. Beltran, what will be your roll in the new Cuba?"

"I came to this country and studied to be an Engineer. This is where I would like to make my contribution. There is much to rebuild in Cuba and I am eager to contribute what I can."

"But why were you chosen to give the speech at the UN?"

"In the past I have worked as a translator for the Cuban delegation at the UN. It was thought that since I know my way around, and I was able to deliver the message in both English and Spanish, that I would be the most effective. There are many who could have done the job but they are all busy back in Cuba. For these reasons I was chosen.

What I want to stress to you is that I am here for the Cuban people. My words, and the words of Lydia Rosales were the words of the Cuban people back home, we were only the messengers.

Now, if you are going to follow me once more, I am on my way to Spanish Harlem. I must win a dance contest there or I will be punished at least a couple of times, gracias y buenos noches."

Liliana had quickly picked up on Angus' suggestion to use the press. Liliana then stepped into the cab while some of the fleas continued hurling questions and others hailed their own cabs to follow.

"¿Cómo estás, Treenie?"

"Muy bien, gracias. I am so excited to dance with you tonight. And now I see that you are a rock star. Are all those people going to follow us to the club?"

"It looks like they are."

"My mother told me that you talked to her while you were in the jail. She said that you told her that Cuba was going to change soon. Of course she has heard these stories her whole life, but when you talked to her she believed that it would happen."

"It is happening now, Treenie."

"And today, everyone was watching as you gave your speech. All my friends in Little Havana were watching. If you come to Little Havana they would put you in a car with flowers and drive you up and down the Calle Ocho."

"I may need that someday, Treenie. Are you ready to do this dance contest? I'm more nervous over this than the speech."

"You will be fine. Just imagine that you are at The Cadillac club in Havana."

As they arrived at the "Green Tangerine" the press had beaten Treenie and Liliana and was waiting at the entrance.

"Liliana," shouted one reporter, "they won't let us in, would you twirl for us?"

At the suggestion Treenie grabbed Liliana and gave her a twirl like a top. The flash bulbs went off as if they were walking into a movie premier. As they entered the club it was Angus, holding down a table and waving them over.

"Do you know what it took for me to get in here? They were waiving hundred dollar bills outside like it was chump change. My next profession is going to be door man at a dance club. You guys had your paid contestant tickets; I'm just a lonely single guy with a three hundred dollar bill. I'll bet there's still a thousand dollars being waived outside at the door. I'll order you guys some drinks if you want to go warm up – what a band, huh?"

Treenie and Liliana retreated to the restrooms to make the final adjustments that would reveal their dancing costumes. When Liliana returned to the table Angus' jaw dropped along with most of the other women in the room.

"Stunning, Liliana, they will not have the nerve to eliminate you. And you, Treenie, you look great as well. You will have your hands full tonight mi amigo."

On the dance floor Treenie and Liliana produced their competitor tickets and with a marker the number "12" was written prominently on their skin. In the case of Liliana the opportunity for skin was plentiful. Liliana's dancing outfit consisted of a top that, although it was not painted on, it certainly gave this illusion. It was a thin, almost sheer black material which was covered in sequins and glued tight to her skin. There was a wide separation down the middle so there could be no buttons or snaps. The back dipped down as well and stayed just above the boundaries of reasonableness. It was basically two halves that were connected only at the neck.

Around her waist were attached long peacock feathers of varying lengths that dangled loosely to above her knee and revealed only black panties when she twirled. Liliana's shoes were black with silver sequins on the heels that were too tall for mortals. In her hair was a single peacock feather. Angus was particularly proud of his peacock contribution. Angus had to be told several times to please sit down and not block the other's view.

Treenie was decked out at the top with a wide brimmed black hat trimmed around the brim with a silver sequined band which held a single peacock feather. He wore a black long sleeved shirt with a silver sequined vest and black slacks. He was the perfect foil for Liliana and had they not had to dance they would have destroyed the field.

The problem was they were not dancing in Little Havana, or at The Cadillac club in real Havana, they were dancing in the Big Apple, home to more professional, and would be professional, dancers than anywhere this side of Las Vegas. And still, fearless, they began to dance, not seriously, but only half speed to warm up, the way a boxer might approach a punching bag. No one wanted to show their moves.

The orchestra was great: Eddie Palmieri and the Afro Caribbean Jazz All Stars.

"You can tell there are some really good dancers here," observed Liliana.
"Just remember," reminded Treenie, "we are only in Havana at The Cadillac club. We will do the best we can and wish the others good luck. Ha, I was only kidding about the last part."

"Yeah, may they all stumble and fall."

The club was huge. It was fashioned after the original Copa Cabana that was the sensation of the forties over at 10 E. 60th Street. Now all the great Latin acts showed up here at the Green Tangerine and the dance contests were a prized ticket.

After their brief warmup they returned to the table and a cheering, whistling, clapping Angus Quin.

"You guys look like a million bucks out there," said Angus, with the enthusiasm of a father watching his son play little league baseball.

"Who are the judges?" wonders Angus.

"Here, you can look at the flyer," offered Treenie, "they are listed at the bottom. There are three: Zoe Saldana: actress, dancer, Mario Espinoza, Broadway choreographer, and Emilio Carmona, owner of The Green Tangerine."

"I am now sitting in the yellow Cadillac back home in Havana," advised Liliana, "I feel no pressure as long as I'm sitting in my Cadillac. Zoe Saldana can dance. She is from the Dominican."

"Hey, Treenie – *the music is starting*," said Angus with a smile.

And indeed it was as the MC took center stage. And after a long winded introduction and commercial for the Tangerine he finally announced the first contestants: No. 9.

"Number nine? That's not right," protested Liliana, "they're supposed to go in sequence."

"That means we could be next," shouted Treenie, as the music started.

"Madre mia, may I please not fall down on the way to the dance floor, wished Liliana. "Thank you Angus for this night – I think one of these peacock feathers is crawling up my culo. My self-esteem was good until tonight. Are you comfortable, Angus, can we get you anything."

"C'mon, you're going to be great. Look at these guys, you can do this good."

The next number was not twelve, nor was the one after that. They all had variations of twirls, dips, and the occasional spin like a top moves. There didn't seem to be any bad dancers. Then, after the sixth couple had danced their number was called – 12.

"Go, kill, have fun," urged Angus, as Liliana and Treenie left the table.

There are times when a person, for reasons that are inexplicable, rises above their station, when reasonable expectations are confounded by circumstances. History is littered with these examples: when the Americans beat the Russians in hockey in the Olympics (the Miracle on Ice), when James Buster Douglas knocked out Mike Tyson in Japan, when Seabiscuit beat War Admiral at Pimlico. Occasionally, when the moon is blue, a person is propelled into a place where they were never expected be. Sadly, this was not one of those occasions.

When all the contestants had danced and the scores were tallied Treenie and Liliana did not finished in the top three.

"You see," declared Angus, "you finished fourth in a strong field. I call that a victory."

"How do you know we finished fourth and not last, Angus?" wondered Liliana as they stood on the curb and tried to hail a cab.

"Well, anyone could see that you should have come in second," said Angus with conviction. "The winners were very good and were probably brought in illegally, but clearly you guys were next.

Treenie, this is where we part. I hope you enjoyed your stay in the apple."

"Wait, look at this picture of little Angus," Treenie said as he pulled his phone. "I'll send more pictures as he grows up. Thank you so much, Angus, and be sure to thank President Clinton also. Goodbye, Liliana. Maybe I'll see you again in Havana."

"Maybe so, Treenie, goodbye," called Liliana as Treenie drove away in a cab. "President Clinton?"

"It's a long story."

"I am so hungry. I want steak, Angus. I want steak like the one we had on the Coyote boat. And I think you are trying to get out of punishing me for not winning. I could have won easily, you know, but the thought of not being punished made me hold back. I know it wasn't fair to Treenie, but I couldn't help myself."

"If you keep talking like that you will have to skip the steak. Driver, take us to Keen's Steak House on W. 36th.

"Angus, I am worried about Lydia and Yolanda."

"Not to worry, I checked on them before I left and they are in good hands at the Waldorf. They were going to have dinner at the Peacock and then spend the evening watching cable TV in the room."

"In the morning I'll take a taxi and pick them up and take them to the airport."

"Would you like to drop them off in Havana on our way to San Antonio?"

"Oh, Angus, that would be such a treat for them. The crowded plane from Miami was hard on Lydia. I'll call them and tell them of our plans."

+++

One of the meetings held at Angus' apartment was with Robert Starr of Pinnacle-Starr Brokerage.

"You know," Robert said, "there was a serious dust up in the Bronx last night. Rioting and looting with police cars set on fire. It could just as easily have been in Spanish Harlem where the two of you were. Things are getting very dicey all over the country."

"What set this one off, Robert," asks Angus.

"There seems to be a common theme: the police try and arrest some criminal, there is a scuffle and the police win, then anarchy ensues. Businesses are looted and burned and the police become more and more reticent to chase the bad guys for fear of ending up in jail themselves.

There is deep social unrest and I don't know how it's going to get resolved."

"You could be socialists like we are in Cuba – make everyone dirt poor and then there is no energy for rioting."

"Well," offers Angus, "I'm afraid this country has turned the corner. The only hope may be to take from the haves and redistribute it to those who can't compete. And it's not just in this country the whole world is migrating; from Africa north to Europe, from South America north to the US.

They already have French-fry machines that can peel, slice and fry potatoes all day long, and the guy that's standing there now is demanding a doubling of the minimum wage? They're just going to bring in the machine and send the human home. I saw where they now have a machine that can brick a house in two days. You feed the machine the plans and turn it on. All day in the hot sun this machine lays a perfect course of bricks. How are people going to compete with these smart machines? What are these brick masons going to do, switch over to orthopedic surgery? There will probably be a machine to do that as well.

If we don't provide some relief for the average Joe we're going to end up with a small portion of the population barricaded behind walls with the have-nots outside throwing rocks and trying to break in. We are going to have to provide relief for those on the bottom rung just to keep the peace. I'll give you food if you promise not to kill me. This is what taxation is going to be in the near future.

Once it was to benefit the elderly and the truly needy, now we're heading for something completely different and this current financial crisis may be what lit that last length of fuse. It's a brave new world we're heading into.

I'm with you Robert; I don't know how this is going to get resolved. I mean, how different is this than when they stormed the castle walls in Europe hundreds of years ago. It is curious that today when they get over the castle wall they choose to leave with a Sony TV."

"In Cuba," added Liliana, "Fidel climbed over the wall and everyone cheered. But Fidel left everyone outside and only a few lived well. This is the fate of humans. We are flawed and we repeat the mistakes of the past. I worry about what kind of mistakes we will make after we get over the wall this time.

Can we discuss our present business and not be fatalistic for a while? This talk depresses me.

Robert, my father was impressed with your enthusiasm when he spoke of baseball on the Coyote boat. We wonder if you could work toward this goal: We would like to partner with one or more baseball franchise owners to construct our baseball stadium complex. With your contacts in Boston, and elsewhere, think about how this could be accomplished."

"I understand and I will make some inquiries. Would you be available to meet with these players in Havana at some future date?"

"Of course we would. Also, as you begin to develop your contacts consider trying to get an audience with the commissioner of baseball. We would like to set up a tour for our Cuban team. We would like to play at least one game in every major league stadium next season. And think about how we could profit from these games. I know there is a complicated system of revenue sharing between the teams, but we believe that a game, or series played against a Cuban team would be a tremendous draw and we would like to participate in the revenue somehow. See what you can make happen. We would also like to do a tour of Japan.

This stadium complex that we imagine would also have a hotel associated with it. We want to approach the best hotelier for this project."

"Would you consider having a commercial sponsor for this tour? This could be very lucrative."

"I don't think so. I would like to keep our own identity, but I will think on it. Maybe we will be sponsored by "Cubana' the new electric car company of New Cuba. It doesn't have to exist in order to sponsor, no? And it will exist someday."

"There have been some impressive stadium projects in recent years," offered Robert, "I'll see if I can find out what kind of numbers we're talking about."

"Good. I think you and Angus and others will soon begin to wonder just how you will profit from all this activity. Put your heads together and present something to me."

"We will do that, and I'm sure we can come to an understanding in that regard."

As Liliana, Robert and Angus sat around the dining room table Robert took on the current state of affairs within Cuba.

"As you must know, Angus and I are risk takers by nature, but we are also careful and studied in what we do. I have contacts at the State Department in DC and they have contacts from various intelligence sources at State and elsewhere. They inform me that there is resistance within Cuba at this time and that factions within the military are not going quietly down your 'New Cuba' road. Do you have any comment in this regard?"

"You must know by now that we too are risk takers, and that we are also careful and studied in our approach. It was anticipated that there would be certain individuals within the military and in the government that would not want to give up their seats of power. Recently certain individuals were lured away from Cuba and are now finding it difficult to return. However, we knew that we could not eliminate all opposition in this way and some would have to be dealt with within Cuba.

Because we had the benefit of knowing precisely when the transition would take place we were able to plan to that moment. There is a military base at Isla de la Juventud. This is the island south of the mainland of Cuba. A conference was scheduled there with certain military attendees receiving awards and medals from government officials.

Enrique Fuente, the friend of your partner, Philip, is counselling this group as we speak. It is anticipated that his negotiations will not be successful.

They have two options: they can remain on this island and become the opposition, or they can board a waiting ship and sail to Guayaquil, Ecuador. The government there has agreed, for consideration, to accept this group.

If they choose to remain we will fight them and overwhelm them within a short period of time."

Angus wonders, "But if these players are within the military won't they have an advantage in the fight?"

"These are army leaders, not air force. We have control of the air force through General Cienfuegos that you met on the Coyote boat. And there is one other thing – about 8 months ago we acquired some significant military assets. We received three so called "Black Hawk" helicopters and three A-10 "Warthog" fighting jets. There will be a sudden show of force and through the use of these assets they will come to understand quickly that Ecuador is their best option. There is no way off this island and any assets that they may use will have no way to reach them. We will make arrangements to bring their families along later."

"When you first started this campaign," asked Robert, "How did you know who to approach?"

"Of course you can never be sure what is in people's hearts and minds, but from the start it was our philosophy to approach people who had children.

General Cienfuegos has eight children. Almost all of players in this movement have children.

This drama on the island will play out in a short period of time and with the exception of a few here and there our goals will have all been met.

What I have told you here today is known only to a few and it would be best to keep it that way. The presence of these assets is sensitive. So, Robert, if you would like to wait a few days before you approach your baseball friends that's fine, but knowing what I know now, I would proceed right away."

"I have two more questions," says Angus, "Who will be the leader of this New Cuba, and is there any office space available in Havana?"

"My father will soon emerge as the President of New Cuba and we will provide whatever space you need, Sr. Quin."

"You know that I require an ocean view, Señorita Beltran."

"When we return Lydia to Havana you can pick your spot, Angus. And Robert, you have my personal invitation to bring your family to New Cuba and be our guest, and you can bring your sister as well."

"Thank you, Liliana. You're approach in these matters does seem careful and studied."

"Those that would have the fruit must climb the tree, Sr. Starr. And I should add: Nadie es profeta en su propia tierra. No one is a prophet in their own land. These little sayings sound more profound when spoken with an accent, don't you think, Robert?

Angus, I think I'd like to go spend a little time with Lydia and Yolanda. I'll just catch a cab and be gone a couple of hours. Adios, Robert, stay in touch."

"Will do, Liliana. Adios."

Angus walked Liliana downstairs to the cab and then returned to his apartment.

"Angus, there is more to this gal than a long inseam. Is there any doubt in your mind that this whole business is of her making? I think this entire architecture was formulated in her head. You need to be careful with this one, Angus. She may be out of everyone's league."

"She is a handful," was Angus' only response. "*Careful and studied*," muttered Angus to himself. "Robert, who do you think would be the greatest prize for this so called opposition? I need to get a hold of Paul," Angus then punches out the numbers on his phone, ignoring whatever Robert's response was.

"Paul, the games afoot; we're off to Havana – ten AM tomorrow. There will be myself, Liliana, and two women of the elderly type, and maybe another player to be announced. And Paul, get in touch with George and dress him up as co-captain. If all goes well we will drop off the elderlies, spend the night, then head for San Antonio the next AM. See you tomorrow, and Paul, make sure we have our special bag of tricks on board. Yeah, that one, I'll brief you on the plane tomorrow."

Angus then dialed another number.

"Treenie, my man on the dance floor, when do you leave the apple?"

"I leave tomorrow morning."

"How would you like to make some good money?"

"Are you kidding? I have booties to buy and college to save for. What did you have in mind?"

"Best case we will just have a one night stand in Havana, worst case you may be needed for some Cuban espionage. I'd like for you to ditch that flight in the morning and join me and Liliana on my plane back to Havana. We leave from Teterboro airport at ten in the morning. Tell the cab driver to take you to Teterboro airport in New Jersey. Allow for maybe 45 minutes to get there."

"You can always count me, Angus; I'll see you in New Jersey at ten."

"Great, see you then."

"Angus, I'm going to head out. You know, Cuba could be a place in flux right now in spite of Liliana's confidence.

You should sleep with one eye open, mi amigo. You don't want to end up as a historical statistic."

"I'm with you on that thinking, Robert. I am a *careful and studied* man, don't you know. You take care as well and don't get mixed up in any riots. I will be curious as to what you can come up with on the baseball front."

"What a prospect this is, huh, Angus? I'll see ya."

Just as Robert was leaving the phone rings …

"Yes, Liliana, how are the hotel guests?"

"Muy, muy, bien, Angus. They don't want to leave. This small taste of capitalist extravagance will ruin them for the rest of their lives."

"I know exactly how they feel. My life has been ruined with extravagance."

"Angus, I was just on the phone with Treenie and he said that he was coming with us on the plane tomorrow. Last night Treenie made a suggestion that I have been thinking about and I wanted to see what you think.

On our way to Havana we could stop in Miami. Treenie thinks that he can arrange for a kind of parade down the main street in Little Havana. We could put Lydia in the back of a car and show her off. Treenie says that there was a tremendous response to her speech there."

"Does Treenie have the kind of connections that could pull something like that off?"

"Treenie says that he is friends with the man that owns the Versailles restaurant on this calle oche and that this man knows the mayor. He's going to make a call and see what he can put together. I think this kind of boost in Little Havana could be a real plus. What do you think, Angus?"

"I think you are right. From what little I saw while I was there this Little Havana is just what the name implies. We'll let Treenie work the deal and see what happens. We need to touch down in Miami for gas anyway."

"Thank you Angus. I'm going to call him back right now. I'll see you shortly."

"Watch your step, ladies," urged Paul from below, as Lydia and Yolanda made their way up the steps of the Gulfstream.

"Here we come, Angus," assured Liliana, "slowly but surely we will get there. Believe me ladies you will like this plane much better than the one we arrived on."

"Welcome to Air Angus, ladies, your chariot waits," said Angus from the top of the stairs. "Our motto is: 'If it's down there, we'll find it.' As you take your seats please notice that we have provided for each passenger one of our local newspapers. And for you Lydia, we have managed to obtain a whole bundle of these papers. I suspect, however, that Liliana will want to buy a few more before you can sell them on your corner."

"Oh my God, look at this!" exclaims Liliana.

There was Liliana – pictured on the cover of the New York Times – being twirled by Treenie like a whirling Dervish at the entrance to "The Green Tangerine." With the headline: 'Cuba – Dancing into the 21st Century.' Next to Liliana's picture was one of Lydia at the podium at the UN.

"Look at this, Lydia. Yolanda, look at our friend standing there proud and schooling those old bastards. I was so proud of you, Lydia."

"You ladies have made the big time," said Angus, "and it is my honor to serve you the beverage of your choice, as long as we have your choice.

Treenie, you might want to latch on to a couple of those papers as well."

"I'm going to frame this picture and put it on the wall at the 'Ball and Chain,' and maybe 'The Cadillac' too, and one for my mother and one for my Isla, and one for my sister. And I will put one up in the laundry room at the end of the block. And I will put one up at the Versailles."

"We may have to land and buy more papers," warned Angus.

Liliana was busy reading the article.

"They are skeptical that we will succeed," as Liliana reads the commentary below the pictures, "all they want to do is plunder and imagine how they can make money. I don't want to read any more of this. I will read what they say a year from now."

Paul and George, the new co-pilot, then emerged from the cockpit and announced that they would now do their walk-around check of the outside of the plane.

"Angus, would you join us? And how about you, Treenie, would you like to come along?"

Now, while standing on the tarmac at the nose wheel of the Gulfstream G280, these four could pull a private meeting.

Angus began: "I first thought we were going straight to Havana but now I understand that we will stop over in Miami for a parade. Treenie, how's that working out? Do you have all the arrangements made?"

"Yes, they are very excited in Little Havana. We are supposed to meet the mayor at the Versailles at six and Liliana and Lydia will join him for a parade. They will probably drive up and down the Calle Ocho a couple of times and that will be it. I think you will be surprised at the turn out."

"Well, this is my concern, says Angus, "while Lydia and Liliana are making their splash here in the states there are still a few skirmishes going on back in Cuba. If I were the opposition I would set my sights on Liliana as a bargaining chip. I don't think she would be assassinated, necessarily, that wouldn't give them any leverage. No, what they would need to do is take her. I would like us all to be vigilant and pay close attention. There may be some bad actors waiting to spoil all this fun, both in Miami and in Cuba.

So, with that said, let's go to Miami. Who doesn't love a parade? George, Paul will fill you in when we get underway and we'll get you set up when we get to Miami."

"Roger that, captain" acknowledged George.

"Everyone buckle up," advised Paul, "we're about to leave the ground."

In a short time they were at cruise altitude and Angus unbuckled and stood to say:

"Congratulations on your speech, Lydia. You told those old reprobates."

"I was very happy to do it," responded Lydia, "and thanks to Liliana for her excellent coaching. She gave me the courage I needed."

"Yes, and for her part she now will receive the surprise that she has probably forgotten about. This was finished and delivered yesterday."

"What are you talking about, Angus?" asked Liliana.

Angus then went to the back of the plane and pulled a box from an overhead storage compartment.

"This is the first piece of your collection," and Angus handed the box to Liliana.

"This is very heavy, Angus, I hope it is the first of my gold collection."

As Liliana opens the box she screams and starts to cry: "Angus, you always listen to me. Mal Tiempo."

This was a working miniature of the old dilapidated steam locomotive that Liliana showed Angus in Havana, the one with the words: Mal Tiempo written on the sides.

"You said this is what you wanted. And you can now start your own model train collection in the basement of your home in Havana. Do they have basements in Cuba? You can add all kinds of cars for it to pull along your tracks. You could even get yourself some chickens to run on the tracks in front of it."

"I know this train," said Lydia, "I have seen this train before."

"Angus, you are such a thoughtful man," declared Liliana. "I will start my own collection and as I watch this train go round and round it will take me back to when Jaime and I would run in front with the chickens. I wonder – do they have mechanical chickens? Thank you Angus."

"You can go on the internet and order anything and have it delivered even to Havana. You can order track, cars, mountains and bridges, anything. And you just put it all together the way I did in my basement. When my trains run I am back on the Calumet heading out with my father, or returning to the yard in Chicago. My trains are my time machine. There is a real train that starts in Calgary, Alberta and travels through the Canadian Rockies of British Columbia and ends up in Vancouver. Someday I will make that trip."

"I'm sure you will, Angus. I can't wait to get the catalogue and see what I want to pull behind my 'Mal Tiempo' engine. I need to have a car that holds sugar cane for sure."

"Angus," asks Treenie, as he reads through the New York Times newspaper, "who are these people 'Fannie Mae' and 'Freddie Mac' and how can they have so much money? It says here that the federal government has just taken over both Fannie Mae and Freddie Mac who together guarantee over six trillion dollars of home mortgages. A trillion is a lot, no?"

"A trillion is a lot, yes. Fannie and Freddie are not real people; they are government agencies that are mixed up in the mortgage mess that's trying to bring down our economy. The government is trying everything it can to bail everyone out. It's a big mess."

"Isn't this your business, Angus," asks Treenie.

"Yes, this was my business and I was up to my eyeballs in this mess. History will note the irony of this time: as Cuba fights to shed itself of its socialist policies the US rushes to adopt them. Before this is over we may all be better off in Cuba. "

"Please, Angus, don't start sending everyone to Cuba," pleads Liliana, "we are not ready."

"I am a capitalist," insists Angus, "and I will always be a capitalist. It's true that I have benefited greatly from this system, but I also believe that it offers the greatest hope for everyone. I am the son of a train conductor and because of the unlimited opportunity that this country provided I can now fly my own plane. You can't give everyone their own plane, it just won't work. You have to provide the opportunity, not the plane. This is the genesis of all these financial problems; the government designed an artificial system through Fannie Mae and Freddie Mac and tried to put everyone in a house, whether they could afford it or not. Something for nothing will not work.

The world is littered with evidence of how not to construct a society: Greece, Spain, Cuba 90 miles away, and instead of learning from these failed systems we're doing our best to emulate them.

This is all too depressing for me. I need to go up and have a chat with Paul and George to make sure they have the plane pointed in the right direction. Once we were heading for Ohio and we ended up in Kentucky. You know you just can't get good help these days."

"Yeah, I'm sure," said Liliana, "if he can find Spain he can surely find Florida."

In the cockpit Angus says: "Hey guys what's our ETA?"

"We're looking to land at 2:10," said George.

"What do you think of my fixed wing beauty, George?"

"I don't see it hovering in place, Angus."

"No, it can't do that, but it can cruise at Mach .80. Can your egg beater do that?"

"No, can't do that. I guess we all have our purpose."

"When we get on the ground you guys should go straight to the FBO and get George lined out. This little pony show will kick off around six and probably won't last too long. So get your coordinates for Little Havana and this Calle Ocho. No doubt they will have some kind of convertible with Liliana and Lydia in the back. So, Paul, we have our box of goodies in the back storage, right?"

"Yep, all the way back," confirms Paul.

"Ok then, carry on."

Angus then returns to the cabin and says: "Liliana, come to the back I want to show you something."

Angus then pulls from the storage a metal box.

"Liliana, it must have occurred to you that for the next few days while you are in Cuba, and even in Miami, you may be the target of those in the opposition."

"I never gave it a thought, Angus – I have you and Paul."

"Well, I've given it some thought and I want to show you something. I'd like for you to wear this little bug pinned to the inside of your blouse. This is a powerful transmitter and when you speak I will be able to hear everything you say and anything those close to you say.

I don't think these people want to harm you, not right away; they would, however, try and use you to bargain their position with your father. So, just as a precaution you should keep this bug attached like this - bueno?"

"You really know how to sweet talk a girl, Angus. OK, I'll wear your bug. This kind of device could be very addictive, I think. I will have to be careful what I say about you."

"Information is a very addictive thing, you are right. It's more addictive than heroin, or so I'm told. Paul, Treenie, and George will also be able to communicate with me and we will take positions along the parade route. So, if Fidel comes and snatches you just remain calm and the cavalry will be along shortly."

"You mean I can't kill them until you get there?"

"Right, don't kill them until I get there."

"Kiss me, Angus."

"Have you noticed that whenever there's the slightest hint of danger your mind turns to sex?"

"Have you noticed that on some airplanes there are beds? Kiss me Angus."

"Have you noticed that on some airplanes the bathrooms are very large?"

"Really? I feel danger now, Angus. Show me this large bathroom."

And so Angus and Liliana casually retire to the bathroom in the back of the plane as Angus laments: "I guess I'm going to have to get a bigger plane. Do you know how much this plane cost?"

When the blood runs quick, and in the heat of such moments, people can overlook little details. Liliana forgot that she had a bug attached to her blouse, and Angus forgot the receiver on the seat in the cabin.

And so off they flew toward Miami at 35,000 feet with Angus and Liliana defiling the cabinet, the sink, the toilet, and the walls of the bathroom, with Treenie, Lydia, and Yolanda glancing curiously at one another. It was Treenie that approached the receiver, reached down to pick it up then decided against it. They all then gave each other a knowing glance and a nod toward the bathroom. Treenie then returned to his seat and they all squirmed to the noises usually heard through the wall of a cheap motel room.

When Angus and Liliana finally emerged from the bathroom Angus declared:

"Now that we've gone over your route just get out there and wave your little heart out. And how about those cigars that you brought for the people in Texas and California, why don't you hand them out along the parade route? We could pick up some more tomorrow when we get to Havana."

"That's a really good idea. You got some good PR chops on you, Peace Pipe."

"I should never have told you my name was Calumet. Do you have a middle name?"

"I have three, and they would only confuse you further."

When they got on the ground in Miami Angus again gave instruction:

"I think it would be best if Treenie and you three ladies go on together in the cab to the Versailles restaurant. Treenie you stay in touch with me. Paul, George and I will work our plan from this end. Liliana, we are going to be in the background and we won't make contact with you until the parade is over and it's time to return to the plane. So don't acknowledge us if you see us. Treenie, you find your way to the west end of the route and Paul will be at the east end and I will stay with the car at the Versailles.

So, here is your cab. You guys can schmooze the restaurant until it's time to kick off the parade. We will follow shortly in a rent car. And again, don't acknowledge us when you see us."

Angus listened on his receiver as their cab pulled away. Of course the first thing Liliana said in the cab was:

"Did you know that Angus' middle name is Peace Pipe? Can you hear me Peace Pipe?"

Angus just shook his head with no ability to respond.

At six o'clock the mayor gave a speech in front of the Versailles restaurant lauding Liliana and Lydia and the recent events in New York and Cuba. And waiting at the curb was a bright red Cadillac convertible with a driver that was grinning from ear to ear.

The Calle Ocho (Eighth Street) is no stranger to street celebrations. Each year the Calle Ocho parade is held and claims to be the largest street celebration in the world. News that Cuba would soon be free spread fast through a population that is attuned to every morsel of news about Cuba. And, this was no general in uniform with medals covering his chest and riding in a tank, this was two women - one old and frail and the other lean and beautiful. Somehow, this made the whole thing more believable.

The streets were lined East and West along the route with well-wishers of every Hispanic stripe. Each would have a story to tell about Cuba, each wanted to get a glimpse of the two women that they had seen speak on TV at the United Nations.

The car pulled away slowly and first headed west with Liliana and Lydia perched on the back seat and the mayor in the front. As they passed the people threw flowers and streamers which soon covered the inside and outside of the Cadillac.

All this merriment was taking place while simultaneously negotiations were still underway on the island 60 miles south of Cuba – Isla de la Juventude, previously known as Isla de Pinos. Curiously, this island, because of its pirate history, has made its way into English literature: Treasure Island and Peter Pan are both based in part on the pirating activity on and around the island.

Enrique was having no luck convincing the army big shots to cease their efforts to return to Cuba. Soon the planed show of force would be necessary. Soon the Black

Hawk helicopters and the A-10 Warthogs would be brought forth in convincing fashion.

Back in Little Havana Angus was left at the restaurant while Paul and Treenie took up positions East and West along the route. George was hovering in a helicopter 2,500 feet above the Calle Ocho.

"George, they are in a red Cadillac convertible. Keep eyes on that car."

"Will do, Angus," answers George, "I'm in good position and I have them in sight."

Treenie had taken up position a few blocks west at Ponce De Leon Blvd. and saw the Cadillac slowly pass by and continue west out of Treenie's view. The street crowd was beginning to thin as they headed west when they finally turned around in the Chevron station at Le Juene Rd. to head back east.

In this gas station a man ran up to the car and threw in a package – "This is for your father, your father. These are shirts from La Casa de las Guayaberas," the man said. A Guayabera is a loose fitting Cuban styled shirt that has pleats and buttons down the front. Ronald Reagan actually came to this store and bought a Guayabera.

After about 5 minutes Treenie saw them pass again in front of him.

"They are heading back toward you, Angus," informed Treenie.

"Copy that, Treenie, I guess you should stay put they may make another lap, I don't know. I see them now coming my way."

"OK, Angus, I'll stay here."

"How are you doing, George," asks Angus, "I see you up there do you read me?"

"I read you, Angus. I have the Cady in sight. I did have a problem when they got under the canopy at the gas station, but I have them in sight now."

"Good, this should be over soon. Paul they are heading toward you."

"I read you, Angus, I don't see them yet. I am down standing near this strange tree. Did you know that they put chicken bones at the base of this tree for some strange religious sacrifice?"

"I didn't know that. Take care that someone doesn't sacrifice you under this tree."

"I'm on full alert, Angus. This stuff gives me the willies."

"Treenie, I want you to find your way down to this gas station where the Cady turned around. George could not get eyes on them under the canopy."

"OK, Angus, I'll get down there."

"Thanks, Treenie, you are a terrific spy if the dancing thing doesn't work out."

The car just passed the Bay of Pigs Museum and headed for The Versailles heading east and still the crowds are enthusiastic.

Liliana and Lydia were having fun as they passed the "Ball and Chain" nightclub on the left and the famed "Tower" theater at fifteenth St.

Suddenly a girl ran in front of the car and forced it to stop. "Liliana," a girl screamed, as she came to the side of the stopped car. "I made this CD for you. I'm from Lily's records and I made this Salsa music CD for you."

"Thank you so much. I will listen to it first chance I get." And the car traveled on.

The mayor explained that they were about to pass Maximo Park where the old timers play checkers and other board games.

"Please stop in front of this park," said Liliana, "I want to give away some cigars to the gentlemen there."

Liliana then gave Lydia a box of cigars to hand out to those in the crowd around the car and she got out and entered the park with two boxes of the finest cigars on the planet.

"Gentlemen, please, take one of these Cuban cigars. I have brought them for you and to tell you that Cuba is now free. Soon our families will be united and the nightmare will be over."

She then proceeded to hand out all fifty of the cigars in a matter minutes.

"Thank you for waiting, Viva Cuba," she said as she returned to the car.

At thirteenth St., and the bags of chicken bones, the car turned around and headed back west. It was the same all the way down past The Versailles and Angus waiving from the curb as they went by.

"Treenie there making another lap and heading your way again, surely this will wrap things up."

"OK, Angus, I'm now outside the gas station."

"George, do you still have eyes on our car?"

"I'm still in position, Angus. I'm still locked on to the car."

"Good, this won't take much longer. Paul, I think you can start making your way back to The Versailles. Maybe we can finally get a bite to eat at this famous restaurant."

"That sounds good, Angus, anything but chicken, these bags of chicken bones have put me off chicken for a while."

"Just call it pollo and you'll be fine."

As the Cadillac headed west the mayor turned and said: "This has been a great day and I thank you for making this possible for all those here in Little Havana."

"My father will be sorry that he was not here with us. Lydia, how do you feel? Are you hungry? We could get a bite to eat at The Versailles."

"This has been a great day for me as well. I am tired and hungry but I will go as long as you want. There will be no more days as good as this for me."

"I wouldn't be so sure about that, Lydia," predicted Liliana.

The Cadillac then turned into the Chevron station to turn around for the last time.

"I see them Angus," offered Treenie, "they just pulled in to the Chevron station to turn around."

"Good, Treenie, maybe you can hitch a ride back with them."

"No, this is not my parade, I'll follow them back."

The Cadillac then stopped under the canopy and the driver turned around, and with that mile wide smile, said: "This has been great day for me as well."

And still smiling he pointed a pistol at Liliana and said: "Get out of the car, now, and he opened his door."

A white van then screeched alongside the Cadillac and two men got out and began pulling Liliana from the car. Lydia then leaped from her perch on the back seat and grabbed Liliana's leg and would not let go. One of the men finally struck Lydia in the head with the butt of his gun.

"What about the Mayor?" asks one of the men.

"Leave the mayor, take the cigars," said the smiling hijacker.

Once in the van Liliana said: "Are you guys sure we couldn't just sit down and smoke a Peace Pipe – you putos, you pendejos? Anyone here got a Peace Pipe?"

"George," said Angus, "she's been taken. Treenie, what do you see?"

"It's a white van, Angus, they are pulling away now. I couldn't get there in time, it's a white van."

As they drove away one of the men then tied Liliana's hands as she said: "Take a good look around you putos, look at the clouds and the birds in the trees. This will be your last day on earth. Think of what you three pendejos will tell God later today: God on my last day on earth I was kidnapping a woman in a white van. Yes, God will be pleased. He will then call you putos and he will send you straight to hell. And you, smiling driver of the Cadillac, como se llamo?"

"Tape her mouth," was the reply.

"George, follow the white van just leaving the gas station. Do you have eyes on this van?"

"I have it, Angus, it's heading west."

"Good, there are three men in the van. Don't give yourself away just keep eyes on them."

"Roger that, captain."

"Treenie, drive the Cadillac back to the Versailles and stay with Lydia. Paul, where are you?"

"I'm coming, Angus, I'll meet you at the car."

"They are turning north onto a side street," advised George ..., now they've pulled into a building and closed the door."

"Paul, I want you to take a cab back to the plane and wait there. There may be a mission for the plane that we don't foresee."

"Wait, George has something more."

"A black SUV, I think it's an Escalade, just pulled out of the building. They're turning west on the Calle Ocho. I think we can assume that they just switched vehicles."

"Hover at the building for a moment then tail them, George."

"Go ahead, Paul."

The Calle Ocho does run east and west. It runs straight from the Atlantic Ocean west through Little Havana and on toward Naples on the southwest gulf coast of Florida. Shortly out of Little Havana it turns into Hwy 41, AKA, the Tamiami Trail (Tampa/Miami), AKA Alligator Alley. This is not the high speed Interstate 75 route, but instead a two lane scenic route giving a more up close look at the everglades and alligators that occupy both sides, and sometimes the middle, of the road.

George proceeded to tail the black SUV being careful to stay in their blind spot and Angus trailed out of sight in the rent car.

While Angus drove he tried calling Liliana's father but had no luck. No doubt these hijackers would soon make contact with those being held on Isla de la Juventud south of Cuba. Again he called but there was no answer. Then he remembered the fellow that liked eggs benedict – Carl Fowler. He must be mixed up in this some way. Carl appeared to be a man who could muster resources.

"Carl, this is Angus, do you remember me?"

"Of course, Angus, are you taking care of our beautiful Liliana?"

"Listen carefully, Liliana has just been kidnapped. She is being driven west out of Little Havana in a black

Escalade. I am following well back. I don't know where they are taking her but I have a helicopter with eyes on them above. If they haven't already they will soon contact those being held south of Cuba. She will be used to gain their release. At least this is how I have this little drama figured. Do you know anything about the happenings south of Cuba? Do you have any assets that you can send to me?

"Angus, you are doing good work, stay steady. I'm here on the island south of Cuba. When they have reached their destination have your pilot mark their coordinates and then call me back on this number."

"I don't think they will hurt her," Angus said, "I just think they are trying to gain some leverage in the negotiation. Soon they will get to their destination and if we can show enough force they may just give her up. I will be back to you as soon as they get to where ever they are going."

"Angus, I have assets located at Homestead Air Base which is just a few clicks from your position. They could be on you in no time. I'll wait to hear from you."

"Roger that."

Well, that was a load off. *These Carl Fowlers, where do these guys come from?* Angus wondered. Angus was pretty sure where they come from: military intelligence. These guys were always in the shadows in every corner of the globe. You're never sure who they're working for, or who it is that cuts their check. They get recruited out of all branches of the service. They were all over Italy where

Angus did his time in the Marine Air Corps flying the Osprey around the Med.

"Angus, they're pulling off the road. There is some kind of business with a parking lot. They've pulled into this parking lot and are now stationary. They're getting out of the car now, Angus. They're transferring to what looks like an air boat. This is the everglades, Angus. There are two air boats and they are heading off into the everglades."

"Keep eyes on them, George. When they settle I'm going to want you to fix their precise coordinates."

"Angus, I think I can set down in this parking lot. The rest of this area is nothing but swamp."

"Understood, I should be there in a few. Just get those coordinates."

"Roger that, captain. I'll stay up here until I get their fix. This is one place you wouldn't want to ditch. There are alligators everywhere. I think I can see where they are heading, Angus. Up ahead there is a patch of land with a cabin on it. This must be where they're heading."

"Good, George, just stay high and then get that fix."

"That's it, Angus, they are pulling the air boats onto the shore of this small island in the middle of the swamp. They are carrying long guns and entering the cabin. This must be their planned hideout – not bad, if I do say so."

"George, lock that GPS location and I'll meet you back in this Everglades Safari parking lot. Just put her down where you can. We'll make our apologies as we need to."

Soon George was hovering over the parking lot looking for a suitable place to light. Angus rushed to the cockpit of the helicopter and entered.

"Here are the coordinates, Angus."

"George, shut this thing down. I need to make a call.

"Carl, I have the coordinates. Liliana is in a cabin in the everglades just off the highway. She is on an island with three men. The only way in is by air boat."

"How big is this island, Angus?"

"Here, talk to George."

"Sir," said George.

"George, how big is this island? Could you land your bird on it?

"Yes, Sir, I believe I could."

"Good, give me the coordinates, George."

"Here they are, Sir: Latitude: 25.729435, Longitude: -80.648070."

"Are you a Marine, George?"

"Yes, Sir, I will always be a Marine, Sir."

"Carry on, Marine; now give me back to Angus. Angus, I'm sending two Black Hawks your way. Is there a place where you could join one of them before they go to these coordinates?"

"On the highway, half a click north of the fix is a business and a parking lot. If you have to you can land on the highway."

"Good, this is what I want you to do. I want you to convey to these thugs that their bosses are now dead. Explain to them that they have no one left to fight for and if they let her go you will not kill them. You only want the woman. If they haven't already tried have them call their boss. They won't get an answer, and if I can find his phone it may be me that answers. Do you understand the drill, Angus?"

"So things on the island have been resolved?"

"Things here have come to a conclusion."

"Understood, what is your ETA at my location?"

"One hour or less, Angus."

"Roger, that, and thanks for the help. Maybe we can do those eggs benedict again someday and you can bring your wife."

"Never had eggs benedict, Angus, but thanks for the offer."

Angus stares at the phone and shakes his head. He then calls Paul.

"Paul, have you got the bird warmed up?"

"Sitting on go, Angus."

"Paul, I want you to punch these coordinates into the system. Here they are: Latitude: 25.729435, Longitude -80.648070. I want you to take off and get up a good head of steam heading west. In only about 25 miles you will come to this fix. I want you to be low to the swamp, Paul. There is a little cabin in the everglades and I want you to rattle the front door. Understood? But don't delay. We have Black Hawks scrambling to this fix as well. If you leave right away they will be well off your tail. Understood? Then return to Miami and we'll be in touch."

"Roger that, captain, rattle the front door."

"We should see Paul shortly. This should set them to wondering. And, it will give Liliana some assurance that we're on the case. I've heard some of their conversations but it's mostly been in Spanish."

"I'm in the air, Angus, see you soon."

Most people never see a plane up close flying at 500 mph. We see them cross the sky and they are easy enough to track, but to see one traveling just off the deck at that speed, even from a quarter mile away, would be very impressive. Actually, you wouldn't want to be any closer than a quarter mile.

"Don't blink, George, he's heading this way."

Inside the cabin, "Smiley," the parade car driver, was trying to get his contact on the phone – this time no answer. It came upon them so quickly and with such a force that part of the roof of the cabin was sucked right off and deposited a hundred yards away. The walls moved violently from the force of air first being pushed, and then pulled. Then, as quickly as it came, it was gone. Nothing that was in the cabin, or near the cabin, was now where it was before. Even the swamp water along the path was sucked up and misplaced.

"What the hell was that?" asked Smiley as his hands now covered his ears and he looked up through the open roof.

Liliana began to nod her head up and down as if to say – yes, I know what that was.

"Do you know what that was," Smiley asked Liliana, and he ripped the tape off of her mouth.

"Yes, I know what that was. That was the Devil and he is coming for supper. He is now feasting on alligators but he will soon be back – he is very hungry."

All three amigos looked at each other and contemplated their fate.

"Who is this Devil that can make such a noise?" demanded Smiley.

"You have chosen the wrong side of the fight," began Liliana, "events have overtaken you and you are lost. Soon you will be given another choice: you may live, or you may die. You may choose to continue to live out your lives with your wives and children, or you can die here in the swamp and become food for alligators. You have very little time to consider. Your plan to hide me here and make your bargain is no more. Think quickly, soon the Devil will return."

Smiley dialed his phone once again – still no answer.

Angus and George are sitting in the rented helicopter waiting when Angus' phone rings:

"Angus, its Carl, I was unable to get the Black Hawks so I'm sending an upgrade. One Apache Long Bow was sent instead. That should be plenty for a cabin in the swamp."

"Do we still have the same ETA?" asks Angus.

"Maybe sooner," responds Carl.

"Roger that, Carl, we're here on the highway in the parking lot waiting his arrival, If he can pick me up here I'll have George trail us to pick up Liliana off the island. After we get her we'll send your Apache on his way."

"Understood, Angus, let me know how this goes. How does it feel to be part of history?"

"I joined the Marines because the man said they had trains in the Marines. Then I found out that the Marines don't have trains, so I flew the Osprey instead. Where have all the trains gone, Carl? I now have eyes on your Apache coming in. I'll be in touch."

"This is one mean machine coming our way, Angus," said George, "this is the most kick-ass helicopter in the world today – state of the art electronics, hell fire missiles, folding-fin rockets and a 30 mm cannon. I never flew the Long Bow. It was after my time. We certainly don't need two of them to take care of this crew."

With all this commotion most of the inhabitants in and around the Air Boat Safari Tour building had accumulated out in the parking lot. Angus and George stood in the highway blocking traffic east and west as the Apache landed on alligator alley, highway 41. When the Boeing AH-64 Apache Attack Helicopter finally sat down it created quite a stir. With a wingspan of 48' and a length of 58' this imposing machine took the entire highway and into the parking lot to get on the ground.

Angus squeezed in and they lifted off with George following close behind.

Back at the cabin the sound of beating blades could now be heard. Liliana had been fending off threats and accusations since her proclamation regarding the Devil. One of the things that worked against her arguments was that these were low level peons that had no idea of the big picture. They were called upon to do a job and they were doing it. Unfortunately for them the big picture was about to unfold just outside the door of the cabin.

Smiley looked out the one front window of the cabin and saw, in the fading evening light, the Apache Long Bow hovering. Its spot lights were fixed on the door of the cabin and it did look as if the Devil had come to visit. Angus was given the microphone and he began his case: "In the cabin, send the woman out. If you send her out we will not kill you. Those that you have been trying to reach by phone are dead. Send the woman out, you have one minute."

The reason the Apache did not land was because a rather imposing alligator was parked near where he would have set down.

"Do the right thing for your children," said Liliana to the three, as she continued trying to make them see the futility of their position.

"You have 30 seconds to send her out," Angus said succinctly, without a clear idea of what he would do when those 30 seconds were up. Angus then directed the pilot: "smoke that alligator with your cannon."

As Smiley continued to look out the window he then saw a blast of light and sound from the Apache's 30 mm canon turning the alligator into a red stain on the bank of the island.

"Send her out," screamed the other two kidnappers to Smiley "send her out." And they combined to push Liliana out the door of the cabin.

"Remove the tape from her hands," said Angus coldly, "there is another chopper behind us that will land and pick up the woman. As this happens you will be inside the cabin."

One of the men cut the tape and ran back into the cabin as the Apache lifted off and George's helicopter came forward and landed with the Apache hovering ninety degrees off its position. Liliana got into the helicopter with George and they lifted off.

The Apache then rotated around to the front of the cabin and Angus spoke again matter-of-factly:

"Thank you for your cooperation. Also, there is a dark blue Ford sedan in the parking lot on the highway. Please see to it that it gets returned to the rental company." And with that the Apache opened up with its cannon on the two air boats that were resting on the bank.

With George and Liliana still hovering nearby, Liliana said: "I hope they will make it through the alligators to tell this story. Maybe in the morning we should send another boat to pick them up. I want them to spread the word about the night the Devil came to dinner."

Both helicopters then left the scene and rendezvoused back at the highway. Angus got out of the Apache and joined Liliana.

"George, why don't you get this chopper checked back in and you and Paul can take a cab and join us at the Versailles. Liliana and I will drive back. In fact, call this number and ask for Rejito. He is our cabby. And when you get to the Versailles have him come in with you. We should buy his dinner."

"Will do, captain, see you there.

And then there was yet another call to make: "Carl," said Angus, "we have reached a successful conclusion and Liliana is safe. Please notify her father."

"Will do, Angus, good work, maybe we can put this drama to bed, or at least turn the page."

"Well," responded Angus, "we should put something to bed. There is nothing but drama around this woman," as Angus smiled at Liliana.

"I can only imagine, Angus. Be safe, maybe we'll cross paths again someday."

"Take care, Carl."

"One more call," as Angus dialed the number, "Treenie, we are all coming back to the Versailles."

"Is she rescued?" asks Treenie.

"Here, you ask her."

"Liliana, are you rescued?

"Yes, I am rescued by my Captain America. We are on our way, Treenie, we'll see you soon.

Angus, kiss me."

"I knew it. That was as predictable as the moon over Miami. Show this woman a little danger and she's all over you.

Please, I'm trying to drive in a straight line. Please, Liliana. Maybe you could wait for a phone booth."

All were then gathered back at the restaurant except Treenie and Lydia.

"You told him the Versailles, didn't you Angus?" wondered Liliana.

"Yes, and here he comes now, the super spy agent for President Bill Clinton."

"Treenie, where is Lydia?" asks Liliana.

"She didn't make it. Lydia died at the hospital."

"What are you saying, Treenie?" Liliana asks.

"When I got to the car the mayor was just standing there and Lydia was unconscious in the back seat. The mayor said that they had struck her with the gun as she held on to you. I drove her to the hospital and they told me she was dead."

"You know, Paul," said Angus in a somber tone, "when we finish this campaign I want to drop all this military 'captain' this, and 'roger' that, crap. I don't want to hear it anymore."

"Angus," said Liliana with fierceness in her tone, "get that helicopter back. I want to go back. Take me back to that swamp now, Angus."

"Liliana, we can't do that," and he held her as she began to sob. "We're here for only a short time – she made her mark."

Two Weeks Later

"Mi Tierra, por favor," was Liliana's instructions to the cabbie just outside the "La Mansion Del Rio" hotel in downtown San Antonio, Texas. "And drive us by the Alamo on the way.

Have you ever seen the Alamo, Angus?"

"I used to pretend that I was Davey Crockett, but, no, I've never actually seen the Alamo."

"There it is, right in the middle of the city. Pull over please, driver. It looks exactly like the pictures in the history books, don't you think? My father and I took the tour when we were here years ago. They have preserved it for all these years. It's an interesting story, the Alamo. This is where the Mexicans kicked ass. All were killed to the last man, they took no prisoners. General Santa Anna and his troops set up camp on the other side of the river right across from our hotel. For thirteen days they assaulted the mission. The Mexicans wanted to retake Tejas, but they made mistakes."

"Didn't the Americans chase him down and kill him not too long after that?"

"I don't remember that. No se puede hacer tortilla sin romper los huevos. OK, you can go on now driver."

"Liliana, you have slipped over into your Spanish mind."

"The lady said: 'You must break some eggs to make the omelet'," offered the driver.

"You guys are ganging up on me.

"No cantan dos gallos en un gallinero," was the next comment from the driver."

"And what did I miss with that fusillade?" asked Angus.

"Ha, the driver tells us that two roosters cannot crow in the same hen house. These are old Spanish proverbs."

"Here's an old Irish proverb: Never wear a metal hat in a storm, how about that?"

"Oh, that's a good one, Angus. I'm sure I will remember that good advice."

"Have you ever stayed at a 'Four Seasons' hotel," asked Angus as he glanced down S. Alamo St.

"I think there are newer hotels but La Mansion brings me back. La Mansion is where my father and I stayed when he brought me here when I was a little girl. From our balcony we watched a parade on the river below. Floats covered with flowers passed on the river just beneath our room with hundreds of people watching from the banks. We had the perfect seat. This is old school, Angus, as is Mi Tierra, where we are going now for dinner."

"You are my Quixote and I am your Sancho Panza. Take me to this Mi Tierra."

"You know when I was in Spain I saw the windmills that threatened Don Quixote in the province of Castilla-La Mancha. There are bronze statues of Quixote and Sancho Panza at the Plaza de España in Madrid. These communists that we are fighting, they are no windmills, Angus, you know that."

"Yes, I know that."

"And did you also know that Don Quixote promised Sancho the governance of an island as a reward for taking on his adventures?"

"Right now I would settle for a plate of tacos," responds Angus.

"They told me at the hotel that this restaurant has not changed for many generations. When I was there it had a bakery case with many Mexican pastries and candies. My favorite was the pecan praline. I must have one of these pralines tonight, Angus."

"Si, it is still this way," added the driver. "We are almost there."

Angus reads the name: Theodore, on the driver's visor then asks: "Theo, how long have you been a cabbie in San Antonio?"

"For only a few weeks, I was just laid off from my job."

"And what was your job, Theo?"

"I was a construction engineer in charge of a project that was cancelled just as it got started. In the mornings I look for work and at night I drive a cab. We are here now. Here is my card, you call me, my name is Theodore, but for you it could be Teddy."

"Thanks, Teddy, we'll give you a call," said Angus as he handed him a $100 bill. "Keep the change."

"That was a nice tip, Angus," as Teddy thanked Angus and drove away.

"It's the least I can do. Besides, we have made excellent use of both cab and cabbie lately. Do you sense any danger now as we enter this restaurant?"

"No, Angus, I feel no danger."

"That's good, because if you do feel danger I will make the necessary arrangements. We could maybe visit the back porch of the Alamo."

"I prefer the front porch, but no, Angus, I feel fine. I only crave a pecan praline at this time. However, I reserve the right to alter my mood at any time."

"This is my concern," stated Angus, "now, show me this restaurant. I should warn you that I'm considering hiring someone to frighten you after dinner."

"You won't need to frighten me, Angus."

As they entered Mi Tierra they were confronted with a very large restaurant that was broken into multiple separate dining rooms. In the front was the 20 foot bakery case and the sound of mariachi music came at them from multiple directions.

In the case were many types of sweet breads – pan dulce; there were sugar coated orange slices, coconut bars in the colors of Mexico, and of course pecan pralines.

"Buenos tarde," was the greeting from the hostess, "a table for two?"

Paintings of Emiliano Zapata hung on the wall alongside those of Cantinflas, Frida Kahlo, and a life size painting of Bill Clinton jogging. There was also a twenty foot floor to ceiling wall mural with the faces of anyone and everyone that is important in Hispanic culture. Lights, streamers, and piñatas hung from the ceiling with such abandon you would think that it was Christmas Eve.

"You are welcome any time of day or night," explained the hostess, "we never close 24/7.

"Someday, Liliana, your face will be on this wall," predicted Angus. "Do you know all these people?"

"I know some. I see Carlos Santana, a great guitar player. I think my choices would be different. I will have your face on my wall, Angus."

"Soon you may be able to copy the one off the wall at the post office."

Groups of mariachi musicians roamed throughout the large restaurant area and bar. And for a bargained price you could be serenaded at your table.

"Did you see those pralines in the case? This is what I want after dinner."

As they settled in at their table and perused the menu they were approached by one of the mariachi players:

"Would you like a song for the lady, Señor?"

"Do I have to sing?" the lady has already decided against my singing."

"No, Señor, we will handle the singing."

"Good, then, sing a song for Liliana."

"Si, Señor, Liliana," and he summoned four more mariachis with violins, guitar and a trumpet. "Cielito Lindo," announced the lead player and they began:

*"Del la sierra morena cielito lindo vienen bajando
un par de ojitos negros cielito lindo de contraband
ay ay ay ay conta y no llores ... "*

As they sang Liliana interpreted the words for Angus.

"That was Magnificent!" declared Angus as they concluded. "You know, Liliana, that part about your mouth – your boca ..."

"Yes, '*cielito lindo, junto a la boca*,' lovely sky next to the mouth…"

"That's the one," agreed Angus, "I have a confession to make."

"Please, Angus, we are not yet through our first margarita."

"It was on the Coyote yacht when we first met," began Angus, "it was your lips, your mouth that destroyed me. You must have noticed me staring throughout the night. I heard only half of what the others said after you first spoke. Even now I am fractured by the form of your lips as they move without a sound. They speak to me even when you say nothing. This is my one half margarita confession."

"I forgive you, Angus, for staring at mi boca. You know that behind these lips there can be a sharp tongue."

"Kings have risked their crown for less."

"Shall I confess to you, father Quin? My confession will require more forgiveness than was required of me. In the beginning I needed a person like you – smart, connected, and so I courted you for my purpose and for my needs. Since then my mind has changed, since we have been together I feel different about you. You are not my Jaime and no one will ever be the Jaime that I have kept in my heart for so many years, but you are Angus, and my heart is changing. There is much to you, Angus Peace Pipe Quin; there is much to make a woman forget here past. And this is my margarita confession."

"And what will become of us, Liliana, as you set about making your New Cuba?"

"Ha, you got to ask the question first."

Angus' phone rings …

"Hello, Robert."

"Well, Angus, I have some serious news."

"Robert, knowing you the way I do it is either about the bond market or baseball and I'm going to go with baseball. Am I right?"

"You are right. Do you have Lilian there with you?"

"She has had one margarita and is working on her second; however, she still seems coherent. I'm going to place the phone on speaker. Here she is."

"Hola, Robert, Hello. How are you?"
"I am very well, thanks. I have news regarding baseball."

"I am very eager to hear, Robert, tell me your news. No, wait, could you let us call you back later this evening?"

"Of course, I'll wait for your call."

"Good, thank you, Roberto," and she hung up. "I didn't want to spoil our evening with baseball."

"Well, that was an unexpected concession," remarked Angus as their dinner arrived: tortilla soup, chicken fajitas sizzling in an iron skillet with onions and sweet peppers, accompanied by guacamole and pico de gallo. "I've really worked up an appetite with all that singing."

"I must save room for my praline."

"And I have to buy one of those t-shirts with the rooster on it."

"More musica, Señor?"

"Yes, sing, make something up."

"Si, Señor," and the violins began once again over fajitas con tortillas de maize.

"You know, Liliana, the real bargain in this restaurant is the tables next to ours. I guess to ask them to chip in would be bad form."

"I know you, Angus, and you would never do that."

Angus summoned the waitress and directed her to bring a tray of pecan pralines and hand them out to everyone in the room.

Angus then stood up and shouted over the music: "I am with the most beautiful woman in all of Cuba! The music and the pralines are on me."

"I can see why you take Paul along with you, Angus, you are a trouble maker."

"I'm just stating a fact," as Angus again stared at Liliana's boca that was now wet with tortilla soup.

When the plates were cleared and the music had moved to a different table Liliana said:

"You know I am still angry about Lydia. I was responsible for her."

"I know; when it comes to mind just think about those guys being chased by alligators through the swamp."

"If the alligators don't get them they will show up and someone will see them then they will wish for alligators."

"Lydia was surely near the end of a long hard life, and at the end she conducted herself in a heroic manner and died for a cause she believed in. Will we be as lucky as she when we are near the end? And how would the rest of her life played out had she not met you?"

"These things are true. She spent her last day in a parade held in her honor. Still, I'm going to do something special for Lydia. I don't know what yet, but something."

"I've given it some thought."

"Tell me your thoughts, Angus."

"I think I would commission a Cuban artist to sculpt a bronze statue of Lydia standing with her newspapers and place it on her corner. There may be some pictures that the New York newspapers would share for such a project."

"That's a wonderful idea, Angus, and maybe one on the Calle Ocho as well. I'm going to get that started as soon as I return to Cuba. You are good to have around, Angus. You are a lousy singer, but you have other qualities which I will test when my praline has settled."

"You will not be able to resist me when I put on my rooster t-shirt."

"Angus – El Gallo – the Irish rooster will crow tonight!"

"Shouldn't I also crow in the morning?"

"You should not exhaust me for my meeting in the morning, Angus."

"When we get to San Francisco what will be your goals for those meetings?

"There is a man there that I have communicated with, a remarkable man. This man has designed a train called 'The Hyperloop' that moves on a cushion of air and can travel at almost 600 km per hour. He has shared with me his design drawings. He has proposed that this train be built from San Francisco to Los Angeles. I want to convince him to help me build it in Cuba."

"This is not my kind of train. This is a train for getting from point to point in a hurry. The trains in my mind are more nostalgic."

"I know, and I love your trains, Angus, but they are of the past. We cannot build another "Mal Tiempo.' Cuba must move quickly into the future; we have been stagnating for too long. I have looked over his drawings and I have ideas and questions. This train must travel in a straight line. Nothing that travels at these speeds can tolerate curves and bumps. Cuba is a long straight shot from Pinar Del Rio in the west to Guantanamo Bay in the east. We could be the perfect beta site for this train.

This same man is also building a car company for electric cars. I want to bring these cars to Cuba. You have seen the way we get around in Cuba; we are like a time capsule from the fifties."

"Well, Liliana, no one can accuse you of looking backward."

"With all that we have come through, and all that we have risked getting to this point, we cannot become lazy and just plod along into some commercialized future of foreigners wandering around with cameras. We have to be bold in our approach. There are people back in Cuba that are excited about these things that I will bring back: a limited amount of drilling that I will discuss tomorrow, trains and automobiles. These people will greet me when I return ready to work."

"Clearly you have much on your mind and having some gringo hanging around would only be a distraction."

"It could be a good distraction, Angus."

"I envy the clarity of your vision. My passion, which has been far less noble, has been interrupted, and maybe ended for good. I need to find myself again; I need to find my own new direction. I have some ideas that need to be thought through. Maybe there is some noble cause out there that my wealth and energy could be a part of."

"Angus, there will be many opportunities for a good man in New Cuba."

"Wherever I am I will see your mouth, your lips wet with tortilla soup, and your skin the color of tobacco leaves."

~ANGUS and LILIANA~
Chapter XXIII
New Beginnings

In the great northwest, where French has not yet given over to Spanish, a train prepares to leave the station. From Vancouver it will first head north toward Whisper, British Columbia, and then on to points further north. The well-to-do seeking a more contemplative, nostalgic journey sit alongside other like-minded passengers and stare out the specially designed windows at *la vue panoramique*. Their excited children, now out of their comfortable seats, will crawl over and around the well-appointed train cars designed for luxury, scenic travel. In the dining car, depending on the level of service, passengers will dine on hot dogs to foie gras.

This is luxury, non-essential, travel at its best. A ticket to ride, even at a modest service level, is out of the reach of most. And the chosen route is no accident; this is arguably one of the most picturesque journeys on earth.

Luxury train travel, like everything else since the arrival of The Great Recession, has suffered of late. Fewer passengers have put a strain on the company's ability to operate these excursions for the well-healed. Nonetheless, this trip is booked, provisioned, and will soon be leaving the station. There has, however, been a slight delay for today's departure. The wait is not for a late arriving passenger, no, the wait is for an additional car that is being attached to the end of the train.

Now, with all cars fully coupled, the train starts its slow predictable motion out of the station. Seven days hence this train having completed its circular route will return to Vancouver.

Picturesque from the start the train follows along the water's edge of Howe Sound, with the islands of Bowen, Gambier, and Anvil sometimes visible to the west. These islands are surrounded by waters coming up from the Salish Sea and the Straits of Georgia.

Continuing north the train travels through Lions Bay to Porteu, Furry Creek, still skirting the waters of the Sound. Now in the dark through Squamish and on toward the Serratus, Mamquam, and Garibaldi Mountains the children now lay sleeping in their seats.

It is at Prince George where the train will finally turn back south. From here the view, as if it could get more magnificent, gets really good. Through the northern Rockies the train makes its way through the valley with the Cariboo Mountains to the west and Mt. Robson Provincial Preserve to the east.

The occupants of the last car of the train will not dine on hot dogs this night; there are no children to demand them. The last car on this train is a private car not accessible to the ticket holding passengers.

Sometime ago a passenger car was selected for transformation. Not an average car but one of the longest passenger cars ever built. The outside was not finished with pinstripes or loud paint, but refurbished to look like any ordinary work-a-day car.

The inside, however, was a different matter. Drawing on the finest Chicago interior designer no expense was spared to create a comfortable living environment. The car was stripped to its bones. The mechanical undercarriage was gone over and oiled and greased sufficiently to soften unnecessary creaks. The walls, floor and ceiling were double and triple insulated to protect from the anticipated harsh winter cold and provide further soundproofing.

There was a lounge area at the rear of the car, a full galley with generous storage for provisions, a master suite with a king bed, a shower, and a closet for storage and dressing.

There was only one identifying external feature: on each side down low and on the top was written the word: "Calumet." This identification was necessary because of its ordinary exterior. When the transformation was finished the car made its way west from Chicago. Hitching rides as it could the car traveled empty as it made its way slowly and calculatingly toward the train yard in Vancouver. Here the car sat on an unused portion of track and waited, it waited for when the time was right, it waited for that time when an old dream could become a reality, it waited for a time when the road ahead was no longer clear.

With a helping investment toward the company's financial future the Calumet insured itself a place at the end of the train; a place away from conversation and paper airplanes. The end of a train is a good place to think and plan your next move, even if that move is to go around one more time.

Now, coming out of a tunnel the train would need all its speed to manage the grade ahead, steam billowing up, the unmistakable *chugging* sound reflecting off the mountain wall, the single car known as "Calumet" obediently followed the train. The train gave a long *whistle* as it again came up to speed.

On the platform in the back of the last car stands Angus Calumet Quin. The flutter of snowflakes swirled behind the car along with the essence of a good Cuban cigar.

The car door opens and Angus is joined by a woman, a lean beautiful woman. They embrace to fight the wind and cold. Then again the door opens and another woman appears and joins the embrace.

Inside the car and out of the cold sits a crystal vase, and from this vase rises a single white lily whose petals are dusted with yellow gold. Beside the lily is a long stemmed rose, a single red opening bud with petals tinged in pink.

Meanwhile, in Havana, New Cuba ...

"If I'm still alive after this, another day I will tell more."

"Oye Lydia ¿Cómo estás? ¿Cuáles son las noticias?"

Many times a day the question is still put to Lydia: ¿Cuáles son las noticias? – *(What's the news?)*. If she could answer she would say: "Si estoy todavía vivo después de esto, otro día mi lengua será más floja." *(If I'm still alive after this, another day my tongue is looser.)*

Across the street in the dining room of the Hotel Sevilla Liliana looks out the window as she waits for her breakfast appointment. From her table she can see Lydia holding her newspapers.

"Father, *¿Cómo estás?*" Liliana says and she kisses his checks as he joins her at the table.

"It feels like rain," her father says, "my shoulder is telling me that rain is near."

"She looks good there, don't you think, Father?"

"She will be there for all of time, Liliana. Long after you and I are gone Lydia will give her message on that corner. You did Cuba, and even Lydia, a good service by taking her to New York."

"Maybe so, this is also what Angus told me."

"Look at how many are lined up to look at her and to read the words she spoke at the UN. Mothers and fathers are bringing their children from all over Cuba and beyond to see her words written there. This is a good thing, Liliana."

"I can't stay long, Father. I have many meetings today."

"How is the train coming along, Liliana?"

"We are trying to slow it down. This is our problem. I think 250 km per hour is enough for our little island. I'm afraid that it will not slow down enough and it will keep going into the sea. Such a problem…, we go from trains that cannot move from the rust to trains we must slow down."

"Liliana, please don't try and run in front of this train."

"Ha, I don't think the chickens would win either."

"Is this little car I saw in front of the hotel the newest prototype? There was a crowd around it as well."

"Isn't it beautiful? By this time next year we will build 20 per day, and the year after 100. We should be exporting cars in two years. I have to go now father. Maybe tomorrow I can stay longer."

"Now, Liliana, tell me what I want to know."

And with a broad smile she said: "The Tragons defeated the Detroit Tigers last night and are now assured a place in the playoffs."

"Liliana, you have made your father a happy man."

Liliana then kissed her father's cheeks and drove away silently and without emissions in her new electric "Cubana."

The End

Epilogue

The following is excerpted from: "The Financial Crisis,: Why Have No High-Level Executives Been Prosecuted?" By: Jed S. Rakoff, United States District Judge for the - Southern District of New York.

"Who was to blame? Was it simply a result of negligence, of the kind of inordinate risk-taking commonly called a "bubble," of an imprudent but innocent failure to maintain adequate reserves for a rainy day? Or was it the result, at least in part, of fraudulent practices, of dubious mortgages portrayed as sound risks and packaged into ever more esoteric financial instruments, the fundamental weaknesses of which were intentionally obscured?

On the one hand, the government, writ large, had a part in creating the conditions that encouraged the approval of dubious mortgages. Even before the start of the housing boom, it was the government, in the form of Congress, that repealed the Glass-Steagall Act, thus allowing certain banks that had previously viewed mortgages as a source of interest income to become instead deeply involved in securitizing pools of mortgages in order to obtain the much greater profits available from trading. It was the government, in the form of both the executive and the legislature, that encouraged deregulation, thus weakening the power and oversight not only of the SEC but also of such diverse banking overseers as the Office of Thrift Supervision and the Office of the Comptroller of the Currency, both in the Treasury Department. It was the government, in the form of the Federal Reserve, that kept interest rates low, in part to encourage mortgages. It was the government, in the form of the

executive, that strongly encouraged banks to make loans to
individuals with low incomes who might have previously been
regarded as too risky to warrant a mortgage.

It was the government, pretty much across the board, that
acquiesced in the ever-greater tendency not to require
meaningful documentation as a condition of obtaining a
mortgage, often preempting in this regard state regulations
designed to assure greater mortgage quality and a borrower's
ability to repay. Indeed, in the year 2000, the Office of Thrift
Supervision, having just finished a successful campaign to
preempt state regulation of thrift underwriting, terminated its
own underwriting regulations entirely.

The result of all this was the mortgages that later became known
as "liars' loans." They were increasingly risky; but what did the
banks care, since they were making their money from the
securitizations. And what did the government care, since it was
helping to create a boom in the economy and helping voters to
realize their dream of owning a home?

Five years have passed since the onset of what is sometimes
called the Great Recession. While the economy has slowly
improved, there are still millions of Americans leading lives of
quiet desperation: without jobs, without resources, without
hope.

Not a single high-level executive has been successfully
prosecuted in connection with the recent financial crisis, and
given the fact that most of the relevant criminal provisions are
governed by a five-year statute of limitations, it appears likely
that none will be."

About the author:

The pony is long gone, but the little boy remains…

I was sitting on the sofa reading Don Quixote when a knock came at the screen door. As I approached I could see an old man, and behind him, just beyond the porch steps in *my* front yard, was a pony! Ponies didn't come to my front yard. Ponies didn't exist in my neighborhood. The old man said: "Would you like to sit on this pony, son?" Then my mother showed up and I knew she would put the squash on this chance of a lifetime. However, to my complete amazement, my mother was down with the program. I would sit on the pony and have my picture taken and my mother would give the old man money.

The man and the pony had parked at the end of the block and walked up to each front door looking for a six-year-old boy like me. They had with them, strapped to the side of the pony, the entire set-up: the camera, tripod, hat, chaps, boots, and even a red handkerchief. And so, under the magnolia tree in my front yard, with my mother looking on and my father at work, Trigger and I posed for this photograph.

During the brief time that I sat in that saddle I felt that Trigger and I had developed a bond, an understanding of sorts, a common sense of purpose: to rid ourselves of this mundane life and head out on our own and find something more – together. But alas, our short time together had come to an end – or had it?

"Ok, son, time to get off," said the old man. Suddenly I was filled with purpose! I kicked the old man in the shoulder, dug in my spurs and shouted: giddy yap! Trigger responded instantly to my bold initiative and bolted out from under that magnolia tree like Secretariat out of the gate. Down the sidewalk we flew toward Spain and the windmills of Cervantes. On we galloped toward adventure and away from our ho-hum life on Hammond Ave on the South-side on San Antonio, Texas. Farther and farther we went; my borrowed hat now off with the wind.

Well, actually, we only got down to the front of Mr. Porter's house, which was three houses down, when Trigger's legs gave out and he came to a full stop. His spirit was there, he felt it as I did – I know it – but his old legs had betrayed him.

Shortly thereafter the old man and my mother arrived to drag me unceremoniously out of the saddle and back to a ho-hum life, albeit now with some time-out restrictions. Back I landed at 1123 Hammond Ave on the South-side of San Antonio, Texas.

It was sad to watch as he was loaded into that trailer at the end of the block - head down, defeated, somehow. As the years have passed I've come to forgive him. There are times even today when I want to bolt forward with some bold initiative only to be brought to a full stop by these old legs. Ride on, Trigger, ride on.

Mike McCarty is an author and portrait artist living in Tulsa, OK. Other books available from the author include:

- Dance of the Incumbent – non-fiction
- The Adventures of Alex the Vegetarian Coyote

www.ingramcontent.com/pod-product-compliance
Lightning Source LLC
Chambersburg PA
CBHW051321250626
47155CB00007B/2407